ADDICTIVE

TJ. NGUYEN

This book is a work of fiction. Any references to historical events, real people, or real places are used fictitiously. Other names, characters, places, incidents, dialogue and events are products of the author's imagination, and any resemblance to actual events or places or persons, living or dead, is entirely coincidental.

Copyright © 2021 by TJ. Nguyen

TRIGGER WARNING.

This content might contain potentially sensitive topics like death, violence, abuse, mental health issues, drinking, substances, trauma, suicide, language, and more.

To sixth grade me; for coming up with this story in the first place.

And to anyone who's had an Eden Brooks or Mina Willow, this book's for you.

"She has the problem so I have to find the solution."

"That's not your responsibility, is it?"

"It can be if I make it."

1
interrogation 1
[JUNE 1, 2019]

APRIL 4, 2016

A dose of panic and adrenaline rushed through my veins. I was only 14.

"No, no, no!" I screamed, "He didn't do anything!"

This is where reality started to come back to me and slap me across the face.

"¡Mierda!" I shouted as I ran over to him.

"You pronounced it wrong." he chuckled softly.

My head was pacing and spinning in circles. I didn't know what to do. I didn't know what was next. I wasn't even sure if *anything* was real.

JUNE 1, 2019

"What were you doing on the evening of May 31st, 2019?" the inspector asked me.
"I was with Mina." I replied softly.
The inspector looked at me wide-eyed. I knew what she was thinking.
"*What?* That doesn't mean I killed her!" I explained arrogantly.
She sighed and put down her pen.
"Mr. Brooks," she sighed.
"Call me *Eden*."
"This would be a lot easier if you would just confess." she continued.
"I have nothing *to* confess."
I looked her dead in the eye. I wasn't angry. I wasn't upset. I was numb. I didn't feel a thing. Mina is dead. Mina was murdered and they all think it was me.
I don't even have a motive.
"Okay." she sighed, "Let's start from the beginning."
I sighed and brushed my hands through my hair in frustration.
"I already told you what happened five times."
My lawyer was next to me eyeing me down like I was a statue in a museum.

"Tell me it again in *full* detail." the inspector ordered.

I looked up at her trying not to tear up. I gulped and looked away for a second.

"It was the last day of school." I said, "We skipped 7th period because there was no point in staying."

I continued to tell her what happened as best as I could. I have been interrogated for hours. I needed to rest even though I knew I wouldn't be able to fall asleep.

Mina was the type of girl who needed the feeling of adrenaline. Mina was the *run from the cops* type of adrenaline junkie, the *run in the empty highways while it rained* type of adrenaline junkie, that feeling was like a drug for her.

The more she had it the more she needed it.

She wanted to run through a sunflower field together. I didn't want to at first but she managed to convince me.

"Why a sunflower field?" the inspector asked.

I scoffed, "She wanted a *peaceful* feeling that day."

She nodded and started jotting notes down.

"We were supposed to meet our friends there after school but Mina wanted to go early." I continued.

"Do you guys usually do stuff like this?"

Yes. Mina loved movies, shows, books. Romance, action, and thriller. She liked to rely on the fictional world. She loved movies to the point where she'd want to live life like one. She's the type to have a thousand problems but never cares enough to go and solve them.

"We were running through the sunflower field and uh.. y'know there's a hill at the end of it leading to a *smaller* sunflower field and the view, the view was mesmerising. She probably wanted to sit at the edge of the hill to watch the sunset or something."

"Then what happened?"

I sighed. This was the hardest part. Talking about it is almost like reliving it.

"And then we reached the end of the hill. I almost slipped off but she grabbed my arm and pulled me up. We sat on the grass at the edge and y'know, her nails were sharp, that explains the mark on my arm from where she grabbed me."

Mina started talking to me about life. I figured she was excited about turning 17 in September, it was her golden birthday. She said 17 was the age she'd pick if she could stay that age forever. She started going from topic to topic like she always did.

"What happened next?" the inspector insisted.
"She sat up and turned towards me."
"But what?!"
"That's when she got shot."

I started breathing heavily but I tried to hide it. Thinking about it just made it worse. Being numb is better than this. I covered my face with my hands and inhaled sharply.

"She died right in front of me." I muttered.

I started tearing up. I hate crying.

"Eden, I understand this might be hard, but you *need* to tell me everything."

I nodded and grabbed the plastic cup of water with both hands.

"The arrow hit her left side. Near her lung."

"My left or her left?"

"Hers."

Everything happened so fast. There were forests aligning the field, the killer must've shot from there.

A sharp pain entered Mina's chest. She fell forward a little and blood started flowing out of her like she was a fountain.

"¡Joder!" she gasped quietly as she turned around to see where it came from.

"¿Joder? Isn't that spanish?" the inspector asked.

10

"Yeah, she was asian but she spoke all three languages for fun, Vietnamese, English, and European Spanish."

Her eyes started tearing up. She always told me she doesn't feel a lot of physical pain anymore. She usually deals with it quietly when she does. She looked down at the wound. The blood was dripping onto her hands and clothes.

The same phrases kept repeating in my head.

She's not dead. C'mon. It'll all be okay.

I kept yelling out words trying to keep her awake. I laid her on her side of my lap for the moment and brushed the hair out of her face. We were showered in her blood.

I panicked. I started hyperventilating as quietly as I could. I tried to keep calm because I didn't want her to see me panic. I wanted to scream. I wanted to cry, but I couldn't. It'd only make it worse. I whipped my hand over to my pocket and patted it quickly. I was trying to find my phone.

Call 999! Shit, I don't live in the UK. 911! Call 911!

I dialed the right number and they picked up.

"911, what's your emergency?"

"Mina! She got shot!"

"What's your location?"

"Erm.. I'm not sure! We're in the sunflower field near the school."

Mina started coughing up blood and it freaked both of us out. It got all over my sweatpants.

"Send an ambulance. Please! Someone shot an arrow through her!" I cried softly.

Mina tapped my leg. I drifted the phone away from my ear.

"Eden." she said, "It's no use."

I raised an eyebrow at her.

"If they send an ambulance it'll take awhile to find us."

"Huh?"

"We're in the middle of nowhere! They'll have to search for us when they get here. By then I'll be dead."

Mina was Mina, she never took anything seriously. Her mind was always somewhere else. This time she had to be real. She was dying.

"Shut up." I scoffed, "Don't say that."

I knew she was right. I just didn't want to accept it.

"Well, why did you call 911 then hang up a few minutes later?" the inspector interrupted.

"Like I said, it was no use. I didn't want to give her false hope." I answered.

Back when it happened I was anxious.

The cops are going to suspect something. They'll think it was me. I'm the last person to be seen with her, I'm covered in her blood. Her blood's on my hands, my face, my clothes now the next thing you'll know I'll be in a jail cell for something I didn't do.

Mina turned her head to a specific direction. She lifted up her hand and tapped my leg repeatedly.

"WATCH OUT-" she shouted.

I looked up and ducked quickly. We both flinched and I turned to my left to see what was behind her.

Another arrow.

I felt my heart drop down to my feet. I tried picking Mina up but it didn't work out. She didn't need me to carry her anyway.

We were trying to hide since the killer was aiming for me. One almost hit my stomach.

She stood up slowly to run with me. She did track in school, she was fast. Seconds later another arrow hit her thigh while running and she fell and cussed again. I swung around and saw her laying on the ground.

"FUCK!" I shouted.

"RUN!"

I jumped over her body and we crawled into the field as I shielded her. One more arrow in the wrong spot would've killed her. I didn't care if I got hit. Sometimes I don't care if *anything* happened to me.

We finally made it deep into the field. There wasn't any way the killer could see us. I kept praying the killer wouldn't run into the field themselves to finish us off. She laid on her side and rested her head on my lap again.

After hiding in the field we waited for the cops to come. I was tensed up waiting for them to yell. I wanted them to come quicker and I'll yell out to guide them to my direction. Every second counted.

I panicked. I didn't know what to do. I kept hoping that she'd be lucky enough to live.

She hated crying as much as I did. She tried covering her face but she didn't have to. She was used to crying around me.

"Just hang on Mina, keep talking to me." I told her quickly, "It's going to be fine. It's going to be okay."

We don't usually soften up like this. Whenever something happens we laugh it off. But in this situation I genuinely panicked, I didn't want to lose her.

I sniffled.

"I promise you I'll find out whoever did this to you." I whispered softly.

She nodded and sighed. Her skin was pale and blue. She looked like a zombie. She smiled lightly.

"Do you know if I'll see fictional characters in heaven?"

"Erm..." I sighed.

I wanted her to live. I wanted her to be with me. I'm not sure if that's selfish or not. I just tried to make her as comfortable as possible. But she's Mina.

"Yeah, you'll see him, but *not soon.*"

"Andres?" she laughed.

She chuckled softly but then hissed silently every time her lung moved.

"I thought he went by a city name."

"Yeah he does, but I don't think *he'll* be in heav-" she laughed softly.

I raised an eyebrow. I turned my head and there she was. She was there laying in my arms covered in blood lifelessly.

She wasn't breathing.

My emotions were everywhere. I didn't know whether to scream or cry. I didn't know if I was angry or sad either. I stood up and looked at my hands.

Blood. Her blood.

I spent the next 5-10 minutes staggering back and forth screaming until I physically couldn't. It's not normal but it was for me.

I paced over to the edge of the hill angrily and screamed at the world. I couldn't stay still. Staggering back and forth, running my hands through my hair out of breath with tears swimming down my cheeks. I think I was going to go insane.

I reached for my phone and yelled at it. I looked crazy. I yelled until my face turned pink and my eyes vibrated.

"WHY COULDN'T YOU JUST *FUCKING* HURRY UP!" I screamed, "SHE'S *DEAD!*"

I threw my phone up in the air in anger and it fell back to hit me on the shoulder.

"OUCH! DAMMIT!" I screamed again.

The inspector was squinting her eyes at me.

No, I'm not sugar-coating, I go through out-breaks like this often. Mina dying was my breaking point.

The inspector looked at me with concern and sighed. This is just how I am, I can't help it. I looked up and the ceiling and winced. The light above was bright.

"On your phone, 911 wasn't the last number you called that night" the inspector said, "Can you tell me who you called?"

I looked up at her.

"Her brother, Jules." I replied softly, "Julian Willow."

I called him right after panicking and tapping her face trying to wake her up. I knew it was no use. I just wanted a miracle to happen but miracles don't really come by when it comes to Mina.

"What happened on the phone between you two?" the inspector asked.

I called him a few minutes after crying. He picked up.

"Jules." I cried softly.

"What? What's wrong?!"

"It's Mina."

"What!? She dumped you? *Finally.*" he snickered, "Took her long enough."

I shut my eyes and inhaled sharply. I hate when he jokes about everything. I never find it funny.

"Don't be a bitch Jules, she's dead."

"WHAT?!" he shouted.

I heard his usual cheery voice turn to heavy breathing and hesitation.

"What do you *mean* she's dead?!" he snapped.

"I'm not joking around. Why would I joke about this?"

"Where are you?!"

I could hear his footsteps on the phone. People were asking where he was going but he continued pacing. He opened a few doors and his car beeped.

"We're in the sunflower field we planned to go to. It'll take awhile for you to find us." I told him softly.

"Is she breathing?" he stuttered.

"No."

It took awhile for the police to find us. By then the sun was almost done setting and the blood on Mina's shirt was almost dry. I held her in my arms silently. It was the last time I could ever do that.

I wanted to run. I wanted to go chase after the killer, they had to be nearby, but I couldn't. I didn't know if they had more arrows to kill me. I needed to be alive to tell Mina's story.

When the cops found us there were flashing lights and people surrounding us. They took Mina away. I stood up as they swabbed my clothes with q-tips cause I was covered in blood. After they were done I turned around and saw Jules. He was frozen, staring at the people bringing away Mina.

I staggered up to him slowly and he hugged me. I dug my face into his shoulder.

Jules was tall, pale, and slim. 6'0. He was toned and had that look on his face. He was the type of person to look friendly and fierce at the same time. He looked like those perfume models with the perfect straight light brown hair and jawline.

"What took you so long?" I cried.

"I had to convince the police to let me come with," he answered.

"I'm sorry."

He started crying and asked me what happened.

"Someone shot her with a bow and arrow."

I kept getting the small hiccups from crying. I tried to act tough but it obviously won't work out if someone I loved just died on my lap.

The inspector looked at me and sighed.

I looked up at her in anger, "Is *that* enough detail for you?"

"Wait- you're friends.." she said.

"What?" I shrugged.

"You said you two were going to meet up with them.."

I nodded, "They never showed up."

"Why didn't they?"

"Don't know, throughout May, Mina hung out with me the most, the rest of the group were acting like douches to her."

"Why is that?"

"I don't know, I don't think they don't genuinely hated her or anything, I think they were just annoyed at her for some reason."

She sighed, "Are your parents home?"

I froze for a second and gulped. My parents are in London. They wouldn't care less if I called about this. They haven't heard from me in years.

I came over here years ago to live with my sister. She's a freshman in college. That means I basically live alone in my house.

"Erm- I live with my sister. She's a freshman in college but she does school online."

I lied. She's far up north in Boston.

"I'm turning 18 soon." I said.

I lied, again, I turned 17 three months ago.

"We got the results from the autopsy and-" the inspector said.

"What?" I shrugged.

"You knew her well, correct?" she asked, "Did you know she was pregnant?"

I scoffed, "*Yeah* I figured, I started to notice something about it weeks before she died."

"Were you two *distant* or *close?* How would you describe your relationship with her?"

"We *were* complicated. We weren't exactly perfect." I explained, "But that doesn't mean anything. I mean, who do you think *the father* was?"

She widened her eyes.

2 HOURS LATER

I walked out of the interrogation room and immediately called my sister. I walked out of the police station and she picked up. I paused.

"Maddie, I need you to get back to Maryland right now." I told her sternly.

There was another pause.

"So...no hello?" she said cheerfully.

"Maddie! It's serious."

"Okay bud, what happened."

"...Mina's dead. The police think it's me. And now they're asking about Mum and Dad and I don't know what the police will do when they realize I'm a minor living alone."

"I mean you're 17, it can't be that bad. But, woah- bloody hell, slow down, what do you mean Mina's dead?"

2
the 7 suspects
[JUNE 8, 2019]

"Damn, I can't believe she's gone." Jules sighed, "Come on Eden, we got to get ready for the funeral."

I've been staying at Jules' house for a week waiting for my sister to come back from Boston. I also wanted to stay in Mina's bedroom because I feel like that's all I have left of her.

Jules' house was huge. Dark interior design, perfect for parties, and straight on top of a mountain. He lived on the extremely rich side of the neighbourhood.

I looked up at Jules, he had a black suit on with a black tie. I didn't have any fancy suits at home, he let me borrow one of his suits but it was a little loose on me. I was skinnier and he was more fit.

"Bloody hell." I judged.

"What?!" he whined.

"You've been living with Mina for how long now?"

"6.. years?"

"How would you not know?"

"Not know what?"

I sighed angrily and stepped out of the room. I went to go get my clothes for the funeral. I put them on quickly while trying not to cry. I went over to the mirror to adjust my tie.

Jules walked up to me slowly and put his hand on my right shoulder. He looked roughed up, he hasn't slept well ever since that night. His blue eyes looked tired. They used to be full of joy.

"Dark--emerald-green--tie?" he said slowly.

"It was her favourite colour, Jules." I snapped.

"*What?* I thought it was purple!"

I sighed. It's not his fault. He has a brain of a chipmunk. Humour is his coping mechanism to everything. Although, no one understands his humour.

"It was green, brown, and black. Now go change your tie." I told him.

"Why?"

"Didn't she tell you this? She said to wear black and a hint of a colour to represent loved ones before she died. We all have a colour of our own to represent us but, we wear *each other's* colours. Not our own."

Mina was extra. She did this type of stuff to see if people actually cared about her.

"What's your colour?" Jules asked me.

"Purple. Mina's was neon green."

"Did she say what colour I represented?"

"No. I don't know why though."

I finished adjusting my tie and went to put on my shoes. Jules took a deep breath and brushed his hands through his light brown hair slowly.

We arrived at the funeral home. Mina's casket was made out of light birch wood. She was wearing a green silk dress that fit her perfectly. Her hair was dyed a light blonde, she had light tan skin and had a toned mean face. Her eyebrows were dark and arched and it made her look intimidating. She had an eyebrow slit right on her left eyebrow.

Mina was wearing winged eyeliner and a small silver hoop earring on her left ear. It was her signature thing.

I stood upon the casket looking at her. I tried not to cry. There was a red apple on the bottom left corner of the casket. She told me to put one there years ago. It was for a fictional character she looked up to.

I turned to my left and saw all the flowers people sent her. They were all red and black roses. She loved those. I turned to my right and saw her picture on the stand. Everything reminded me of her. It was eating me up inside.

"What is she doing here?! Mina hated you." someone yelled.

I turned around. It was Michael Cooper, he wanted everyone to call him Miles. He was in a black suit with a pastel yellow tie. He was taller than me, around 6'1. He had dark brown hair and he was slim, a little tan, and in-shape. He was yelling at someone down the aisle near the entrance.

"What?? I just want to pay my respects!" the girl protested.

"You didn't even respect her when she was alive, Evelyn," he snapped, "and you're not even wearing black!"

I walked over to him. He turned to me and his dark blue round eyes were ice cold. He had eye-bags and looked angry. Really angry, Miles never gets angry.

"What's going on?" I asked.

Miles huffed and motioned his head towards Evelyn.

Evelyn was tall and skinny. She had a body-figure like those swimsuit models, the only difference was her height. She was 5'6. Her grey eyes showed no emotion and her light blonde hair was up in a bun. It didn't seem like she cared about Mina. Her facial expression gave it away.

She stood there awkwardly caressing her opposite elbow.

"What are you waiting for? Get out!" Miles shouted.

I flinched lightly, Miles never shouts like that. I looked over at Evelyn. It was true. She rarely talked about Mina and when she did, it was never in a good way.

"I- I- never did *anything* to Mina." she said softly.

Miles scoffed.

"Didn't you tell her to go eat a dog *a week* before she died?" he snapped.

"What?!" I gasped.

"Oh? She didn't tell you?"

He was about to break down and cry. His voice started breaking up and his frozen eyes started melting.

"She would humiliate Mina every chance she could. She's only here to do it one last time." he explained gently, "Riah told me about it."

Riah was his girlfriend, they've been dating since 7th grade.

I started firing up. I didn't want to get involved that much but I was on Miles' side. I didn't want to say much because I knew I'd go too far. I wanted Evelyn out as much as he wanted. Everyone did. She clearly wasn't welcome.

I sighed.

"Evelyn, get out." I said softly.

She scoffed and walked out slowly.

"Fucking bitch." I whispered.

Miles inhaled sharply and grabbed my shoulder.

"C'mon, let's go sit down." he whispered.

We walked down the aisle of chairs and sat in the first row.

Mina didn't have a family that was blood related. Jules' family adopted her from Vietnam when she was twelve. She already knew how to speak English when she moved.

The first row on the left was Jules, his parents, and Lily, his blood-related sister. Lily was older and had an attitude. She wasn't fond of Mina, but that doesn't mean she hated her.

I went and sat down on the first row on the right. A blonde girl trotted over to me quietly. I turned and flinched cause I thought it was Evelyn again. She smiled softly.

"It's Emily. Evelyn's less *hostile* twin." she explained.

They did look pretty similar. In fact they looked exactly the same, only Emily's hair was longer and lighter. You could easily tell who is who from their personalities. She had a tight black dress on and a black bucket hat. Her hand-bag and accessories were in white.

"I'm sorry for what happened." she said softly, "I can't imagine how hard this must be."

I looked up at her. Her eyes were different from Evelyn's, they were like my eyes but had more of a grey tint to it. Her eyes showed emotion unlike Evelyn's, her eyes showed sorrow and sympathy.

She patted my shoulder softly and walked away promptly. She went to the fourth row behind me and sat down quietly. Emily used to be Mina's friend back in 8th grade. Ever since Evelyn hurt both of them, they sort of *grew apart.* They tried reuniting once and a while. They were there for each other when they truly needed it.

Miles moved quickly and sat on my right.

"Why'd you move?" I whispered.

"I don't want to be near Jules," he answered.

I raised an eyebrow.

"Why not?"

"I don't know. He gives me a bad vibe."

"He's on the other side of the alsie!"

"But *still!*"

I scoffed and moved down a seat. I didn't know what that was about. Maybe they just had something going on. I looked over at Jules, he was rubbing his eyes with one hand and taking shaky deep breaths.

Miles moved down a seat and we both looked forward to get a good look at Jules. Jules glanced over at us and noticed the clueless look on our faces.

"What?" he snapped quietly.

I didn't even notice the look we gave him. Jules glanced over at Miles. Miles raised an eyebrow as Jules rolled her eyes and glanced forward again.

"He's a bitch." Miles whispered.

"What happened between you tw-"

"What did you just call me?" Jules asked loudly as he turned completely over to Miles and I.

Miles widened his eyes and smiled lightly. He leaned forward with a cheeky grin.

"Oh I called you a bitch." he grinned.

The annoyance started caving in. I blinked slowly and took a deep breath. Miles and Jules gave each other the same look, the *"Can we not do this right now?"* look.

Even though Miles was known to have his priorities straight he couldn't help but break through once and a while.

A blonde girl walked over quietly. She sat down next to him and laid her head on his shoulder and sniffled softly.

"Hey Riah." I sighed.

She had converses on, they were a light gentle green and it covered her ankles. Her shoulder-length blonde hair was straightened and silky. She had high-waisted black baggy jeans and a t-shirt on. She wore a red zip-up jacket over it.

Riah was 5'6. Her grey eyes were glistening and sore from crying. She looked tired. I don't blame her. Hours of interrogation, crying, no sleep, we all went through it too.

Kai and Parker walked over. They're not the type to wear dresses either.

Kai was wearing black overalls with a dark grey t-shirt underneath. Her curly dark brown hair was up in two dutch braids and she had black stud earrings on. Her glasses were bold blue and squared, the glass was tinted a very light and faint pink. Her sneakers were a little roughed up. They were dark grey and looked like it was bought years ago.

    Kai was around 5'9. She's usually hyper and energetic. This time she was calm and tired. Her green eyes described her feelings too. She was sitting down next to Riah nervously while bouncing her right leg up and down. She was fidgeting with her fingers while looking down trying not to look at Mina and cry.

    Parker was wearing all black. Ripped jeans, a comfy sweater, converse, and a beanie. The only colour shown was her beanie and jewelry. They were neon green.

    Parker was around 5'8. She had strokes of pink, purple, and dark blue in her blonde curly hair. She had an eyebrow slit just like Mina but it was on her right eyebrow. Her green eyes looked like she was hurting really bad, worse than how she was before.

    All three of the girls' attires weren't what people would picture wearing to a friend's funeral. It wasn't their fault. None of their wardrobes had fancy dresses.

    It was time for the speeches.

    Jules went up first for his speech. I can't say he wasn't a salty person. He was still confused on why he didn't have a colour. I mean, he was her brother, why wouldn't he have a colour?

Jules stood upon the podium staring at the index cards he wrote the night before. Jules had a bad memory. Although he usually remembers the unimportant details.

"Mina was- uhm-" he paused while looking up from his cards.

He inhaled sharply and continued his speech.

After a few minutes it was my turn. I stood up promptly and stood behind the podium silently. I cleared my throat and thanked everyone for coming.

"So erm- I was Mina's...um...*boyfriend*, Eden." I said.

I looked at the crowd and sighed. I heard someone murmur.

"He was the last person to be seen with her." they gasped quietly.

I tried to ignore it and continue my speech.

"Thank you everyone who followed the dress code, although I think Mina wouldn't have minded if you forgot. Some of you were wondering what colours represented who. *Neon green* for me, *red* for Miles, *pastel yellow* for Riah, *neon orange* for Kai, *royal blue* for Parker," I said.

I continued explaining the colours as normal while trying not to sob in front of everyone. I was shaken up because that night kept replaying in my head.

I told them how confusing I could be and how Mina would spend hours trying to figure me out. She'd text me for hours every night because that's when she'd think I'd open up and show my true colours.

I told them how much she loved the spanish TV-shows she always talked about. I told them funny stories about when she made me do reckless things with her and how ruthless she was.

Eventually my speech was done and half of the crowd was crying and the other half was trying not to cry. I wasn't sure if they were being genuine or just putting on a show. I've heard of everyone who attended the funeral. Mina told me her opinion of them.

I went and sat down. It was Miles' turn.

He stood up slowly and went to the podium. He rested his hands on each side of it and bent his head down to hide his face. He took a deep breath then stood up straight.

The whole group hasn't been sleeping. We all looked roughed up but Miles... Miles looked the worse. His face was pale and his eyes were showing crazy emotions. His eye bags showed he hadn't slept in days. His hands were shaky and his shoulders were tense. He looked like he was about to explode and we wouldn't know if it would be tears or aggression.

He stood there silently as the rest of the crowd waited for him to speak up. He looked up at me and inhaled sharply. He looked back down again.

"I- I'm sorry, I c-can't do this right now," he said quickly.

By now tears were streaming down his face and his heart was racing. He walked out of the room and into the hallway of the funeral home.

Riah was about to stand up and go comfort him but Kai grabbed her shoulder before she could move. They exchanged a look. Riah nodded and looked over at me. She motioned her head over to the hallway then stood up and headed over to the podium. I stood up and walked into the hallway.

It was beautiful. There were chandeliers above me and the walls were painted a faint blue. There was another room on my left and I saw the back entrance with a small coffee table next to it. There was a flight of stairs on my right. The wood was old and chipped and the carpet was stained.

I walked forward through the hallway to find Miles. He was sitting on the floor with his legs crossed. His back was leaning against the stairs and his head was in his hands.

"Miles?" I whispered.

He inhaled sharply and wiped his tears casually. He stood up quickly and brushed off the dust off his shoulder.

"Yeah?" he coughed.

"You okay? Don't say you're fine because we both know you aren't."

"Why didn't you carry her?" he asked.

I froze. I took a deep breath and went over to him slowly.

"Why didn't you carry her dammit!" he sobbed.

He slammed his hand on the wall on his left and I flinched. He started crying and crying as he used his right hand to cover his face.

"What are-"

"You *know* what I'm talking about man.." he cried, "You could've carried her! You could've picked her up and ran! The *police* could've found you guys quicker and *she* could've had a chance to live dude!"

I felt bad because he didn't know. He didn't know the whole story yet.

"The murderer tried hitting me too, Miles. I also didn't want to tear the wounds."

He gasped softly, "Shoot, did you tell the inspector?"

"Yeah. I couldn't pick Mina up. We crawled into the field to hide away."

He took a deep breath.

"Sorry Eden, all of this is driving me crazy."

We both sat down on the floor together. I gave him a few minutes to calm down.

"It's okay. Let's go back in." I said softly.

I put my hand on his shoulder and we went back into the viewing room.

We sat down and by then it was Kai's turn to talk but a duo stopped her.

They were in leather jackets and fancy shoes. They tapped Kai's shoulder gently and she jumped. She shrugged her shoulders then trotted back to her seat awkwardly. The pair stood behind the podium together.

"Sorry for interrupting." one of them announced.

The other cleared his throat.

"If your name is... Eden.. Brooks, Emily... *Clarins*, Zariah Jones, Michael Cooper, Karina Murphy, Parker Smith, or Julian Willow, come meet us in the hallway we need to talk." he said sternly.

All our heads lifted up slowly in confusion. We all stood up and went into the hallway. Jules told

Lily to make a speech in the meantime as he stood up.

We stepped into the hallway and the two looked at all of us carefully.

"I'm Detective Maxwell Clarins, you all can call me Detective Max," he said as he showed us our badge.

Clarins?!

"and I'm Detective Toby Lenz!" the other one said.

He was patting his pockets to find his badge and show us. He was full of energy but tense at the same time. We all stood in a circle watching him awkwardly trying to find it.

"It's on the floor." Miles said.

"Huh?"

"Y-You dropped it on the floor.."

Detective Toby turned around.

"Ah! Thank you!"

He showed us and put it in his back pocket promptly.

Max looked tough and intimidating. He looked young as well, maybe late 20s. He was tan and had charming brown eyes. His hair was straight and was a dark cherry brown. It looked like bangs going down to his ears. He was wearing blue jeans and a button up shirt. He had a brown leather jacket over it with pens, a notepad, and his badge in the pockets.

Toby looked energetic and friendly. He looked young, maybe early 30s but he acted like the type that tried to be *cool* for the teens and to be honest his act worked. His black hair was styled with gel and he had a smile on his face. His blue eyes seemed full of energy. He looked like a kid who just drank three cups of coffee but tried to hide it.

The inspector walked into the room as well.

"I'm Inspector Alex, most of you have already met me." she said.

She was a green-eyed ginger with freckles. She had a grey suit on and looked fancy. Her hair was in a low pony-tail with a few strands left out on the sides. She was calm. She didn't look intimidating like Max did. She looked welcoming and caring.

"We need to talk to all of you." Max announced.

"You couldn't find a better time to do this?" I asked.

"Yeah, why do this in the middle of her funeral?" Parker said.

Max huffed and looked over at Toby. Toby just shrugged his shoulders and looked over at Alex. Alex looked at both of them in confusion.

Our group was pretty quiet unless we were all in the same room. We were all troublemakers only when we're together, that's why you never catch any of us alone. We were good at minding our own business. Our opinions usually grew in our heads because we all had our own problems. But, since this case involved each and every one of us, the more we talk, the faster this ends.

It was good to ask questions.

"We found the murder weapon. A bow and arrow." Max explained.

"Wow. That's new!" I said sarcastically.

I looked over at Miles. He was standing there swaying side to side, brushing his hand through his hair while analyzing the trio. He looked a bit annoyed. Riah was trying to listen while biting her nails without zoning out into space. Jules was still waiting for their point to come across. Kai was fidgeting nervously with her fingers. Parker looked over at her and nudged her shoulder.

"Dad, why did you bring us here?" Emily asked.

"Dad??!!" we all gasped.

"Yeah, Detective Max is my Dad." she said, "Well, my *Step*-dad."

We all looked at each other and shrugged. Kai hesitated a little.

39

"H-How do we know it was a murder?" Kai asked, "What if it was an accident?"

We all looked over at her.

"Well- no one would go shooting bows towards a sunflower field for fun." Riah answered.

"Plus, the killer tried hitting both of us." I said.

Kai nodded nervously and let Max continue.

"The bows used to *murder* Mina was a custom made bow. A bow that all *seven* of you had access to." Max explained.

Our facial expressions went from tired and sad to nervous and full of adrenaline.

"So- *one* person in this room is the killer." Jules commented.

"Not necessarily." Alex explained, "You seven are the *main* suspects but the people living with you *could've* done it."

Why are they telling us this?

"It depends on your connections, motives, profiles, alibis." Max continued.

"What were you guys doing with *custom made* bows and arrows anyway?" Toby asked us.

"We made custom made ones for films." Riah answered.

"Films?"

"Yeah it was going to be a summer project. Mina was going to direct them." Riah explained.

It was just a small group project for school at first. Once it ended Mina told us we should continue it because she was going to miss us all spending time together.

"We all planned to act in it so we got arrows to make it more special. Each one of us got a stack of nine arrows and a bow." Riah continued.

Inspector Alex turned to Toby.

"Are they even allowed to do that in the first place?" she whispered, "Don't they need to learn archery first?"

"I don't know," he shrugged.

He turned and looked at us.

"How did you guys even get the arrows?"

"We all have connections." Parker answered, "Friends who have friends that could do anything you can think of."

The arrows were black. There were two neon green stripes at the tip and neon pink feathers. The bow was plain. It was just black with neon green stripes at each end.

"Although," Riah continued, "I don't remember *Emily* joining this project."

We all looked over at Emily and she turned to us and raised an eyebrow. Emily is a gentle yet energetic person. She wouldn't hesitate to stand up for herself. She would have a small attitude even if she didn't intend it.

"Miles didn't tell you?" she pointed.

Miles grunted softly and winced up at the ceiling. He sighed quietly.

"I let her join the films Riah, seriously your grudge against her is stupid." he explained.

She scoffed softly.

"Do you realize who that is? That's Evelyn's sister!" she whispered.

She pointed at all of us and forced a laugh.

"Did you guys agree to this?!" she scoffed.

Technically we *didn't* agree to it, we just didn't want to get involved or start a fight. We were just as pissed as Riah was that Emily was there. We all looked at each other awkwardly and then to the ground. Miles however, looked her dead in the eye.

"Evelyn and Emily are two different people. We'll talk about this later." he said sternly.

Miles was intimidating. Riah was calm and smiley. So I guess you could see how that *talk* worked out.

Parker wanted to change the subject.

"Did you get any fingerprints from the arrows?" Jules asked.

"No, probably not, all of us would be smart enough to wear gloves." Parker interrupted.

We all looked at each other closely. There we were.

The 7 suspects.

Julian Willow, also known as Jules. 68% Irish and 32% European Spanish, tall, blue-eyed, Mina's older brother by a year. Mina got pushed up a grade because of her scores. That's how they were in the same class. Jules could've gotten mad at her for something. Jules holds grudges frequently. Jules also had secrets. Many secrets. Mina could've found them out and planned to tell me. So Jules took the bow and arrow and shot her before she could. Obviously he didn't know if she told me yet since he shot from a far angle. That's why he aimed for me.

Or it could be Michael Cooper. A quarter jew by blood, christian but hasn't been to church since 8th grade, tall, intimidating, blue-eyed. He's been best friends with Mina since he was nine. They were close. They fought often, but they were always *Mina and Miles*. They always found a way to come back to each other but, maybe her liking me hurt him? No. Miles wouldn't. Miles *never* gets jealous. He's strong. He has his priorities straight. Miles didn't have any motive.

Riah Jones. Miles' girlfriend. Italian blood, grey-eyed, bold. She was a quirky and hyper person. She was outgoing and quiet at first, once she warms up to you she'd be the girl who never stops laughing and goofing off. She had trust issues. Really bad trust issues. She was also an overthinker. Riah became Mina's friend when she got with Miles. They've been loyal friends since 7th grade. Riah was a troubled person. Home issues, school issues, mind issues, but she would never pull a stunt like this. She had no motive.

    It could be Parker Smith. A little german, green-eyed, curly, long haired blonde. Parkers' teachers had sky high expectations for her. *The role model.* Funny to assume Parker's perfect and well behaved over her grades. She was obnoxiously funny, only intimidating when she was mad. Nobody knew whether she was serious or not when she joked about death, fights, or even murder. She was a maniac, one time she slipped and told us she and her cousin made specific murder plans for everyone they knew, even us, *even Mina.* She cared about Mina as far as I knew. She was protective of her and would back her up whenever she needed to. She was like an older sister to her but, if she *really* wanted to kill Mina this wouldn't be her plan. She's smarter than that, *she's more creative than that.*

Maybe it was Karina Murphy, Kai for short. A little Irish, green-eyed, curly long dark-haired brunette. She was more laid-back and open minded. She looked like a teen growing up in the 80s. Remember her question about whether it was an accident or not? Maybe it *was* an accident. She always pulled stunts like this. Joking around, pranking, play-fighting, sometimes her clumsiness gets *herself* crippled. It was her way of showing she cared. Although we often forget since she's either hitting the back of our heads or throwing oranges at us. Maybe she shot arrows at us as a prank. Maybe she meant to hit the area beside us to scare us. But when it hit Mina she freaked out. Why wouldn't she run and help us if it was an accident? I don't know. She doesn't have a motive but her being anxious the whole time the detectives were talking made me think. Maybe *I'm* the overthinker. Kai wouldn't do that. She's funny and dumb but she's responsible in her own ways.

Maybe it was Emily Clarins. British blood but carrying an american accent, skinny, grey-eyed blonde. Maybe she did it to prove Evelyn something or maybe *Evelyn* did it. Evelyn had the bigger motive. Overall, if it was either one of the twins, Detective Max could've helped them cover it up. He's their Step-dad.

There's always a chance.

Or maybe it was me. Tall, british, fluffy blonde hair, freckles, and my eyebrows are dark and flawless. I had a matching eyebrow slit with Mina. It was on my left eyebrow. I'm skinny, toned, blue-eyed. Maybe I hated Mina for hanging out with Miles so much. Maybe I suspected something between them.. or maybe I only texted her out of pity so she wouldn't be sad. Maybe the more paragraphs she sent the more I judged her. Maybe our relationship was forced. Maybe when she was so close to me that I could feel her breathing, I took an arrow and sliced it through her heart. Maybe I didn't even need a bow. Maybe I just stabbed her and left her there to bleed.

They all say I'm capable of doing that, right?

But no, that didn't happen.

Mina was smart. She'd never do something with Miles. Never.

I looked around the room. I knew it wasn't me. I was tense because I knew. I knew I was in the same room as the person who killed Mina.

"That means- we can't trust anyone in this room." Miles said, "One of you guys tried to kill Mina and Eden,"

"and it worked, well, *halfway.*" Riah continued.

We all looked at each other nervously. Tensed up and about to explode.

3
the fiesta
`[JULY 7, 2019]`

"Damn." Jules chuckled, "Eden! Where have you been dude?"

We were in a graveyard. It was a cloudy day. A bit foggy.

"I come here everyday." I replied.

I was sitting against the side of Mina's gravestone. I went to her grave to talk to her like she could hear me. I'd tell her about what lame drama she missed.

"How'd you find me?" I asked.

"Riah and Miles figured you'd be here," he said.

He went over and sat in front of me.

"I miss her," he said.

"I do too."

I didn't have the heart to tell him how much I missed her. I knew he was going to make fun of me for it. In reality I'm slowly going crazy but it turns out he didn't need me to tell him.

I reached into my pocket and took out a pack of cigarettes. I opened it and put one in my mouth. Jules widened his eyes and gasped quietly.

"Since when do *you* smoke?" he gasped.

"It helps me calm down." I answered.

We both knew the real reason why I started.

I pulled out a white lighter out of my pocket. I lit the cigarette and inhaled. I leaned my head back and exhaled the smoke out of my system. Jules sighed.

"Y'know, your coping methods are getting worse." Jules said.

"Okay?" I answered.

He shrugged, "I'm just worried about you man."

I looked at him and raised an eyebrow.

"First it was video games all day, then it was intense partying *alone* and falling asleep drunk every night,"

I giggled, "Now *that*, that was fun."

Jules rolled his eyes, "next was just sleeping all day, and now smoking."

I sighed. He was right.

"Not to mention the night it happened," he scoffed.

I widened my eyes, it's been a while we actually talked about that night. The night Mina was murdered.

"You were trapped in your room, blasting music, chugging down bottles of booze while dancing around obnoxiously." Jules explained.

I raised my eyebrows.

"Not to mention you were crying uncontrollably."

I didn't really know what to say to that. Jules tried changing the subject.

"Y'know Marina's hosting a party tonight in her basement. You should come." he said.

I was surprised at first. The first couple of weeks the group has avoided each other all tensed up trying to find out who the murderer was. We were all awkward around each other, sometimes we would almost get into arguments and now we're going to party?

"Do I look like I'm in the mood to party right now?" I asked.

"You love it when you do it in your room every night. Dammit Eden, you keep my whole family up."

"I'm sorry! I'm still waiting for my sister to come back home."

He raised an eyebrow.

"Where is she? It's been a month."

"I don't know, she hasn't been answering my calls."

He nodded and tapped my shoulder.

"Gimme a cigarette."

I chuckled softly, "Since when do *you* smoke?"

He smiled and took one.

"Y'know, Mina wouldn't want to see you like this," he explained as he lit up his cigarette.

"I'm literally doing what she would do everyday."

"But she's *at ease* when she does it. You're doing this because you miss her. Plus, Mina didn't *smoke* cigs, she would only hold lit ones to look cool."

I paused. Mina *did* smoke once and a while, she only did it when she walked alone in streets because she thought it'd make her look tougher. She had a fear of kidnappings. Maybe Jules didn't know.

I decided to confess. I couldn't hold it in anymore. I've been avoiding him, I've been avoiding everyone.

I sighed, "Jules I'm going in circles. Every time I close my eyes I see her. Everytime I go to sleep I dream about that night."

The rush of regret grew inside of my stomach quickly. I knew he was going to say something to make it about himself. It's what he always does.

"I'm going in circles too, Eden! But, *I* have been coping differently." he said with a small cocky tone.

I rolled my eyes. If only he could see what I saw that day.

"We all cope differently, Jules."

"You should really come to the party, Eden. The group has been worrying about you, alright? *I* worry about you."

That sort of caught me off guard.

"Since when does the group worry about me?!" I scoffed.

"Marina pointed it out to them. They know you're clearly not doing okay."

He stood up and looked at my shirt. He raised an eyebrow.

"Heya- is that Mina's flannel?" he asked.

I looked down at my shirt. It was an oversized green flannel with a grey hood and white buttons.

"Yeah, it's Mina's, found it in her closet."

"Why are you wearing it?"

"I don't know."

"Huh-" he replied, "What exactly does she *smell* like?"

I paused to think.

"I don't know, she smells good though." I answered.

He turned around and started walking towards his car.

"Need a ride?"

"Nah, I'm going straight to Marina's."

"Okay dude, I'll see ya at home."

He got into his car and drove away. I stood up and tossed my cigarette. I started walking to Marina's house. It wasn't far away. The walk was peaceful. I blasted alternative rock music on my phone as I walked down the sidewalk to avoid having people talk to me. I winked at random strangers who gave me dirty looks. It amuses me when they give me that confused look afterwards.

I eventually made it to Marina's place. It wasn't big but it was nice. I knocked on the front door and it swung open.

"*HEYYY* DUDE- have we met before?" she said sarcastically.

I scoffed playfully and walked in.

"Damn, you good?" she asked with her eyes wide.

Marina always told me my resting face made me look like an angry lunatic, she said I'd look like a sociopath and extremely intimidating. It's my secret weapon.

    Marina was almost as tall as me, around 5'9. She had round black eyes and red hair. She's been dying it bright bold red since she was 14, surprisingly her hair was still soft and silky. Her eyebrows were dark and perfect and she had a matching eyebrow slit with Parker. It was on her right eyebrow. She's always been like an older sister to me. Marina was spanish. She'd always mumble "¡Joder!" or "¡Mierda!" under her breath when she's frustrated.

    Marina lived with two roommates, Kai and Jordan. Since Marina's 19 and the oldest, she's been the legal owner of the house. All of them have been orphans since birth. When they met each other they figured they could just live on their own together in a small house. They didn't need any contracts or anything, they never fought enough to kick each other out.

    I remember seeing Marina and Jordan at the funeral. They were the ones who wore black ripped jeans and jackets with hints of yellow and orange.

    "Where's Jordan?" I asked.

    Jordan just graduated high school. He was a tall black guy, around 5'11 and calm at most. He'd have outbursts of energy every once in a while. He had brown eyes and black curly hair. He was born in Hawaii but the foster care system dragged him all the way over to the mainland. He loved nothing more than the ocean.

"He's working." she replied as she jumped onto the couch in front of her.

"He got a job?"

"*Yeah!* By the shore- he's a lifeguard." she exclaimed excitingly, "Proud of him."

We live near the coast of Maryland. It's a 15 minute drive if we wanted to go to the beach.

"Cool- where's Kai? Is *she* working?" I asked.

"Nahh she's downstairs hanging up decorations." she explained.

I nodded and looked around. They decorated their house uniquely. Records on the wall, fake vines hanging everywhere, license plates on every wall, they had no adults to tell them no. In each room you could easily tell who decorated who. Kai's rooms had an 80s vibe to it, Marina's rooms were modern, full of black and red interior design and white marble floors, and Jordan's rooms were full of thrifted items and stuff he found on the shore.

"I need to talk to her." I said.

Marina nodded and pointed to the basement door.

"I have to go to work. Someone's gotta pay for all the *booze* we're buying tonight!" she cackled as she walked out.

I went down. It looked like an *ordinary* basement that would be perfect for throwing parties. There were couches, televisions, record players, and marble counters that worked like a snack bar. There was a door leading to the backyard.

Kai was sitting next to the counter taping fairy lights under the edges. I knocked on the fame of the door and she jumped and hit her head.

"Ouch!" she yelped as she bursted into laughter afterwards.

"Oop- erm- sorry." I replied.

I didn't want to stay long. I wanted to go home and get some sleep. I only came here for an explanation.

"Where were you that night, Kai?" I asked.

"What?"

"You never showed up. We were all supposed to meet."

"OH." she said as she stood up, "I was with Parker."

She jumped up over the counter and fell.

"Ouch!" she yelped again.

I chuckled softly and walked towards her. She stood up and grabbed her phone.

"Parker and I snuck out of class and got doped up."

I scoffed playfully, "Why?"

"For fun? It was the last day of school!" she explained.

I meant why didn't she invite me?

She showed me a few video clips she took on her phone. In the videos, they were running around the halls laughing their heads off.

"What time did *it* happen?" she asked.

"Around 2:15."

She nodded and showed me the time the video was recorded.

2:13PM.

"Why were you two a no-show *the whole* night?" I asked again.

"Parker wanted energy drinks so we went to the supermarket to buy a bunch of junk for all of us. By the time we were done shopping we got called into the station." Kai explained.

I knew she was telling the truth. Kai was energetic and lively. She was clumsy and hyper. But when she explained what happened she was calm and serious. She'd usually talk in a higher-pitched voice unintentionally if she was lying. I looked into her eyes for a moment. They were full of trust.

"Alright." I sighed.

We paused for a moment. It was most likely because I barely talked to anyone anymore, not even Marina or Jules. I was a little distant from the whole group, to be honest I've always been.

She shrugged, "Wanna see the lights?"

I nodded. She walked around the counter and towards the door to the backyard. She kneeled down and pressed the button plugged into the outlet.

Poof!

All the edges of each door, each corner of the wall, each edge of the ceiling, and all the areas underneath the counters and cabinets were shining white.

"Bloody hell Kai, how long did this take?"

"I don't know, a few hours?"

"Nice." I said while looking down at my watch.

I didn't feel like making up an excuse so I decided to be straightforward.

"I gotta go home."

She didn't really care.

"We're hosting a party here, you coming tonight?"

"I dunno, we'll see."

I signaled goodbye.

"Wait." Kai said.

I turned around.

"Hm."

"Why do you always do that *thing* when you walk away from someone?" Kai asked.

"Do what?"

"Y'know, *that* thing. That thing where you salute but you *don't?*"

"Huh?"

"You curl your hand and leave the pointer and middle finger up but not completely *stiff and straight.* Only a little curved."

I raised an eyebrow and held up my right hand. I did what she said I *usually* did.

"Then, you salute but your fingers aren't on your forehead. It's near your nose. Then you do a messy salute, a sloppy but neat one. No stiffness but you're also not flopping your hand." Kai explained.

"Huh.. I never noticed." I smiled softly.

I did the saluting thing *again* then I found my way out and walked home. Jules and his family were having dinner in the dining room. I didn't feel like interrupting.

I walked into the room I was staying in. I was looking around the room. I saw frames of photos of

Mina and Jules together, polaroids of her, Riah, and Miles, photos of her, Parker, Miles, Riah, and pictures from her track meets with Parker and Kai. They were all hung around the beige walls. I looked down. It was her old black backpack. I noticed something was sticking out of it, something white.

    I kneeled down and opened the backpack slowly. I knew I shouldn't have snooped but I just had a weird feeling.

    It was an envelope. It had my name written on it.

    I held the envelope in my hands for a few seconds. Moments later I started to hear footsteps coming towards the room. I spun around to try to hear who it was, all I heard was footsteps growing louder. I quickly folded the envelope and slipped it in my pocket. Seconds later the person opened the door as I awkwardly stood up.

    It was Jules.

    "Hey dude- I got an idea," he said.

    He wanted us to share a room. He wanted to move Mina's bed and furniture over so we could watch movies together every night or play video games until our hands became sore.

    "Why?" I asked.

"Well my parents want to turn this room into a guest room since, y'know, no ones really going to *own* it anymore." he explained.

I gave him a look. Erasing Mina already?

"Hey, I didn't agree to it either." he said.

So we did what we had to do. We moved her bed and nightstand over. Each time we went back in and out of her room carrying things I noticed Jules looking back scanning the room. I figured he was trying not to step on any junk that could puncture his feet.

Jules' closet is huge. He let me use half of it when I didn't need to. The room looked a bit wonky, Jules' bedframe was brown and Mina's was black.

I laid down on Mina's bed and looked up at the ceiling. I was exhausted from moving all the furniture across the house.

"It's almost 6:00." Jules said while laying on his.

"So?"

"I'm going to the party, are you *sure* you don't want to go?"

"Yeah, I'm sure."

He nodded and walked out. His room was big but it looked smaller now with two beds almost next to each other. His closet was next to me and the TV was in front.

I sighed and sat up. I took a shower and walked into the closet with a towel wrapped around my waist. I sighed and got dressed. The silence was caving in. All I heard was my thoughts. I even started to hear them in Mina's voice. It sounded just like her. Her voice was deep and soothing, you could fall asleep to it.

Dude, you've been like this for weeks.
They just care about you, appreciate that.
Go to that party! Don't disappoint them.
You're alone now.
All you do is stay in your room all day and cry.
Don't be lazy, you're never lazy.
Go live!
Just move on.
JUST MOVE ON!
The group thinks you're a slump.
They think you're a total bitch.
You should've tried harder.
You should've carried her.

"Just shut up." I murmured quietly to myself. The thoughts stopped.

I sighed and covered my face with my hands for a bit. I paced over to my nightstand quickly to grab my keys. I hopped down the stairs and jumped over the railing near the last few steps. I got into my car. I haven't used it in a while.

I sat in my car alone in silence. I checked the time. *6:45PM.* I started driving.

After a few seconds I started to hear things. I ignored it because I thought it was just my head messing with me.

"Eden!" the person yelled, "EDENNNNNN!!!!!"

I started to slow my car down a little to hear it clearly. The voice was extremely loud and raspy, it was scary.

Silence.

I shook my head and kept driving.

"EDEN!" the person yelled again, "EDEN, STOP THE CARRRR!"

I hit the brakes and got out of my car quickly. I stood and looked over at my right to see who was calling for me.

BAM!

"OUCH!" she screamed as she ran into the streetlight.

"Parker?" I asked.

"Eden, I've been chasing your car for three blocks now."

"I- I'm sorry! I thought my mind was messing with me."

We both got into the car and I continued driving. She rolled her eyes. I was a little startled, Parker and I went way back but we drifted apart.

We haven't had a stable conversation in years. It was awkward.

"Where are *you* going?" she asked.

"Marina's party." I replied, "Are *you* coming?"

"Yeah," she replied.

I drove her to the party and she hopped out of the car. I followed. She dodged the front door and walked past it.

"Wait Parker!" I said, "Where are you going?"

It felt like the old days, we'd go on little adventures knowing damn well we were going to get ourselves into something.

"Around the back!" she yelled as we continued walking.

We finally arrived at the back door that connected to the basement. The music was so loud we could hear a muffled version of it from outside. She swung the door open.

We walked in confidently. We got a few stares and some girls whistled at me.

"Looks like some girls got an eye on you Eden," Parker chuckled as she jumped over the counter on my left.

I continued walking around trying to find someone I recognized.

The basement was crowded with Marina's college friends. Marina lays low, she made a small circle of friends at first, then her friends introduced her to *their* friends. She wasn't popular but people knew her.

People knew her because of her past.

The music was pounding and the colourful lights were flashing in every direction. Seconds later Riah jumped in front of me and I flinched.

"HEY GORGEOUS!" she said cheerfully.

Her eyes were red and she was happier than usual. She was dancing along bubbly with the music.

"Hey Riah." I said, "Hold on,"

I leaned in and looked closer at her eyes, she noticed and jumped up and almost bit me playfully. I flinched and moved back. She purred in a feisty way and continued dancing obnoxiously.

"Are you high?" I asked carefully.

"*Maybeee.*" she said happily.

"Bloody hell Riah, where do you get that stuff?"

"From Marina's spanish college friends!" she danced.

"Does Miles know?"

"Do I know what?" Miles asked as he walked over to us.

He was happier.

"Of course he knows, it's only just this once." she said cheerfully, "I just wanted to try it!"

Miles chuckled and grabbed my shoulder. We both knew it wasn't just this once nor it wasn't her first time either.

"Come on, let's get a drink!" he said.

We went and sat among the tall counters as Riah danced away from us. Kai put red stools at the edge to make the area look more like a snack bar than before. There were blue coolers at the opposite side of the counters. Kai was standing there pouring out drinks while singing along with the music.

"You came!" Kai smiled.

I smirked lightly.

She gave each of us a purple-ish liquid in a red plastic cup. We gulped it down in seconds.

"Hey, give us something stronger!" I told Kai as she gave us the strongest drink she had.

"What's in this?" Miles asked.

Before Kai could answer he interrupted.

"Ahh who cares,"

He gulped it down and slammed the cup on the counter and sighed.

Parker and Jordan walked over to us to grab drinks.

"Hey Parker! Did you see your room yet?" Kai asked.

Miles raised an eyebrow.

"New room?" he asked.

"Yeah, Parker might be moving in." Jordan joined.

"How are you guys gonna handle the bills and Marina's tuition?" I asked.

"Jules." Kai, Jordan, and Parker said at the same time.

Jules was loaded with cash. He wouldn't mind helping them out until Marina gets a proper job.

Miles chuckled and turned to me.

"How are you man, I haven't seen you in *ages.*"

"I don't know. I just feel like total-"

"Hm," he interrupted me, "I know what can help!"

I looked up at him in confusion.

"I know something that's better than *smoking.*"

How does he know I smoke now?

"You need to move on, get some closure, or at least find a way to escape." Miles sighed.

He stood up and motioned his head towards the couches. I stood up and we walked over to my right.

"Who wants to play spin the bottle!" he yelled.

"Oh c'mon! We're not kids anymore dude!" a random college friend yelled.

"Too bad!" Miles laughed as he plopped on the couch.

There were three couches facing each other. On the last end, there was a TV streaming a random spanish TV show. Miles sat on the long couch facing the TV, I sat on the couch on his left. The couch I was sitting on could only fit two people, whilst Miles' couch could fit around five. I looked at the couch in front of me. It was a single couch and one of Marina's friends was sitting there smiling at us.

"What's up dude!" Miles said to him.

He looked up at Miles cluelessly, "Hola."

"*Ahh!* You speak spanish? Oye, ¿quieres jugar a girar la botella con nosotros?"

"Woahh." I mumbled under my breath, "You speak spanish now?"

"Yeah! Mina made me learn it." he laughed.

Parker walked over with drinks, she handed one to the spanish friend and another one for Miles. She looked at me and paused for a moment then asked me if I wanted one. I shook my head no because I didn't finish mine yet. She nodded and sat down next to Miles.

"Uh, no gracias, tengo 22 años," the college friend replied.

"¿Eh? ¿Qué estás haciendo en una fiesta de la escuela secundaria?" Parker asked.

"Huh? You know spanish too??" I exclaimed.

"Yes!" Parker replied.

"¡Sí! Le dije a Marina que sería extraño pero ella insistió en que debería ir." he explained.

Marina walked over to us, "Hola Arón."

She started leaning against Arón's couch while sipping her drink.

Arón was tall, around 6'1. He had short curly dark brown hair and brown eyes. He had a charming big smile and a loud laugh. His voice was deep and soothing. I could listen to him talk for hours even though I could barely understand him.

He's known Mina since he was 19. They were like siblings. I remember seeing him at the funeral. He was wearing a black suit with an emerald tie.

On his left ear he had the same earring as Mina did. Mina's earring was originally his earring. He gave his other earring to her years ago so they could match.

Marina took a glance at me and laughed, "Were you guys all speaking spanish without translating it for Eden?"

"Yeah!" Parker laughed.

She, Marina, and Miles started laughing together. Arón just started laughing along awkwardly.

"Don't worry, I just asked him if he wanted to play *spin the bottle* with us, then he said no thanks because he's 22." Miles explained.

"Then I asked why a 22 year old is at a high school party and he said he thinks it's strange as well but Marina insisted on him coming." Parker continued.

"Oh.." I said.

"¡Oh cállate Arón! ¡Acabas de cumplir 22 en marzo! Además, la mayoría de las personas aquí tienen poco más de 20 años." Marina told Arón.

Parker turned to me, "She just told him to shut up and that he just turned 22 in march. And Plus, most of the people at this party are in their early 20s too."

I nodded and continued listening to their conversation. I *could* recognize a few words they were saying but I wasn't completely fluent like they were.

Parker asked Arón why he didn't look like a frat guy you'd usually picture. He said it's because he's a foreign exchange student and he stuck with the style he had in spain.

Riah came dancing over again. She jumped over the couch I was on and fell and we all laughed with her as her face went bright red. She got up slowly and crawled onto the couch. She sat next to Miles and laid her head on his shoulder. She was so high she couldn't stop smiling.

"Hi Arón!" she smiled.

Arón greeted her and drank his drink.

"Alright! Who wants to spin the bottle? Last chance anyone?" Marina yelled.

"I gotchu!" Jordan said as he jumped over the couch and sat next to me.

I immediately noticed he was a little tense around me. I didn't think much of it at first.

"Hey, where's Emily?" Parker asked us.

"She's at work getting bail money." Miles replied as he zoned off into space.

"*Bail* money?" I asked.

"*Yeah...* hold on, do you have *any* idea what happened?" Parker asked me with concern.

"No?"

"She's been trying to get bail money for Evelyn."

"Evelyn got arrested!??"

My eyes widened and my voice got a little higher.

"Yeah?" she said with an attitude.

71

Riah chuckled, "The police arrested her for killing Mina."

"WHAT?!" I shouted.

Arón and Marina flinched.

"Why haven't I heard about it?" I asked.

"I don't know, prolly cause you sleep in your room all day and never answer texts." Parker scoffed.

"Shut up Parker, you never have the energy to answer texts either." Riah giggled as Parker threw a pillow at her.

"Yeah apparently Evelyn couldn't *tell the police* where she was and *her fingerprints* were found on Emily's bow and arrows. Plus, she had the biggest motive." Miles explained, "She refused to take the polygraph test too."

I took a few seconds to process it.

Evelyn? Evelyn killed Mina. Shit I thought they were targeting me.

Seconds later Emily came pacing over to us all stressed out and out of breath. She was wearing a maroon red fast food center uniform. It was a button up t-shirt and leggings with black borders. She took off her cap and her ponytail was slick but messy and frizzy.

"I'm here, I'm here!" she sighs.

"Damn, you really bust your ass everyday do ya?" Jordan chuckled.

She rolled her eyes and sat down next to Parker. She looked over at me as she saw my worried and shocked expression.

"I'm guessing you guys told him?" she asked softly.

We all nodded. Well, except Arón, he was watching the TV sipping his drink slowly.

Jules walked over to us confidently, "So I heard we're playing spin the bottle."

He set down a light wooden plate on the coffee table and placed an empty wine bottle on it.

I started to take a sip of my drink, it was sugary, too sugary. It was the sweetest thing you can imagine. It was strong too, maybe too strong. I figured Miles drank a few of these to get used to it.

I decided to drink the whole thing quickly. It affected me in a matter of seconds and I could rarely remember anything. I wasn't lightweight, I never was. I figured the reason why the drink affected me quickly was because I was already drinking before the party.

Jules went and sat next to Emily and wrapped his arm around her.

"Alright, let's start!" he chuckled, "Kai playing?"

"Nah, she's handing out drinks for the night." Miles answered.

Jules spun the bottle. It landed on Riah. She giggled.

"You wish." Riah scoffed playfully, "I'll pass."

She sat up and grabbed a cup from the coffee table, "Who's drink is this?"

Miles shrugged.

"Ahh, who cares," she laughed as she gulped the whole drink down.

She spun the bottle. It landed on Miles. They laughed at their luck.

Next round.

Marina spun the bottle. It landed on Arón. They only laughed at each other.

Next round.

Parker spun the bottle. It landed on Emily. They laughed. It was just a friendly peck.

They were just messing around.

"What's the harm?" Emily snickered.

Next round.

Jordan spun the bottle. It landed on Riah. She paused for a moment.

"Aren't you 18?" she asked.

She passed and finished her drink.

By now I was as drunk as everyone else was. As we played the game cups and cups were gulped down. I'm not even sure if the story I'm telling you now was real. Maybe it was just in my head.

Next round.

Miles spun the bottle. It landed on Marina.

"No. Way." Marina said as her eyes widened. She chugged her drink at the speed of light.

Riah and Miles giggled at each other.

Next round.

It was my turn.

I spun the bottle. My eyes focused on it and I started hallucinating again. By the time it stopped spinning it landed on-

"Emily." Parker gasped.

"At least it's not Ev-" Jules said.

"Shush!" Riah interrupted.

"I mean they'd make a good couple!" Jules laughed, "Although Mina would probably cry. She would've never gotten over that."

"Shut up Jules." Miles scoffed.

"Yeah honestly it's not funny." Riah said.

Jules kept throwing remarks like that. *Over and over again.* It's not the first time something like this has happened but it still pisses me off.

I quickly sat up and picked up a random drink on the coffee table.

"Here Jules, shut up and drink this." I sighed as I shoved the cup into his mouth.

75

His eyes were widened, caught off guard because of how sweet the drink was. I knew if I spoke up and defended Mina, Jules would've just laughed it off because of how drunk he was. I just decided to forget about it.

Emily and I started looking at each other awkwardly. We didn't say a word. There was tension but I'm not sure what type of tension. I don't think I have an answer.

Jordan and Marina started chuckling awkwardly under their breath.

"Oye, OYE, tienes que ver esto." Marina said to Arón.

She was just telling him to witness the tense situation. We had an audience watching every move.

Jordan started shifting off the couch and Emily looked at him confusingly. He motioned his head towards the couch and she slowly shifted over and sat next to me awkwardly.

We didn't break eye contact. We were so quiet the only thing that came out of us were heavy breaths. The rest of the group was dead silent as well, the only sounds around us was the music. It was *those* types of love songs.

Great timing, am I right?

By now the drinks got to our heads. I kept seeing Mina in the room. One second she's next to Arón trying not to laugh at us then the next second she's the one next to me. I kept hearing her voice too. She kept telling me what Miles told me earlier.
"You need to move on, get some closure." she echoed.
I don't remember much during *this* time frame. I remembered partying hard for the next few hours. Jumping on tables, dancing obnoxiously and shouting, spilling drinks. Miles sneaking up behind Kai, swooping her up off the ground carrying her like a baby and swinging her back and forth extremely aggressively. He did so fast and repetitively to the point where both of their laughter could make her throw up. Riah rolling around, Emily swinging her hair around, Parker being soft and having Jordan carry her back to her room safely, Marina's college friends trying to flirt with me, and laughing our heads off acting like everything was okay.
But it wasn't, nothing was okay.
Mina's voice kept echoing in my head. I remember standing on the counters mumbling gibberish with a drink in my hand, seconds later I blacked out. Noise started to fade away and I couldn't see anything.

6 HOURS LATER

What time is it? 1:00AM? Oh crap! It's 4:00AM.
I woke up in Jordan's room with his sheets covering me. It was almost silent in the house, the music wasn't playing anymore. Most of Marina's friends have left, I just assumed I passed out and Jordan let me stay in his room for the night.

I had a weird taste in my mouth. My head was pounding and I felt insanely dizzy. My body felt heavy and warm. Especially my chest. My ears were ringing and I could only hear faint conversations from the basement. I tried to sit up but I realized-

Bloody hell.

There she was. Emily, right next to me her head rested on my chest and her arms wrapped around me. She was sound asleep. She was so close to me I could hear her heartbeat and her slight snores.

I laid there staring at her cluelessly trying to process everything, when I realized my arms were wrapped around her I gasped quietly and quickly let go.

OH WHAT?????

I moved her off of me gently and laid a blanket on top of her shoulders. I got off the bed and almost fell. My head felt like someone just smashed a load of bricks on it.

I got dressed quickly. I wanted to get out of the house. I almost fell trying to put my pants on. I panicked. I felt horrible. I slipped on my jeans then I realized Emily was wearing my t-shirt. I ran into Jordan's closet and snatched a random tee trying not to wake Emily up. I had an urge. My stomach was doing cartwheels.

I ran into the bathroom and hovered my head over the toilet. I threw up. I don't remember how many drinks I had. I figured I kept drinking more and more during the spin the bottle rounds.

I ran out of the room and ran back down into the basement. It was a mess down there.

I saw Marina and Arón holding trash bags and picking up empty bottles and cups. Jordan was awake too, he was sweeping the floor neatly.

Arón was telling them a funny story.

"Tenía un amigo llamado Val, una vez estaba tan drogado que se miró en el espejo y dijo ¡Oi! ¡Te pareces a mi!" he laughed.

```
Translation: I had a friend named
Val, one time he got so high, he
looked into the mirror and said: oi!
You look like me!
```

Marina laughed with him as she picked up a couple more cups.

"Hola." I said nervously.

I saw a fresh bottle of booze sitting on the counter near the snack bar.

"Mind if I take this?" I asked.

"I don't care." Marina answered as I ran out the back door with the booze in my right hand.

I ran and I ran. I didn't know where I was running. I didn't know where I was going. I just remember running for what seemed like an eternity.

I felt like crying. I didn't know what I just did. I felt like crap before the party and now I feel ten times worse. I felt like melting. I felt the tears stream down my face as I ran.

I stopped running. By now I've been running for about 15 minutes. I looked up at the sky. The sky was a deep dark blue and the stars were extra blinding that night. The air was clear and fresh. I was standing next to the railing of a small light stone bridge. The road was extra busy that night. I needed to throw up again. I leaned over the edge and let it out. I heard the cars honk and the drivers yelling as my vomit splattered onto their windows.

I felt like the world was caving in on me. I lifted the bottle of booze and chugged it down and threw the empty bottle on the ground.

Mina's dead and I think I just hooked up with her ex best friend. Who even does that? Not a good person! I brushed my hands through my hair in frustration.

I wanted to jump. I couldn't take it anymore.

Ah jeez what are you thinking Eden.

Are you mad?

"EDEN!" someone yelled.

I turned around quickly before my thoughts could get the best of me.

"Miles?" I mumbled.

He drove my car over to me and rolled down the passenger side's window.

"Get in before you do something stupid." he scoffed playfully.

I got in and slammed the door. I leaned against the window and rested my head in my hand.

"How'd you find me?" I asked, "And how'd you get my car keys?"

"You had your location on and you dropped your keys in Jordan's room."

"My phone's *dead.*"

"I mean your smart watch, stupid." he chuckled, "Do you want me to drive you home?"

"No, can I stay at your place? Jules is the last person I want to see right now." I replied.

"Yeah.. I get *that*. Aren't Emily and... Jules dating?" he asked.

"No. There were a few flings between them but no, they don't consider themselves boyfriend and girlfriend." I answered.

Miles started driving, "You drank a lot tonight. Do you even remember anything?"

"No."

"*HA!* Well, what *do* you remember?"

"I blacked out and woke up in Jordan's room."

"And?"

"Emily was next to me."

"HOLY-" he shouted as he hit the brakes.

I flinched and lifted my head up.

"You screwed *Emily* Clarins??!!" he gasped obnoxiously.

I scoffed as I watched his jaw drop down to his feet.

"Don't be stupid." I told him, "That probably never happened."

Y'know I hate lying but at least it made me feel better.

Even though I hate it, somehow I'm always good at it.

"What do *you* remember?" I asked.

"Well it was your turn to spin the bottle and it landed on Emily. Then, there was tension then you guys started making out like crazy." he giggled.

"Very funny Miles. That definitely DID NOT happen." I told him.

"I'm just joking, I don't remember anything either. You gotta ask Kai, she was the only one who didn't drink tonight. She'll remember what happened."

"I'd rather not figure it out."

4
the letter
[JULY 8, 2019]

"I- uh- oh dang that's a lot of-" Miles gasped, "Hey, hey, you okay?"

"Do I *look* okay?" I winced.

I spent the night hugging the toilet. Miles figured I've been throwing up because of the drinks but I knew what I did. I was sick to my stomach because of guilt. I sat up and wiped my mouth with a tissue. I thought I was done. I wasn't. I threw up again.

"Ah jeez- do you need any medication?" he asked.

MARCH 30, 2016

We were sitting at a small diner round the corner. The walls and tiles were a dark burgundy, the tables were a polished dark oak, the light sources were from dull warm white lamps covered in cobwebs scattered across the room. I was resting my head on my hand. I had that look on my face. He could tell.

"What's wrong, Eden? You're not upset because of what happened, right?"

"No it's not that, I just have a migraine."

"Hm." he replied as I watched him stand up.

He was classy and elegant. He talked slowly and proudly, walked with pride, and he wanted to make a good impression. I figured that's why he always wore suits and bow-ties. He came back to the table with a small zip-block bag filled with ice.

He kneeled down next to me. He was tall. 5'11. When he kneeled he looked like he was my height. I turned to him.

He gently placed the bag of ice on my forehead.

"Better?" he asked.

"Yeah, thank you." I said as I gently grabbed the bag from him. He stood up and sat down in front of me.

"Now let me tell you something," he smiled.

I looked up with the ice bag resting against my forehead.

"If it doesn't hurt more than a gunshot, *don't* complain, *don't* whine. You don't even need to acknowledge it sometimes." he explained, "This works for mental stuff too, obviously if it really hurts you should treat it but, don't waste time. *Time is money.*"

"Why are you telling *me* this?" I asked softly.

"Because *you*, little one, you speak your mind. You have a thought and you say it right away. I noticed that about you." he smiled, "But, if you follow my advice, it'll make you seem stronger."

JULY 8, 2019

"No, I'll be fine." I answered Miles.

Miles nodded and went to get me a water bottle. By now I basically threw up everything in my stomach. I was starving. I walked into Miles' room and sat down.

I pulled out the letter from my pocket. It was still folded up. I opened it carefully trying to prepare for what I was about to see.

```
hey pretty boy, it's alright.
i understand, so don't worry 'bout
it.
you can move on. never stop fighting.
te quiero, eden, no matter what.
-mina<3
```

I didn't know how to react. Millions of thoughts rushed through my head at once. Miles walked in with a water bottle. He handed it to me and sat at the end of the bed. I shifted over next to him.

"Hey dude, what's that?" he asked.

I showed him the letter. He started chuckling.

"Pretty boy?" he scoffed.

He quickly skimmed the whole letter in his head.

"Whoa." he mumbled, "Where'd you find this?"

"In Mina's backpack."

"Holy- do you know what this means??"

I shrugged. I was still trying to process it. Nowadays my head hasn't been working as fast as I want it to.

"What if... what if she knew she was going to die?" I asked.

Miles scoffed, "¿Qué dices?"

"I mean, before she died we were sitting at the hill watching the sunset, but she spoke weirdly."

"Well she's always weird."

"Well I mean *weirder*." I explained, "She spoke as if she knew what was going to happen. She kept recapping her favourite memories and saying how much she'll miss this. I didn't notice it was weird until now."

"Damn-" Miles whispered.
"Well.. I don't know."
Maybe I'm just overthinking it.
Mina wouldn't write something like this. Maybe it was forged.
Miles rarely talks about Mina too, maybe he was guilty of something.
"I mean c'mon Eden! *Maybe* you're right! This is Mina we're talking about. She wouldn't write you a corny letter like this for fun! She doesn't open up like that." he exclaimed.
"Well why wouldn't she?"
"Cause she's *Mina!* She wouldn't write something like this to please you. She'd think it's too *sappy* and that you'd judge her. She'd probably overthink it like crazy then never end up sending the note! Like saying *you can move on* but *never stop fighting?* She knew!"
Miles knew Mina would've felt that way, not because she told him, but because he knew her. He read her like a book.
I sighed. I folded the letter back up and slipped it in my pocket.
"Are you going to tell the inspector?" he asked me.
"Yeah, yeah I will. Eventually."
I needed to ask him something.

"Where were you that night?" I asked.

"What?" he gasped.

"Where were you? You never showed up."

"I- uh- I-" he panicked softly.

He paused for a second.

"I was at school."

"No shit, but you never showed up to the field." I replied.

He stopped pacing slowly. He brushed his hand through his hair and sighed.

"I can't tell you."

"What?"

"I just can't. Ok? But, *I* didn't kill her and you know that."

I stood up slowly.

"Well if you didn't kill her then why can't you tell me?"

He covered his eyes and grunted.

"Look- I- I- just *can't* okay? I can't tell you."

I could tell he was hiding something. Something big.

Miles usually told me everything. Everything about him and Riah and his issues. This is one of the first times he has hid something from me. I could tell he regretted it deeply.

"It's a *simple* question." I said sternly, "Do I sound like I'm speaking chinese?"

He sighed again and started tearing up slightly. He blinked them away.

"Or do I have to ask you in spanish?" I continued.

"Look! It's none of your business anyway! I *didn't* kill her."

We started fighting. It wasn't a fist fight but it wasn't just those small fights boys usually get into either. It got pretty heated. I told him he should just stop trying to save his own ass and tell me where he was. He told me it's nothing small *nor* big enough for me to know and that I should stop acting like a saint. I kept yelling that the more he stuttered and sighed the more I suspected that he killed her. After a while I grabbed my keys and stormed out. I needed to calm down.

I needed an explanation. *The letter.* What if we were right about Mina knowing what was going to happen to her.

I got into my car and pulled out my phone. I looked through my contacts.

Parker Smith
Kai Murphy
Riah Jones
Jules Willow
Miles Cooper
Marina Murillo
Jordan Covey
Emily Clarins

I haven't talked to Jules since that party. I don't know how he's going to react when I tell him I think I hooked up with Emily. He'd probably tease me and joke about it for eternity.

I didn't want to talk to Emily as well and I wouldn't think she'd want to talk to *me either*.

I looked at Parker's name, like I said, Parker and I went way back. I hesitated a little but then I called her. She picked up after a few seconds, I was surprised.

"What!?"

I paused for a moment.

"Heya- do you know which jail Evelyn's being kept at?"

"Erm... well she spent the first two weeks in juvenile *detention-*"

She told me which jail Evelyn was kept at. I thanked her then hung up the phone. I took a deep breath and started driving slowly. When I arrived they let me come in to talk to her. I was mad. I wasn't even sure I was ready to face her.

She was sitting at the opposite end of the glass as I walked in. She looked up at me slowly. Her eyes still didn't show her empathy. If anything her eyes just showed me she wanted to get out and get everything over with.

I swung the chair open and sat down. I looked her dead in the eye showing her I wasn't going to take up any of her bullshit.

"Hey." she said slowly.

"HEY?!" I shouted as she flinched.

She shut her eyes, she looked scared. I couldn't tell if it was because of the situation she was in or because of me, maybe both.

"Waiting to get out of here, right?" I scoffed.

"I- they- they might charge me as an adult." she muttered, "I'm 17 turning 18 next January."

I pulled the letter out of my pocket and slammed it on the table. She opened her eyes and raised an eyebrow cluelessly.

I opened it and she widened her eyes.

"Damn. *Mina Willow* writing a love letter." she chuckled, "I never knew she could be *this* soft."

I rolled my eyes.

"Explain it." I said.

"Explain what?" she replied.

"She knew, didn't she? She knew you were going to kill her."

She slammed her hand on the table. Her knuckles were red and she had small cuts and marks all over her arm.

"I didn't kill her!" she protested.

"Then, *WHY* are you here, huh? Why didn't you tell the police where you were that night? Why were your fingerprints found on Emily's bow and arrows?" I shouted.

She looked down past my eyes and down to the table. Her eyes started fluttering and she gulped.

"Y'know," she gasped softly, "shouting at me isn't going to bring her back."

I scoffed, "I know what you're trying to do."

Evelyn switches back and forth when she tries to act genuine. Her act never works on me.

She paused for a moment. She smiled and looked up at my eyes without budging her head. She looked like a sociopath.

She smirked, "Like *you're* such a saint too, right?"

I raised an eyebrow as she lifted her head up slowly.

"What are you talking about?" I snapped.

She smiled.

"You're *behind the glass* shouting *at me* for *your* dead *girlfriend* but you *still* had a go for my sister yesterday night, right?" she snarled.

I inhaled sharply and gulped. I stared into her eyes as she smiled at me, amused at my reaction. I stood up and slammed the chair in as she giggled at me. I snatched the letter and crushed it into my pocket.

"News flash!" she snickered, "My sister is *also* Mina's *ex* best friend."

I didn't have enough energy to fight with her anymore. I stormed out. I drove around for a while avoiding the urge to crash my car myself. I just drove home afterwards, home, I mean my *actual* home. The one where I used to live with my sister. I took out the house key I haven't used in ages and went inside slowly.

Memories started flowing in as I walked through each room. I walked into my bedroom slowly. My eyes wandered all over the pictures of Mina and I on the walls, items on the tables, clothes and empty bottles of booze scattered along the floors.

I laid down on my bed, thinking. I remembered how Mina would spend the night here every now and then, she was basically my roommate at that point. I remembered how I'd wake up with notifications from her if she wasn't staying the night there. I remembered how much she'd get nervous around me, she couldn't help but smile whenever she spoke to me even though she *hated* me. Once she felt like I was finally letting her in she felt okay. I never knew what she saw in me.

She's gone now.

I remember how I spent the night *it* happened. After being interrogated for hours I went home. I couldn't take it, I gulped down booze while rivers of tears streamed down my face with loud obnoxiously party music playing. After throwing up I wouldn't sleep nor eat the rest of that night. I just cried while trying to hold it in while reading all the texts she sent me wishing I could answer her back.

But when I laid there that day, the same day I fought with Miles and confronted Evelyn. I felt at ease. I felt alone, I *was* alone, but I didn't really care this time.

I decided to call my sister again. I gave up a while ago since every time I called it just switched to her voicemail. I called her and waited.

Hey it's Maddie Brooks. Leave a voicemail. I'll call you back later.

I sighed and waited.

Beep.
"Hey... Mads, it's me again. *Your* brother. *The* brother that has been living on his own... waiting for you to come home. Call me." I sighed.

After I hung up I set my phone down on my nightstand. I ended up dozing off from the silence a few minutes later.

5 HOURS LATER

I woke up. My phone was ringing. I checked the time.

7:23PM

I reached over to my nightstand and grabbed my phone.

19 missed calls from Anna Cooper.

Joanna Cooper, Miles' twin sister. She looked exactly like him but she had hazel eyes instead of blue and she was shorter, 5'7.

I called her back and she picked up, "Hello?"

"Hi Eden, is Miles with you?" she asked.

"No, I haven't talked to him in hours."

She paused, "He said he was going to be with you before he left, it's been hours and he hasn't been picking up my calls."

"He hasn't spoken with me, Anna." I replied.

5
19 hours missing
[JULY 9, 2019]

"*Can't* be true, he isn't dead is he?" Riah asked.

"Psh- no way," Parker replied.

Miles ran away. No one has seen or heard from him since yesterday, *4:00PM.*

"Wait," Kai asked, "How do we know he's not *kidnapped* or *human trafficked?*"

"He left me a note, I found it on my window sill." Riah said gently.

She pulled out the note out of her pocket and unfolded it carefully and showed it to us.

```
hey riah, don't worry about me. i'm
okay.
i just need to disappear for a while.
- miles
```

We were in Marina's basement. Everyone was there except Emily, she was at work. We were sitting on the couches discussing whether we should tell the inspector or not.

"Why do you think he did this?" Parker asked, "Why'd he run?"

Riah sighed and rubbed her forehead.

"I- I think it's my fault." she said.

We all looked over at her in confusion.

"I think he found out what I did."

She stood up from the couch slowly and started pacing back and forth in front of us.

"On May 31st, I didn't show up because I was with Jordan." she explained.

As she was explaining her story Jordan was walking downstairs patting a towel on his neck. Riah stopped pacing.

"We made a mistake." Riah continued as she made eye contact with him.

He slowly stood up taller with his shoulders broad and gulped. He didn't really look sorry, he was just surprised she told them.

We all looked at her wide-eyed.

"That came out of no-where." Parker mumbled.

"Wait, you're pregnant?" Kai gasped.

"What?! No!" Riah scoffed as Kai immediately bursted into quiet laughter.

We all thought Riah and Miles were endgame. They *were* complicated but not as complicated as Mina and I. Riah and Miles still made it through years and years of heartbreak while Mina and I just forced ourselves to work out because we knew we couldn't stay away from each other.

Maybe we were wrong.

Jordan was standing there awkwardly while we studied him.

"Wait," I said, "Maybe it was *my* fault."

"Why? Did you hook up with Jordan too?" Jules giggled.

Marina and Kai snorted but quickly controlled their laughter by covering their mouths tightly.

"Very funny." I scoffed, "I had a fight with Miles before he went missing."

They all stopped laughing completely.

"What was the fight about?" Jules asked.

"He wouldn't tell me where he was that night and I assumed he was hiding something." I explained.

Jules stood up and started walking back and forth slowly.

"Well I mean, *what* if he *was* hiding something?"

"*Obviously!*" Parker scoffed.

"*Guys,* the point is, the fight got pretty heated and his excuse for not showing up might be tiny anyway." I explained.

They all stopped.

"Miles was the same with me, when I asked him where he was he wouldn't tell." Riah confessed.

A few seconds later the doorbell rang. Jordan sprinted upstairs.

"It's the inspector!" he shouted down the stairs.

Inspector Alex walked down the stairs promptly. She had a black suit on and a notepad in her hand.

Riah and Jules went and sat down on the longest couch.

"Hello all, Miles' family called me."

She started to ask us the usual questions like where were you and what happened before he left. She suspected that the killer might've killed him and that we might've needed to look for a body instead of him in general. We started to suspect too. What if he was the next target? What if the note he wrote was fake?

Why was he the next target?

Riah explained why she thought it might've been her fault that Miles was gone. After that, I explained how Miles and I got into a fight before he went missing.

"What was the fight about?" the inspector asked.

"He wouldn't tell me where he was that night."

She was jotting everything down. She could write quickly and still make her hand-writing readable.

"Hm, he didn't tell me either." she sighed.

"Look, we *can* find him! Just don't send police or search warrants!" I told her, "It's probably not that deep!"

"Why not?"

"Because he'll run further, he'd think he's in trouble. Let *us* find him, he'll come home to us more easily." Riah explained.

"Okay fine," Inspector Alex replied, "but Detective Toby is going to come with you guys, just in case. He's arriving in--"

She looked down at her red leather-strap watch.

"Five minutes."

"Which one's Detective Toby?" Kai whispered.

"The one with the spikey hair." Jordan giggled.

"Oh, and Miles' sister is outside too."

She walked back up the stairs and left.

"Anna!!" Parker and Kai exclaimed excitingly.

"So what are we going to do? He's been missing for 19 hours." Jules asked.

We started sharing ideas of where he could be. We also needed an idea of how to find him without scaring him away. We waited for Detective Toby to arrive. When he did, Jordan ran upstairs as we followed.

We met Anna upstairs, she was around 5'7 with dark brown hair and hazel eyes. She was skinny and slim like Miles was.

"Hi Anna!" Parker exclaimed.

Parker sorta had a soft spot for the Cooper twins. She was protective over them.

Parker, Kai, and Mina were all close to Anna as much as they were with Miles.

When Marina came up she went into the kitchen area to grab a drink. The kitchen area was small and didn't have any doors. She could just stand in front of the fridge and listen to us clearly. In front of her there was a row of counters. In front of the counters was a few more couches and a TV on the wall of the stairs.

The rest of us came up and huddled around the couches again.

"Okay so what are you kids thinking we should do?" Detective Toby asked brightly.

"You guys can take my car and drive around. Jordan, I can use your car and can drop you off at the shore before I go to work." Marina explained.

"Okay!" Detective Toby replied.

"As long as y'all don't get my car dirty, you guys are good."

"Wait, I don't think we'll have enough space." Jules pointed out, "There's only five seats in a car and there's seven of us."

"Here, two of you can take my car and follow us. I'll drive Marina's car around with the rest of you." Detective Toby explained.

We nodded.

"Wait, are you even allowed to do that?"

"Sh! Don't ask too many questions!" Kai said as she hit Jules on the back of his head.

"OWW!!"

Anna started giggling loudly while Kai took the Detective's car and started it up. His car was a dark steel grey and looked fancy. Marina's car was red and it was a tall Jeep. She had furry red dice as decoration on the mirrors.

Detective Toby hopped into Marina's driver's seat and turned it on. I was about to go hop into the passenger's seat.

"SHOTGUN." Riah shouted.

"My foot's already in the seat."

103

"Nope nope nope!" she said as she moved my leg off with a cheeky smile on her face.

We fought and tried to pull each other off the seat for a good *five* minutes.

"My leg's already on the seat, Riah!"

"I yelled shotgun first!"

"*No!*"

"*Yes!*"

"No!"

"Yes!"

"See now my body is on the seat!"

She grabbed onto my waist and threw me off of it.

"You're light as a feather." she laughed.

Parker, Jules, and Detective Toby were in *their* seats watching us fight awkwardly. Riah jumped back onto the seat.

"I may be *light* but that doesn't mean I'm-"

"You're what?" she interrupted.

I picked her up and plopped her onto the ground.

"Jeez- you're-"

"Ah! I got the seat." I smiled.

"No you didn't"

"Yes I-"

"Parker-- flip a coin." she grunted as we both tried to pull each other on and off the seat aggressively.

Parker reached into her pocket and pulled out a quarter.

"Eden, call it," she said.

I widened my eyes for a split second. I didn't expect her to talk to me. For a second I forgot we were distant and we were close again, just like the old days.

"Heads!" I blurted out.

She threw up the coin, caught it, then slapped it on the back of her hand.

"It's tails."

"YES!" Riah shouted happily as she jumped onto the seat celebrating.

I rolled my eyes jokingly and then went into the backseat. I sat next to Parker. She turned to me with the coin still laying on her hand.

It was heads.

I chuckled, "Ah whatever, let her have the seat."

She smiled lightly as I snatched the coin and threw it out the window.

"H-HEY!!" she gasped, "You owe me 25 cents now."

We laughed as Detective Toby started driving. Jules pulled out a black and yellow walkie-talkie.

"Kai gave me this, she has the other walkie."

Kai and Anna were in Detective Toby's car behind us.

"Why can't we just text her or Anna when we need something?" Riah asked in a snarky, sarcastic smart tone.

"I *don't know*, this way is more fun." Jules replied in the same tone.

He fidgeted with the talkie for a few seconds to figure out how it worked. He pressed the button to talk and held it up to his mouth swiftly.

"Kai, you there?"

"Yes!" she answered, "This car seems expensive.. damn."

Toby chuckled as Jules held onto the button to speak.

"Where should we search first?" Riah asked.

"Mina's gravestone, he *might* be there." Parker answered.

"On it!" Anna said.

Anna always had that bubbly, energetic vibe to her.

"Ok where else would he be?" Parker asked.

I thought for a moment.

"Maybe.. he might be at our treehouse." I answered.

"Treehouse?" Riah shrugged.

"Yeah, the treehouse Jules, Miles, and I used to hang out in everyday after school. Right Jules?"

He nodded and smiled softly.

"Let's check there, it's behind my house." I said.

I suddenly remembered I didn't live with anyone. My sister hadn't come home yet. I didn't need Detective Toby to suspect something.

"Address?" Toby asked.

"17 Willow street."

We arrived at my house in minutes. When we stopped, everyone awkwardly looked at each other to see who was going to check for Miles. We were all afraid we were going to find something we didn't want to.

Like a body.

"It's your house, Eden." Jules shrugged.

I hesitated a bit. I had to toughen up a bit, it's nothing I haven't seen before.

"Alright," I sighed.

Parker looked over at me, it's been a while since she looked me in the eye. She sighed.

"I'll go too," she spoke up, "just in case."

Parker and I hopped out of the car and walked in as Jules, Riah, and Detective Toby waited in the car.

We walked into my backyard.

"Where is it?" Parker asked, "I haven't been inside that thing since freshman year."

Parker and I used to hang out daily. We were just kids. Eventually life caught up to us again.

"Further back behind the fence. It's not deep into the woods though." I replied.

We walked fast through my fence and into the woods dodging the branches and sticks. We found the tree house eventually.

"Damn, it's just how I remember it." she sighed as a smile grew on her face.

The treehouse looked old and most of the brown and white paint chipped off. It was shaped like a hut and there were zip-lines coming in and out of the doors. We heard the floor faintly creak inside.

The sun was beaming on us as the clouds glided by. There were short breezes brushing through our blonde hair. Parker looked up at me and hit my arm.

"Ouch!" I yelped.

"Sh!" she whispered, "I think he's in there!"

We stood there trying to listen for any other noises and signs but we heard nothing, just light breezes with leaves brushing by. Parker started walking over to climb the latter.

"Be careful!" I whispered, "This is old and it might fall on yah!"

"Shut up!" she whispered back.

She slowly climbed up carefully and peeked into the door.

"Oh shit!" she whispered.

"What?!"

"Mina?" she gasped.

I scoffed.

"That shit ain't funny!"

She started snickering under her breath. She peeked further into the door.

"Nothing. He's not here." she said, "Wait,"

"What?" I said with my hands in my pockets.

Ssssss

Parker and I both heard the sound. She turned around slowly for dramatic effect and gave me a look. She turned back around and opened the door a little.

"It's a snake." she laughed quietly, "It made itself at home in your hangout."

Ssssss

"*Get--back--down* here Parker!"

109

I was scared for her even though I didn't need to be, she's Parker, she can handle anything.

She was about to climb back down but the latter collapsed and she started laughing hysterically as the wooden pieces fell on top of her. The snake started hissing louder and louder. She stood up and brushed the dirt off her shoulder.

"Run!" I shouted as the snake slithered out to bite us.

She turned around, scoffed, then grabbed my wrist. We ran and ran. We ran back up the hill and into my backyard again.

I turned around to close the fence door but it was too late. The snake was still slithering towards us at the speed of light. It was a light yellow and was as wide as a shot glass.

"Go! Go! Go!" I giggled as we ran around the corner and back to the front of the house.

The feeling was amazing.

"Open the door!" Parker shouted as Jules cluelessly flew open the car door.

Parker jumped in as I followed. I kicked the door in and it closed right when the snake was going to bite me. We sighed in relief and continued laughing loudly as the adrenaline faded away.

"What happened?" Jules asked, "Did you find him? Your faces are bright red!"

"Nah, we found another version of Evelyn though." I laughed.

Parker snorted and wiped the sweat off her forehead.

"Just like the old days, right?" I chuckled.

Parker let out a sharp sigh and looked over at me.

"Like the days we'd get in trouble together?" she asked.

"In *deeepp* shit." I snickered.

"Escaping detention?"

"Damn, the teachers secretly hated us."

"But we were the best of the class!!" we both said at the same time.

She laid back and cackled loudly as smacked the side of my face.

Just like the old days.

She used to pull out my chair to watch me fall, slam my head against the windows on the school bus, beat me with my own lunchbox, and shove me into mailboxes. She was like any other aggressive 14 year old.

She made sure she was the only one who could pull stunts on me like that. Whenever someone laid a finger on me she wouldn't let them see the light of day again because she knew I would do the same for her.

Damn, we were just kids.

"Did Kai and Anna check Mina's grave yet?" Parker asked.

"Yeah, they did," Jules answered worriedly, "They found nothing."

Jules picked up the walkie-talkie and held onto the button.

"Kai, where do you think he might be now?" he asked.

"Kai's driving, this is Anna." Anna replied, "But, I don't know... did you guys check Eden's treehouse?"

"Yeah they did, they found nothing more than a snake."

You could hear feedback on the other side of the talkie.

"He *BETTER* not be dead," Kai exclaimed, "He's too cool to die!"

Jules smiled lightly then set the walkie-talkie down in his lap.

Riah was sitting in the passenger's seat thinking while holding Miles' note in her hand. Judging.

"Let's check his workplace." she suggested, "He works at the local subway."

"Kai and Anna already checked, his manager said he hasn't shown up." Jules replied.

We all sighed. By now it was 2:00PM and we found nothing that could help. All this search gave us was the movie feeling.

"What does he mean by *disappearing?*" Detective Toby asked as he looked over at the note.

"He means he wants to take a break with the world I guess.. but not leave completely." Riah answered, "I- I don't know, he's never acted like this before. It's not him!"

We spend the whole afternoon driving to places we'd think he'd be. We even drove to the shore to check even though Jordan would've called if he saw him. After a while we were all exhausted but we couldn't give up on Miles. We needed to know if he was okay.

We needed to make sure he wasn't dead.

All of us had pretty solid alibis, I was at home sleeping, half of the others were too, the other half was either at work or *out of town.*

We sat in the car through long drives while taking turns getting out to search for him. We waited as the puffy clouds went by and the sun melted us slowly. We listened to music with the windows down as Detective Toby told us stories about his three daughters and how he used to be a history teacher. He even taught us how to analyze clues better.

Kai and Anna would check in with us as they searched for him. Anna said they looked through most of the restaurants in our area and most of the places they thought he'd be. We live in a small town where everyone knows each other. We'd usually meet up at pizza places or thrift stores that were all used to us.

It was 9:00PM now. The sun was preparing to set and the temperature was getting cooler. The air was fresh but moist, it felt like it was about to rain. The roads were damp and the clouds were grey and puffy. We were all car-sick and about to give up, we hadn't eaten in hours. Riah however, insisted on driving the whole night to find Miles. Parker secretly agreed with her but she was being *the usual Parker*. Of course she cared about Miles but she doesn't consider herself a *softie*.

We were driving across bridges and highways until we went over something we thought was a speedbump. That made *all* of our attention shift back to the real world.

We heard a squishy, crunchy noise come below the tires. Toby hit the brakes and gasped quietly. He sat there with his eyes widened and his hands on the steering wheel.

"*What*---was--that?" Parker asked arrogantly.

Jules sat up from resting on the car door and raised an eyebrow.

"Did we just run over something?"

"No shit."

We all sat there in silence. The same thoughts rushed through our heads.

Did we just run over a body?

Miles?!

Riah took a deep breath.

"I'll look!" she suggested as she opened the door. She slowly went around the car and as soon as she saw it, she flinched as she gasped and covered her mouth with her hand.

Jules rolled down his window and stuck his head out.

"What is it?" he asked.

"We just- we just ran over a bunny." she gasped.

Parker slapped her hand over her mouth and her eyes widened. For an odd reason she was trying not to laugh.

"Joder." Jules sighed as he rubbed his forehead.

Toby however, looked like his eyes were bulging out of his head.

Me? I felt bad for the bunny of course, poor thing.

"I just killed a bunny- I just *killed* a bunny!" Toby kept repeating to himself.

He started hyperventilating and Jules tried to calm him down.

"It's okay, the bunny is in a better place now!" he sighed.

Riah was still in front of the car staring at what we've done. She turned around and gasped again. There it was, the bunny's baby sitting at our far left staring at its mothers remains.

"Bloody hell-" I whispered.

Once Toby saw it his breathing got worse.

"I just killed that *baby* bunny's *mother!*" Toby hyperventilated.

He turned around to us.

"How are you guys *not* freakin- I- um-"

"We all saw things worse before." I explained.

Riah quickly jumped back into the car and shut the door.

"Let's go." she sighed as Toby started to drive again.

In five minutes he started to calm down and get over it. Jules was sitting in the car with a confused look on his face.

"Aren't you a trained detective?" Jules asked.

"Yeah, why?" Detective Toby replied.

"You saw and experienced things worse than the roadkill situation, correct?"

"Yes,"

"Then why'd you react like that when the bunny was killed?"

"Jules!' Parker whispered with her eyes widened.

"Because, bunnies are my favourite animals." Toby sighed.

Jules sat there with his mouth open and a judgy look on his face. His walkie-talkie started to static.

"Kai?" he asked as he held onto the button.

"Yeah Jules, I'm at the gas station near the middle school." she said.

"Okay?"

"Miles is here." she said.

Riah and Parker immediately sighed in relief. Parker turned swiftly and snatched the walkie out of his hand.

"What is he doing? Have you talked to him?" Parker asked repetitively.

"No, I parked the car right near the building. If I talk to him he'll run!" Kai sighed sadly.

"I'm looking at him right now, he's in black sweats with his hood up and wearing red and white sneakers. He's sitting on the curb eating...*potato chips.*" Anna continued.

"Which gas station?" Toby asked while driving towards the middle school.

"7-Eleven." Kai answered.

We were already near the middle school. It was a seven minute drive from where we were.

"Oh crap!" she said, "I think he saw me!"

"How do you know that?" Riah asked.

"He looked over at my direction then stomped into the shop."

Toby started driving faster. We were almost there.

"Stay in the area and keep an eye on him, Kai!" Riah said as we drove.

"Shoot!" Kai shouted into her walkie, "He's running out! He's running out of the shop!"

"Chase him with your car!"

We arrived quicker using a shortcut and saw Miles running from our left to right at the speed of light. We almost ran him over but Toby hit the brakes in time. He ran over to our right as Kai's car zoomed behind him.

"We need to figure out a way to cut him off!" Parker exclaimed.

Toby backed up the car and started to drive parallel to Miles. The rest of us looked over at our left watching Miles through the window, running and running like he was being chased by demons. There were groups of trees on our left. On each side of the trees had roads.

Kai was chasing him on the left road as we drove on the right road. We could see Miles through the trees running and almost tripping over himself. It was so quiet the only thing we could hear were crickets chirping, the cars running, and Miles' rapid footsteps and him breathing heavily. The car lights helped our vision more because most of the streetlights were broken.

Riah looked up forward. It was an intersection.

"Turn left!" she shouted, "Toby turn left!"

Toby spun the wheel quickly and the rest of us in the back seat almost slammed into each other. We drove and cut Miles off as Kai's car didn't give him the option to turn around.

He didn't give up. He was Miles.

He stopped running with the look of tiredness and exhaustion on his face. He turned around and blocked his eyes from the bright car lights. He turned to his left quickly and ran into the dark group of trees.

"Shit!" Riah shouted as she threw open her door to run after him.

I threw my door open and followed. We ran through the trees with no sight of him. We could only hear faint footsteps although we weren't even sure if they were his. I caught up with Riah as she sprinted towards Miles.

"Miles!!" she shouted, "EDEN, CUT HIM OFF!"

I ran. I ran past her and around the trees and back onto the road. I ran parallel to Miles and once I finally caught up to him I turned to my left and ran right towards him.

"RIAH, I GOT HIM!" I shouted as she ran towards him too.

I finally found him. I jumped and tackled him onto the ground as he grunted softly. He fought with me for a few seconds to stand up and run again. Riah caught up to us and kneeled down. She pulled out her phone to use as a flashlight.

"Miles.. Miles!" she whispered.

I let Miles turn over as Riah brushed all the dirt off his face. He looked terrible. He had a black eye, cuts on his face, eye-bags, and he had watery eyes but no tears managed to escape. He was breathing heavily and he smelt like straight alcohol. Whoever punched him in the face must've hit hard, black eyes don't usually form in minutes.

Riah's eyes started watering.

"Miles.. Miles.. get up." she sniffled.

He sighed.

"Come."

"What?" she gasped gently.

"Guys, just lay here with me." he mumbled as his eyes shut slowly.

I nodded and laid on his left as Riah took his right. The stars were beautiful. The moon stood out to me. It was a half moon. It reminded me of Mina. About how she'd act like a different person when she's with me, she was happier. She was able to be her normal self around me.

I was her other half.

"I'm sorry." Miles mumbled.

Riah lifted her head up and laid it on his chest. She wrapped her arms around him and sighed in relief as she looked up at the stars.

"What happened, Miles?" she whispered.

He turned his head and looked at her.

"I ran *away,* got jumped by some *thugs,* and got the adrenaline I needed." he chuckled softly.

"You're so stupid," I scoffed, "We thought you died."

"You didn't get my note?" Miles asked as he turned his head over to Riah.

"Yeah I did. We were still worried to death, Miles." Riah answered.

Miles sighed and shut his eyes again. He took a deep breath and sat up slowly restraining his grunts. We did the same. We stood up and walked back to the car together. I can tell Riah was debating on telling Miles about the hook-up with Jordan. She had that expression on her face and kept mumbling stuff to herself.

As Miles reached the car Parker ran out and paced over to him. She bent her neck down to look at his eyes. He had his hood on and Parker scoffed empathetically and brushed the hood off.

"Michael! Your eye, it's bruised." she said gently, "Who did this to you? *Kill them.*"

Miles chuckled, "You never answered me."

"Answered what?"

"That question I *always* ask you. What's wrong with you?" he asked playfully with his hand in his pocket.

"EVERYTHING!" Parker laughed.

"I've met *sarcastic* Parker, *funny* Parker, *playful* Parker, and *bossy* Parker, who am I going to meet next?" Miles chuckled.

"Murderer Parker." she cackled as she opened the car door.

Anna jumped out of the detective's car and ran over to Miles.

"Miles!" she exclaimed as she hugged him tightly.

"Anna?"

"The hell would you do that for!?"

"Oh shit, Anna cussed." Parker mumbled.

Miles chuckled and Anna followed.

"I was worried sick." Anna muttered as she dug her head into his shoulder.

She sniffled.

"Did Mom ask about me?" Miles asked.

Anna lifted her head up.

"Not really, she thought you were at a party."

Miles scoffed lightly. He looked over to Jules, who was still in the car looking at him and cocked an eyebrow.

"You went searching for me?" he asked.

Jules turned and shrugged, "Of *course* I did! Why wouldn't I!?"

We all crawled into the car. Miles went with Kai and Anna. We all drove to the gas station again while Toby asked Miles the usual questions through the walkie-talkie. Kai and Anna met us there and they swapped cars with Toby.

"Hey do you guys need a ride?" Toby asked.

"No, we're fine." we answered.

"Wait, I do." Anna said as she jumped up on the curb.

Toby nodded and he stepped into his car, Anna turned around.

"Miles, what do I tell Mom?" she asked.

"Tell her I'm not on speaking terms with her."

She nodded gently then hopped into the car. After Anna and Toby drove away, we were all still sitting on the edge of the curb on the outside of the gas station. We were all aligned with each other, silent, each thinking about something different.

"Eden, do you still have those cancer sticks?" Miles spoke up.

"Yeah." I smiled as I pulled one out for him.

"No, I don't want one." Miles smiled, "Throw them away for me."

I widened my eyes and slowly got up, shaking the package lightly, and tossed them into the bin. I mean, he was right for that. Smoking was going to ruin my head *and* lungs.

"Why'd you do it?" Kai asked, "Why'd you run away, Miles?"

"I needed some distance from reality," he answered, "for peace."

We were sort of stunned at his answer, he seemed out of character. But he continued his explanation and we listened.

Parker seemed like she was thinking the most, she gave us an idea. An idea that would help us all. An idea that could end this nightmare and spend the summer better. An idea Mina would've wanted us to follow.

Riah couldn't come home.

"My parents forbid me to get out of the house." Riah explained, "I had to fist-fight and bitch-slap my way out. If I come home now-"

"Just stay at my place," Miles said while wrapping his arm around her, "Anna can convince my parents."

She was still hesitant.

"I can't, if my parents find out we'll both get in trouble. I don't want to piss them off more."

Parker made the idea because she couldn't come home either. She ran away to find Miles because her mother wouldn't let her out. She had to climb out of her window and escape to search for him.

"You guys shouldn't have sacrificed *anything* for me." Miles said.

"No, we really *did* need to." Parker scoffed.

We got into Marina's car and drove.

"If we're going through with this plan, should we get Emily?" Jules asked.

Miles raised an eyebrow, "Uhm-"

"Sure." Parker answered as she drove to Emily's workplace.

I felt a sense of panic run down my spine. I haven't seen her since the party and I certainly didn't look forward to it.

Once we arrived at Emily's work place we all got out of the car and walked in.

"Should we order something?" Kai asked.

"No cause then we'll have to pay." Parker rolled her eyes.

"Awh man, we haven't eaten *lunch* yet!" Kai sighed.

Emily saw us from behind the counters and trotted over to us. She sat us down at an oversized maroon leather booth with light oak wood tables. Miles had his hood up again and he was resting his head on his fist.

Emily leaned onto the table, "What's wrong? Why are you guys here?"

"We'll explain later, just meet us outside when you're done closing up." I said quickly.

I was being awkward as usual. I didn't want to make eye contact with her. She raised an eyebrow at me then turned to Miles. He was on the left side of the booth sitting closest to the wooden window.

"What's wrong with *him?*" Emily asked.

Miles turned slightly and brushed off his hood as Emily gasped.

"Black eye." Miles smiled.

A couple minutes later Emily met us outside in her normal shorts and teal tank top instead of her uniform. It was faintly raining

"Okay.. what did you guys want to explain to me?" she shrugged.

"We're running away together." Parker explained.

6
turn your back against the world and <u>it'll do the same</u>
[JULY 9, 2019]

The silence was loud.

Emily panicked, "Can someone explain to me what the hell is going on?!"

We were in Marina's car driving back to her house. We didn't have enough seats so Parker drove with Riah beside her, four of us crammed in the back, and Emily just sat on her knees in front of Miles and I.

I was awkward the whole time, I kept getting flashbacks from the party but I couldn't tell if they were real.

I hoped they weren't.

I could tell Emily was nervous too, she kept making eye contact with me then looking away immediately. She was breathing heavily and failed to hide it, everyone noticed. I was afraid someone was going to suspect something.

"We're driving back to Marina's," Parker explained, "*then* we're going to discuss this idea out before doing anything *stupid.*"

"But, what did you mean by *running away?*" Emily mocked

"Which *part* don't you understand?"

Emily shrugged, "Uh, alright!"

We arrived at Marina's house again, hopping out of her car and walking in. It was late and raining. We all went and sat together in the living room as we heard the rain falling against the windows. Marina walked over.

"What are you guys up to? Eden sent me a confusing text."

"Predictable." Jules murmured.

Parker chuckled under her breath as she sat down on the couch.

"I think we should run away together. Make this summer the best one we've ever experienced."

"It can't be a good summer if one of your best friends was murdered." I said as I sat down, "That *friend* also happens to be *my* lover."

"*And* my sister." Jules pointed out.

"*The murderer* is locked up now! Wouldn't Mina want us to live in peace after this nightmare?" Jordan asked as he walked over to us.

"Honestly speaking? No, she wouldn't." Miles said.

"Wow." I chuckled as Marina started laughing along with me.

"Yeah, she would, deep down below her twisted humour she really would. As long as we don't forget her then she'd be cool with whatever we're doing." Parker answered.

Emily was sitting in front of the coffee table facing towards us nervously. She had her hand on her forehead and she was looking at us worriedly.

"It wasn't Evelyn." she spoke up.

Parker immediately turned her head towards Emily and gave her a look.

"*Okay,* who else would it be then?" Parker asked.

"Explain the fingerprints, her motive, and her alibi then." Riah joined in.

She was sitting right next to Parker giving out the same look.

Emily sighed and laid her head onto the table. She couldn't explain. At least not to all of us.

"*Anyways,*" Parker scoffed, "If Emily's right about Evelyn *not* being the killer, we should spend the rest of the summer together and see who'll spill."

She was right. Spending the summer analyzing clues, gathering hints, and connecting our stories would help figure out who *actually* did it. Plus, summer 19' had a ring to it. We needed to spend it perfectly. It's what Mina would've wanted.

Miles was sitting next to Riah staring off into space, he suddenly looked up and eyed all of us.

"We should do this," Miles said, "The killer is in the room. I know it's not Evelyn."

We all turned to him confusingly. Miles? Defending *Evelyn?*

Riah narrowed her eyes.

"How *do you* know?" Riah questioned slowly.

"I just do." he answered calmly.

Riah would've known if Miles was lying. He's not the type to. Every time he lies he smiles uncontrollably and he turns red.

He'd only lie if it was serious.

Emily looked up from the coffee table and brushed the hair out of her face. She sighed.

"Evelyn was with someone. She told me."

We all looked at her then each other.

"When?" I asked.

"I don't remember, she just told me when I visited her in jail."

Emily took a deep breath as she eyed all of us.

"She wouldn't tell me who she was with. It's not my place to say if I *did* know." Emily continued.

Riah scoffed. This is where she shows us her *not so friendly side.*

"All *I* know is, she was with one of *you* guys." Emily finished.

"How do *we* know you're not making this up?" Riah asked.

"Why would *I* make this up?"

"I don't know," Riah snarked, "To gain our trust, to screw with us, to get your twin sister out of jail?"

Emily took a shaky deep breath as Riah interrogated her.

"*Or* to have a go with Eden," Riah finished, *"Again."*

Kai and Parker's eyes widened and they quickly slapped their hands over their mouths at the speed of light. Marina stood and looked at Riah, then Emily, then me. She started hysterically laughing. The rest of the group was just dead silent trying to restrain their laughter. Eventually Miles broke his silence, he snorted then laid his head back on the couch smiling wide, laughing til his face turned red. He always did that every time something happened.

Riah and Emily were giving each other the death stare.

"How'd you know?" I asked.

Riah looked over at me with a proud look on her face.

"It was obvious, the tension on the drive home gave it away,"

I stood there awkwardly with my eyes widened not knowing what to say.

Emily reached into her pocket and slipped out her phone. She looked through her camera roll and showed us a video. It was a video caught on the security cameras at school, she downloaded it into her phone.

She played the video, it was only a few seconds long. We all tensed up since we all had the same image of her in our heads. In the video Evelyn was running around laughing, she kept turning around every once and a while. It looked like she was waiting for someone. The video stopped.

"What time was that recorded?" I asked.

Emily tapped her phone a few times.

"2:07PM, if she ran to the sunflower field it would've taken her 9-10 minutes." she explained.

"What if she drove?" Riah asked with a smart tone, "She's a fast sprinter too, she did track."

"She doesn't have a license."

We all looked at each other. We had more questions.

"Okay, that doesn't explain the fingerprints and motive." Parker said carefully.

Emily looked up at us.

"I don't have any explanations for that," she said, "I don't even know why she hated Mina,"

"*Okay* then... well guys, let's get to the point, if Evelyn wasn't the murderer who would it be?" Parker asked.

She didn't give us a chance to answer that question. It's not like we could anyway, none of us had solid motives.

"See? That's a good reason to *pack up* our shit and *leave!* We can figure this out on our own." she continued.

While listening to Parker's suggestions a grin grew on my face. It was just like the old days, her giving me ideas while I can't help but do them. I already wasn't doing okay, maybe this stunt will help me distract myself.

"Wouldn't that hurt the investigation more? All of us leaving at the same time would make us look suspicious, the police would overthink it and think it's all *connected* or something." Jordan said.

"Who *cares?* We're NOT the killers! They'll figure that out eventually."

We sat there and listened to what Parker had to say. She sounded like the *usual Parker* more than anything. She stood up from the couch and walked to face us.

"How are we ever going to get out of this? I mean look at us! All of us together seems like a blueprint of multiple disasters left and right." Kai explained.

She was right. We're all unstable crazy teenagers, nine in the same room? Disasters. Especially when we each have our own way of finding our way around.

Parker had the solution for that, she just needed us to follow it.

"Be like me and you don't have this stuff happen to you again." she explained, "Well, don't *be like* me *mentally* but lay low."

We all went silent while listening to her. Breathing in every word she said.

"After that, nobody cares what you do. Stop talking to random people. Make everything a joke. *Get over people.*" she continued, "Say *fuck you* to the world. Be an ass, be smart in what you say, don't ignore open chances."

Most of us couldn't understand half of the things in her lecture but we loved it. Every word she said engraved into our brains. It was movie fuel.

"Somebody talks smack? Fight 'em or laugh at 'em. Don't care about what others think." she said, "Laugh everything off and say fuck it. You guys have to *not* care, but only to the world. When you're alone, deal with it then walk with dead eyes."

We all wanted her mindset. She was that adrenaline junkie everyone wanted to hang out with. She's the type of person who only exists in movies.

"I hate this town, I hate this world, matter of fact." she ranted, "But, you don't see me crying ever, do you?"

"No, unless you're laughing-crying." I spoke up.

"Yeah, see? I don't act all upset do I? No."

"So, be like Dally Winston?" Kai asked.

Parker chuckled, "No, push yourself past caring but don't let others see."

"Parker's right. We're going to have to pull ourselves together next year. Worry about bills and jobs, we're 17. We should live like the movies, like Mina always wanted." I said.

"We won't see anyone past high school, no one will care about our screw ups. So what if I screwed up when I was a teen? Hm? No one will care."

"Didn't you tell Mina all this when she was 13? She ended up six feet under three years after this pep-talk." Jules said.

"She only ended up there because she followed the advice better than I did." she scoffed.

"Why not take the risk? We need to find out what happened to her so it won't happen again." Marina explained carefully.

Parker also told the same pep-talk to me back when we were close, the only difference was I was already living like her.

So they heard her. We agreed to run away together, why? To honour Mina.

Me, Miles, Riah, Parker, Kai, Jules, Emily, Marina, Jordan, *together*. We had nothing to lose. Even if we *did* have enough to lose, we wouldn't have enough energy to care. Even though Marina and Jordan were adults now, they never acted like one. Plus, why not wait until 20 to pull ourselves together?

We discussed the main reason to run away. Mina. But we also had other reasons, Riah and

Parker kicked themselves out of their houses to search for Miles. They needed a chance to escape their homes so they took that one. If they came back home, who knows what would happen to them? Sure, we can let them stay at our places but that-

That takes the fun out of it.

We started packing. Riah and Parker snuck home carefully to gather clothes and supplies they would need. Miles and Jules had their backs just in case anything bad could've happened to them. They manage to look like they give out beatings once and a while. Kai, Jordan, and Marina started packing their belongings at their home.

It was just me and Emily. I drove her to her house and she packed up her stuff. We stopped at Jules' and my place to gather my stuff. We were tense the whole time not knowing what to say to each other. We tried to focus on the important things, like packing to run away with the group but we couldn't stop the urge. Emily broke the silence first. We were in my car driving down an empty street towards Marina's place.

"Eden," she said.

"Hm."

"Are we ever going to talk about it?" she asked.

I looked over at her with a hand on the steering wheel. I shrugged.

"There's nothing to really talk about." I said slowly, "What do you want me to say?"

She turned and smacked my arm. It hurt. I just looked forward and continued driving. She started hyperventilating silently and fidgeting with her fingers.

"Bitch. What *do you* mean there's nothing to talk about?!" she ranted, "We got drunk, *trolled around* and now, I *can't* get you off my mind."

It's not the first time I heard that.

I think she said too much. I sat there driving with my eyebrows lifted. It was obvious that she got caught up in the moment. She started stuttering and covered her mouth with a hand softly. She's the type to speak before thinking especially when it comes to boys.

I tried to laugh it off like Parker told me to. Emily obviously didn't get used to Parker's way of life yet. No one did. It was hard at first.

"Look it was a mistake alright? Some things are just meant to be let go." I explained softly.

I glanced over at her and she took a deep breath. She nodded softly and we continued the painfully awkward drive to Marina's. I couldn't blame her. She hasn't left my mind either since that party.

We arrived at the house meeting everyone there with their bags ready. We discussed how it was going to work. We were only going to use two cars. We didn't have a lot of options with cars, some of us didn't own one. There were only nine of us, we didn't need a lot of space. Jules said we couldn't use his car, Riah asked why.

"I'm a troublemaker, alright? My parents never trusted me *or* Mina," he laughed, "They put trackers on our cars. We'd get busted if we used mine."

Busted for... what exactly?

A vacation?

There was our solution. Marina's red Jeep and my white convertible.

"Do we go now?" Miles asked.

"Nope, too tired." Kai replied.

Miles scoffed lightly.

We all decided to all stay at Marina's house for the night and leave tomorrow afternoon, but we were ready.

We were prepared for the truth to unfold.

7
freshman homecoming
[JULY 9, 2019]

"I need to tell you something." Kai told me.

It was 4:00PM now. Last night, Marina, Kai, and Jordan slept in their usual rooms and the rest of us scattered around the couches in the basement.

4:00PM, we were all scattered around the house but Kai pulled me aside. We were in the laundry room in the basement.

"Why are you telling *me* this?" I asked.

"Cause I trust you and you seem the most responsible for this." she answered as she closed the laundry room door, "It's about Mina."

I doubted it, Kai barely spoke to me. I just continued to listen to what she had to say.

"Remember freshman homecoming?" she asked.

"I think." I replied, "Why?"

"Do you remember what happened? Did anyone tell you?"

I shrugged. I genuinely didn't know.

"Mina, Evelyn, and Emily got in a huge fist fight," she explained, "and I think it's linked to why Mina was murdered."

"*Ahh,*" I chuckled, "I remember hearing about that. I mean, how big was the fight? They were 14-15 years old, maybe it didn't mean anything."

"You *know* Evelyn, she's the type to not hold grudges unless it's Mina."

She pulled out her phone and tapped it a few times. She scrolled down videos and pictures then found what she was looking for.

It was a video, I remember it now. We were filming clips for a small documentary of our lives. We decided to record some at homecoming for fun. Kai played the video as she showed it to me.

We were all at the entrance of the cafeteria giggling. When Mina first showed up on the video my heart sank, hearing her laugh made me want to throw myself off a building. It was hard to accept that the person you used to talk to daily is no longer here. It was unsettling. I felt like I could've prevented something.

We all tried to dress up for that dance. It was the only day we could show up to school without our traditional grey and red uniforms.

  Mina had her dyed golden hair straightened and pearl dangle earrings on instead of her silver hoop. She looked *sorta* the same, especially with the winged eyeliner, she just looked a bit younger. She showed up in those traditional Vietnamese dresses. It was a pretty burgundy colour.

  The camera's point of view moved and faced me. I turned to the camera and smiled. Miles and Jules were next to me too, they were closer back then. They had their arms wrapped around each other's shoulders while laughing their heads off. I was wearing a white suit and a black bow-tie. Miles and Jules decided to match that night, they wore black suits and coloured ties to tell them apart. Miles wore a blue tie and Jules wore a red tie.

  "Eden, you better hope no one spills anything on you." Riah giggled off camera.

  The camera moved over to Parker. She had black cargo pants on, a white long sleeved shirt under a black graphic t-shirt, black converse, and an orange beanie. She was waving her hands around her, she had silver chain necklaces and masculine rings on. She said herself she was proud of the outfit. She loved it. She got to express herself and have no one tell her no.

Beside Parker was Riah. She had rose quartz earrings and a velvet yellow dress on. She was smiling at the camera as her face grew pinker and pinker. She was super excited that night.

"What's with the face, bubble gum?" Jules cackled off camera.

Miles started cackling, he was still next to Jules, laughing as his *face turned red as well.* The camera moved over to Mina and I. We were just standing there with blank faces awkwardly watching them laugh at something that didn't amuse us.

"*Bubble gum??*" Miles cackled.

Riah's face grew even more pinker and she scoffed.

"Nothing! I'm just hella excited, do you guys know how *hard* I convinced my parents to let me come?!" she exclaimed.

Jules and Miles continued snickering. Riah scoffed playfully.

"Don't be a dum dum!"

The camera turned around and it was Kai. She was the one recording. She had blue denim overalls on with a baggy maroon t-shirt underneath. Her hair was in two dutch braids. She was smiling at the camera as her glasses reflected the camera lens.

    We all walked into the cafeteria and met up with Jordan. He was a sophomore at the time. He had a navy suit on with silver stud earrings. We met up with Marina as well, she was a junior, she didn't dress up at all. We were surprised she even showed up. Mina must've convinced her well. Marina was wearing grey sweatpants and a black spaghetti strap tank top with a zip-up jacket over it. Her bright red hair was in a low pony-tail with two strands hanging out the sides of her face. She was by the drinks snickering while pouring booze into the punch secretly.

    The music was loud and the lights were flashing everywhere. Everytime one of us tried to talk in the video we could only hear a faint version of it back.

    The video cut to the point. The whole fight. There was a crowd circling Mina and Evelyn. They were around 2-3 feet away from each other. The music was still playing but they were shouting at each other loud enough.

    Music genre? Rock. Alternative rock. Perfect timing right?

Mina was next to Emily asking her about something that had absolutely nothing to do with Evelyn. Evelyn however, sparked a fight.

Typical.

It was towards the end of the dance. I remember because Mina was changed into her grey crew neck and joggers instead of her dress. She had her silver hoop on again.

"Go eat *your dog* or *your cat*, or *whatever* you have just go eat it!" Evelyn snapped as a smile grew on her face.

She was the type who spoke quickly with *that* voice to avoid laughing. Emily gasped.

Mina cocked an eyebrow and turned to her. Before she could do anything Emily ran in between them and broke them up.

"Evelyn stop- STOP-" she told Evelyn.

Emily's facial expression made my blood boil a little. She was smiling after each word, everyone knew she was secretly laughing along with Evelyn. What do you expect? She wouldn't scold her own sister to defend a person like Mina.

It seemed like no one would do that.

Emily tried covering it up to save her own ass. She turned to Mina.

"I- Mina I have nothing to do with this- um-" she said awkwardly while trying not to smile.

Evelyn didn't knock it off. She was *that* type of girl. The girl who craved male validation. The girl who needed the other girls to be jealous of her, to be honest that dream of hers failed because no one could stand her. She acted like she didn't care about anyone's thoughts about her but deep down she did. She needed it. It feeded her ego.

She was the type of girl to ask stupid questions and play dumb just for boys to answer and react. The type of girl who spoke in that tone, that whiny tone but it sounds a bit mean at the same time. The type of girl to play video games with boys for their attention.

Even boys would get tired of her sometimes. She just wanted them to pick her.

Emily was a little different. She enjoyed the quietness and peace. She couldn't control the fact people knew her *because* of her problematic sister. Sometimes she enjoyed the validation and attention just as Evelyn did, she just tried to hide it. She was hard-headed. Even though she rarely got involved in things or enjoyed the peace she couldn't help the fact she cared about people's thoughts about her. *She really cared.* That's why people usually hate her more than Evelyn because she tries to act all innocent.

"She can't do anything to me." Evelyn scoffed confidently, "Look at her, she looks like a twig."

The majority of the crowd was rooting for Evelyn. They underestimated Mina. They always did. They thought she couldn't fight for shit. They were waiting for Evelyn to humiliate Mina more and more. The grade didn't like Mina. Funny because Mina didn't know anyone's names but they knew hers.

"I don't think you have any friends to back you up, what a shocker." she continued.

Mina snickered softly.

A smirk grew on Evelyn's face and she turned to Emily and sighed happily. Emily looked at her cluelessly then narrowed her eyes.

"I love fighting with people. It's so fun! Especially when you know *you're* right and she's wrong."

Emily's eyes narrowed even more. She made a judgy face then rolled her eyes. The crowd looked at each other with the same look Emily made.

"Notice how she's not saying anything." Evelyn laughed.

Mina smiled. Throughout Evelyn's remarks Mina didn't break eye contact once.

"You're not even cute. LITERALLY GO EAT YOUR DOG-" she shouted as she bursted out laughing.

She covered her mouth to restrain her laughter. She didn't get the reaction from Mina that she wanted. She wanted her to cry and be humiliated but in reality she was asking for a beating.

"Shut the fuck up." Mina smiled.

"What?" Evelyn gasped sarcastically.

"Shut the fuck up before I rock your shit-"

She clearly was thinking through all of the bad things to say to her. Every insult that popped into her mind, she said it. She walked to the end of the crowd and snatched a drink out of a random person's hand.

Evelyn raised an eyebrow. Mina's face grew meaner and meaner, to be honest she looked less human.

"*Clumpy* mascara, *wonky* eyebrows, *crooked* teeth, what *do you* use to floss? A *brick?*" Mina snapped, "Imagine waking up next to *you!* I'd fucking scream."

She was 14, obviously she'd come up with better insults if it happened to her when she was 16.

Evelyn tried acting cool. This was where Emily started to act up. She kept eyeing the crowd as Mina waited for Evelyn to respond.

"Honey, your face is wonky, I mean look at your eyes-" Emily shouted as she couldn't finish the sentence because of laughter.

"PSH- HAHA- she can barely see!" Evelyn joined.

They took a few seconds to laugh. Emily calmed down quickly.

"O-kay, I *did not* mean that, let's go Evelyn." Emily said as she tried to pull Evelyn away, "*Don't* take that seriously!"

"If you're going to try to insult me, bring up something other than race." Mina scoffed, "Unless you want the same energy back."

Mina didn't have one bit of emotion on her face besides satisfaction. No sadness, no angryness, no fear. She was amused. She's been in fights before. She had experience through the years.

"We didn't even bring up race, we were joking." Evelyn snickered.

"Mhm," Mina scoffed, "Then go eat your unseasoned casserole bitch, try not to stick your nose into the bowl, it makes you look like a pig."

The twins gasped. Obviously if Mina made fun of one of their looks it'll count as insulting both of them.

"How about you go ask your *Daddy* to pay for your boob job? Hm? *Oh wait.* He left you cause he didn't want to deal with two screw-ups like you! *What. A. Shocker.*" Mina finished as she splashed the drink onto Evelyn's face.

You could hear Marina off camera. She was standing next to whoever was recording the video.

"Now that was uncalled for." Marina giggled.

The sticky drink dripped down Evelyn's dress in a heartbeat. Obviously that wasn't enough to satisfy Mina. She could hit hard if she wanted to. She learned it from Marina. She also had Parker's mindset. Parker's Dad told her this before he moved to Germany.

"If you're going to get in trouble for hitting someone, at least hit them hard." her Dad said.

Parker told that to everyone.

Evelyn scoffed, she paused for a second.

"You do realize we're british right?"

She started laughing as Emily followed along. Mina narrowed her eyes as she figured out something to say.

"Doesn't change the fact *your tea* is gross and your *biscuits* are bland."

151

MARCH 31st, 2016

We were in an empty field with perfect green grass and barely any trees around. He was there. He was the whole reason why we were there.

"What are we doing here?" I asked.

He was in front of me admiring the sky. He took a deep breath. He pulled out a gun. It was a revolver.

"Holy-"

"A-A-Ah!" he teased.

"B-Bloody hell!" I exclaimed.

"Good." he mumbled.

"Why do you have a revolver?" I asked as I stepped forward slowly.

"To play *russian roulette.*" he sighed happily.

He turned his head to me with a cheeky smile as my eyes widened. I had that look on my face. The face where I was intrigued and a little frightened at the same time. He started chuckling.

"I'm teaching you how to use a gun," he finally explained.

I narrowed my eyes and nervously smiled.

"Why?"

"You'll need it, *little one*, you'll need it." he smiled as he gave me a pistol.

He taught me how to use both. I'm a quick learner. I was amazing at it.

SEPTEMBER 29, 2016

Mina waited for a reaction from Evelyn. She knew there was a small chance of Evelyn hitting first, but she did.
The crowd gasped as Evelyn ran forward and grabbed Mina's neck. Mina's head flew down immediately as Evelyn pulled her hair. Mina grunted softly then punched Evelyn, right on the jawline and nose. Hard. She did that to make Evelyn get off of her. She could barely see because her hair was down covering her eyes. Evelyn fell back and regained her balance and tapped her face gently.
Blood. By the eyes and nose.
Damn.
Emily lightly jumped and her hand flew to her mouth, she gasped silently. Mina looked over at her and smiled.
BAM.
She smacked her as her face turned bright red and her head turned the other direction.

This was where they realized Mina didn't have a scratch on her. The twins were all talk. Mina used objects and fists.

Evelyn went over to throw a punch. She missed.

She ended up getting a punch on the jawline instead.

Emily went over and shoved Mina. She fell back a step. After that Emily got a punch on the right eye.

It started getting worse.

The twins obviously didn't miss every time. Everything went too fast. They were clinging onto each other throwing punches while dragging themselves around the circle. Mina would've easily won the fight in five minutes if the gang would've helped her but at that point she gave up on the group being there for her for any situation she was in. She tried not to rely on them. I knew it secretly, she only told me how she truly felt.

She didn't want to complain to them so she made up an excuse saying she always wanted us to let her fight her own battles because we'll know when she truly needs us.

But we were never there.

They started punching and bitch-slapping. The twins kept the usual facial expressions you'd think of. They were petty and cared about their reputation. They needed to keep their image even though they shattered it years ago. Mina however, she didn't care. Her facial expression was either satisfaction or that look of toughness you'd see on mugshots. Every punch she threw her smirk grew more evil.

Marina was still next to the person recording.

"Alright, I gotta step in and help." she chuckled.

She didn't. The person recording was Parker.

"No, no, no, don't, she got this. It's not worth it." she said as she grabbed Marina's wrist tightly.

As the fight got worse and worse Miles started shouting out of nowhere. He ran into the circle and pulled Mina apart from them. Mina had Evelyn pinned to the ground punching her to the point where no one knew Evelyn was still breathing. Evelyn was hitting her shoulders, face, and pulling her hair to get Mina off of her. Miles ran into the circle and tore Mina off of her. Mina tilted her head forward and threw it back to get all the hair out of her face. There was blood on her bottom lip and a few marks on her jawline and nose. There was a huge red mark on her cheek and the knuckles on her fists were red and a little bloody.

"JULES!" Miles shouted angrily, "Damn it, where is the group when you need it?!"

"Oh my god!" Parker exclaimed, "He cussed!"

Marina started cackling.

Jules sprinted and grabbed both of the twins with each arm. The twins looked much worse. Bloody nose, bruised faces, messy hair. The three girls were still squirming trying to throw another punch.

"You'll regret it *bitch*, you're only digging a deeper grave for yourself!" Emily shouted.

Miles held Mina tighter and jerked her away before she could escape.

"¡Joder! ¡Cállate a las dos, por favor!" Jules shouted.

```
Translation: Fucking hell! Shut
up, both of you, please!
```

Jules tends to speak spanish when he's nervous.

Mina got fired up and escaped Miles and she ran into the crowd. She came running back with-

A chair..? Oh c'mon, she could do better than that.

She picked up the foldable steel metal chair and walked back into the circle fiercely. She ran

and slammed the chair on the twins faces as hard as she could. Miles snatched her and dragged her away from the crowd before she'd kill them. She was still squirming and mumbling angry Vietnamese phrases under her breath. The twins started crying uncontrollably because they just got what they asked for.

"Mày bị điên à! Mày nghĩ mày là ai?" she shouted.

"Mina.. NO ONE CAN UNDERSTAND YOU!" Miles shouted as he continued dragging.

```
Translation: Are you crazy? Who do
you think you are?
```

The camera moved over to Mina and Miles outside of the crowd. She was sitting alone by the stairs silent with dead eyes. She was breathing heavily from how angry she was. Miles walked over to her with a bag of ice. He started quietly chuckling at her. She smiled lightly.

"Is your lip okay?" Miles asked.

"Mhm." Mina replied.

Parker turned the camera around. She was laughing quietly as well. She turned the camera towards the door. I was walking in with a intrigued look on my face.

"What happened?" I asked.

The video stopped.

Kai put the phone down.

"Why'd the video stop so randomly?" I asked.

"Camera died." Kai replied, "That fight was-"

"*Interesting...*" I said, "Why can't I remember any of this?"

"Because you have the memory of a fish. Plus you weren't there, " Kai said, "You, me, Miles, and Jules were out in the parking lot waiting for our ride. The rest of them were inside."

"Where was Riah?"

"Bathroom."

"Oh... did Mina get in trouble for this?"

"Suspended for a week. Although she didn't care, she just stayed up and slept in every night. She was just defending herself. Evelyn hit first." Kai explained, "Did you hear what Emily said?"

"Hm."

"She said, you'll regret it *bitch*, you're only digging a deeper grave for yourself!"

"Well I mean, this was years ago, they were young, they were *really really* young. Maybe she said that out of anger."

"Is there a way to make sure?" Kai asked, "You do know we don't live in a big town right? Her family is powerful but that fight made them a laughing stock for months."

I thought for a second then walked out of the laundry room.

"Stay here." I told Kai.

Everyone out there was still tidying everything up and getting their bags ready. I saw Miles in front of the couches, I went over and grabbed his arm. I pulled him into the laundry room.

"What?" he said.

We showed him the video and he laughed.

"Oh yeah I remember that." he chuckled, "She beat her ass."

"You cuss??!" Kai gasped sarcastically.

Miles rolled his eyes.

"Do you reckon this means something?" I asked.

"What do you mean?"

"What if Emily wanted revenge or something? Maybe this is her motive."

Miles gulped and rubbed his forehead.

"Uhm- I guess so, you should get closer to her and find out what she wants from us." Miles suggested.

"What do you mean get closer? Gain her trust?"

"Yeah, do whatever you can to get her to spill. *Hook up* with her if you have to."

"Uhm- we don't even know if Emily's the target here."

"I mean think about it, why did she want to join the films? Why is she hanging out with us so much?" Kai joined.

"Well, if the killer *was* her, why'd she want to kill me too? Jealousy?" I asked.

Kai shrugged.

"All I know is, she definitely knows why Evelyn's prints were on her set of arrows." she responded.

8
the tunnels
[JULY 10, 2019]

Very cautiously, Miles told Riah about it.

"She says you should pretend to fall in love with Emily to get her to speak up, I agree with that too." he suggested.

"That'll make me feel like a bad person dude, you know how Emily gets when she gets hurt in relationships." I explained.

"*Oh c'mon*, it's not the first time you've been a heartbreaker."

I rolled my eyes.

All our bags were completely packed up. We made sure we didn't forget anything. We all called our workplaces and quit. We all hated our jobs anyway. We knew we weren't going to come home and settle until we found out what actually happened. Jordan however, couldn't quit his job.

He called in and said he's going to take a few weeks off.

"Is this really going to take weeks?" Kai asked.

"Depends on how bad the truth is." Marina replied.

Miles and I were in the basement going over our plan to get Emily to speak up. Miles kept suggesting the same thing. I knew that was the best idea. I had to.

We walked upstairs and into the living room. Jules and Jordan were carrying our bags into the trunks of our cars. I saw Riah and Emily talking to each other on the couches, it was an odd sighting. This time they weren't trying to bite each other's heads off. I figured Riah was trying to get on Emily's good side to get something out of her.

Everyone eventually got back into the living room. We formed a circle around the coffee table. All our stuff was in the trunks.

"Are you sure we should do this?" Miles sighed as he eyed all of us.

"Yeah. We're doing this. They arrested the wrong person." Parker replied.

"I may hate Evelyn as much as you guys do but she doesn't deserve 20 years in jail for something she didn't do." I explained, "They rushed the investigation. They missed a lot."

"Where are we going to go? Once the police realize, aren't they going to search for us?" Riah asked.

"Why would the police search for us? This just looks like we're going on a vacation." Kai replied.

"Our *families* don't know anything. Once they realize we disappeared out of the blue, they'll report it." Miles continued.

"Eden's parents are across the world and his *sister's* M.I.A, Parker and Riah got kicked out, my parents are in Cancun for the next *month*, and then three sets of your parents are dead." Jules explained, "We just gotta worry about Miles' family."

"I called my sister, Anna. She's covering for me."

We continued to discuss it a little more. We didn't want anyone to interfere with the plan. We just needed to run away and figure out a way to find the real killer.

"Again, where are we going to go?" Riah asked.

"Somewhere far away. We needa disappear for a while, go on a big adventure, use our heads, let's go to New Jersey. Our adventure starts there." Parker suggested.

We all agreed. Atlantic City sounds amazing.

"Okay, should we leave *now?*" Jules asked.

"No." Marina joined in.

She was standing in the kitchen mopping the tiles aggressively.

"We leave at night. Leaving in the afternoon where there's light out would cause attention." she continued.

"We don't have anything to hide." I said.

"It's easier this way."

So we listened to her. We laid around all day binge-watching shows, showering, and preparing. I was distracted. I was trying to figure out a way to get closer to Emily. We were tense all day. Eyeing each other, awkward eye contact, whenever we would accidentally touch, we'd flinch. It made me wish I never went to that party. I could've just stayed home and slept.

It was 7:00PM. It was time to go. It wasn't dark out yet. Today was extra sunny because it was raining last night. We were all squinting and covering our eyes from the sun.

We all scanned the house to check for last minute items to pack. We started to discuss the seating out in the front yard. I decided it was a good idea to be in the same car as Emily. It was risky but I needed a chance to speak with her.

"Eden, the keys." Jules said as he turned to me. I raised an eyebrow.

"I'm driving."

I nodded and tossed him my keys.

He caught them with one hand and hopped into my car and turned it on. Miles, Riah, Jordan, and Kai went into mine as well. Riah and Miles sat next to each other in the backseat and Jordan hopped into the passenger's seat. Kai sarcastically stomped on the ground with two fists clenched on each side of her body.

"Oh really?" Kai groaned, "You're gonna let me third-wheel in the back?"

"Yeah unless you wanna go with the *potential love-birds.*" Jordan snickered as he looked over at Emily and I.

I winced softly. I didn't even realize Emily was standing next to me. Kai turned around and widened her eyes and immediately jumped into the car.

"Nice one." I replied.

We got into the cars. Emily and I sat in the backseat in Marina's car. Parker sat in the passenger's seat as Emily scooched over to the farthest seat. I debated on sitting directly next to her in the middle seat or sitting on the other side near the other window.

I thought about it then scooched to the middle seat as casually as I could. We started driving. My car was driving behind us. We reached the highways a few minutes later. It reminded me of Mina.

It was painfully awkward with Emily in the car. Marina kept eyeing me in the rearview mirror every once and a while to make sure I was okay. She'd raise her eyebrow slightly and I'd nod to tell her I'm fine.

She's always been protective of me. She's a better older sister than my actual sister.

Parker kept cracking gay jokes and she and Marina would laugh at them together as Emily and I pretended to know what was going on.

"Tell me Eden, were you ever hot for Miles?" Parker teased.

"Huh?" I replied.

Her question caught me off guard.

"Do you find him attractive or sumn?" Parker chuckled.

"I mean-"

She didn't let me finish. She and Marina bursted out laughing together before I could say another word. I looked over to my left. Emily was looking out the window with her earbuds in. Her phone in her hands as she fidgeted with it and her right leg bouncing up and down repeatedly. I could tell she was nervous. I just didn't know if it was because of me or because we're about to go somewhere we don't know where we'd end up. I turned my head over to Parker and Marina.

"*I mean* I'm not going to say anything, Riah will *slaughter* me. Mina would haunt me too." I chuckled.

Parker laughed.

Hours flew by. I was stuck listening to Parker and Marina goof around like the car was a bouncy house. They blasted Marina's playlists full of spanish hype music. They'd even have private conversations in spanish knowing Emily and I couldn't comprehend anything they were saying.

They'd try to help engage us in the conversation. I was being too awkward and Emily was being too nervous. She started warming up after Parker tried starting conversations with her. 20 minutes later, we reached our destination. I turned to my right and saw the WELCOME TO NEW JERSEY sign. I used this as an opportunity. I turned to Emily, she wasn't looking, in fact, she had no idea what was going on.

I tapped her lightly on the shoulder. She quickly turned her head to mine. I pointed to the sign as we drove by.

"We're here." I smiled.

She sat up and looked out the window. I leaned forward a little to look at her. I put my right hand on the top of Marina's seat. My arm guarded her and the only thing she saw in front of her was me. She scooted back a little with that nervous and intrigued look on her face. She looked out of the window beside her.

We saw tall buildings behind the streetlights. She glanced around the stars and the other cars driving by for a few seconds then turned back to me. Our eyes met.

She smiled.

We drove till we reached the tunnels. It was 11:00PM. Hardly any cars were driving in the tunnel with us. It was just my car and Marina's. Marina rolled down all the windows and stuck her arm out of the car. Jules drove my car to the lane next to us. We continued to drive parallel to each other. Jules took the stack off my car. Riah was sitting on the right side of the car, Miles in the middle, and Kai on the left.

"I SHOULD'VE WENT WITH-" Kai shouted.

"SHUT UP!" Jules interrupted, "Anyways."

We all snickered.

"Parker! Where are we going?? We've been following you for the past four hours!" Jules shouted.

"I don't know." Parker shrugged cheerfully, "Doesn't matter right now."

Jules scoffed then tapped on the GPS. Jordan slapped his hand.

"Eyes on the road!"

He tapped on it a few times.

"There's a Spotify playlist called the tunnels!" he shouted.

I leaned over Emily.

"Yeah Mina and I made that together a year ago." I explained.

"Aight-"

He played it. He turned it on full volume and it echoed through the tunnels. The tunnels were long and wide-ish and the walls were beige. On the ceilings there were warm white lights lining the middle of it with cobwebs scattered everywhere. Every 20-40 meters there'd be a short exit out of the tunnel and an entrance to the next tunnel.

The air was clear. It felt amazing. It wasn't warm, it wasn't exactly chilly either, it was perfect. The sky was pitch black, the only things we could see were the lights and logos in and on the buildings and the stars floating about. Marina and Jules took a look at each other. They nodded lightly and smirked then started zooming the cars at the same time.

Jordan turned to us.

"Eden, how's it like being in a car with all girls?" he teased.

I raised an eyebrow. I didn't think much of it.

"Oh please, Marina and I are into girls." Parker snapped back.

She turned around and looked at Emily.

"Oh wait, are *you* a little fruity too?" she asked.

Emily shrugged and smiled nervously.

Music blasting, perfect air and time, not knowing where the hell we were. It felt amazing. It felt like time stopped for us. Parker unbuckled her seatbelt and opened the sunroof. She got on her knees and stuck her upper body out of it.

She didn't say anything, she'd not the type to, everything always lives in her head. You could easily tell what she was thinking, she tilted her head back and let the wind flow through her hair. She took a deep breath. She loved the feeling up there, it looked like she wanted to scream,

GUYS- THIS IS AMAZING.

She threw up her arms and let the wind flow through her body.

I looked over at Emily. She was smiling. She felt at peace. I looked over at my car. The other car didn't have to do much. The top of the convertible was already down, all they had to do was unbuckle, stand up, then hold on. Riah and Miles went up first.

"DUDE-" Riah chuckled.

She was speechless. Miles was smiling non-stop.

"We could use this to cope. Let everything out." Riah laughed.

Miles turned and looked her in the eye, "Okay."

"What do we do?" Parker asked as she turned to them, "I'm slow."

"Just shout everything you've been holding in. I'll go first!" Riah shouted, "I--*hate*---my Dad."

All of our eyes widened. It was unexpected. Riah continued shouting.

"He almost *killed* me!" she screamed.

She screamed so much her voice started breaking and her eyes started tearing up slightly. It showed us how much she was hurting. It looked like her trauma was replaying in her head as she spoke. She tried to hide it.

She's usually the quirky, loveable, happy person in the group. Turns out she was just good at acting okay.

"He keeps trying to get back into my life! He says he's going to be a better person but I can't forgive him." she shouted, "I just can't!"

Her voice completely broke as she stood there slightly swaying side to side. She sniffled and took a deep breath as the air flowed through her hair. Miles' smile faded. He grabbed her gently as she clung onto him and cried silently into his shoulder.

"You good?" Miles asked.

"Yeah." Riah sniffled, "I just needed to get that out of me. If the world won't listen, I'll make it listen."

Miles nodded.

Jules and Jordan were eyeing each other while the rest of us listened to Riah.

"My Mom hates me. My Step-dad hits me. My siblings defend them whenever I call for help. I'm *trapped* Miles, there's no way out." she cried quietly into Miles' shoulder.

"Hey- hey, there *is* a way out. We'll figure it out together." Miles said gently, "One more year Riah, one more year and you'll be with me."

Riah looked up and Miles used the sleeves from his black hoodie to wipe her tears. She smiled. Miles was the only one who could do that. The only one who could make her stop crying instantly and make her smile after. He knew he couldn't help that much, 17 years of trauma, he couldn't make that vanish right away even though he'd go through hell to make that happen.

Everyone in the group knew Riah's backstory except Emily. We tried helping her in the past but it was no use. We didn't have enough power. We were only startled because we didn't expect Riah to talk about it. I could tell Emily felt bad when she found out.

"My turn." Miles winked.

He doesn't really take emotional or mental stuff seriously. He didn't want or need to cry. His voice was intimidating and it only showed how angry and annoyed he was.

"My Mom favours Anna over me. She starts fights with me. Sets dumb expectations and expects me to follow." he scoffed, "I ALWAYS ask myself why am I not like Anna."

He sighed.

"It doesn't matter."

Riah smiled. He turned and smiled back.

"My Mom insults me a lot. I can't talk to her for *five minutes* without having an argument! She told me to pack my stuff up and leave, and that I was a waste of supplies and space." he yelled.

"That's why you went missing didn't you?" Riah asked.

"No." Miles sighed, "*That's-* a different story."

His voice was raspy. His eyes were dry and red. He turned to Parker. She was still standing out of the sun-roof listening to him.

"I'm proud of Anna. She's the sweetest girl I've ever met."

He turned to Riah.

"No offense." he smiled.

"None taken." Riah giggled.

Miles was protective of his sister. He was only a minute older but he was the older brother everyone wanted. He'd murder anyone who hurt Anna. One time Anna had a crush on a douche. That douche hurt her feelings and later that night, Miles gave him the biggest beating the douche ever asked for.

He cared about Anna even though it didn't show.

"Your turn." he told Parker.

Parker winked.

"I HATE MY MOM TOO!!!" she laughed.

Parker crying? No. Parker doesn't cry, at least not in front of us. We all knew that.

"My brothers ruin everything. My Mom messed me up. She's most likely the reason why I'm like this. She's the reason why I have issues." she laughed.

She threw her head back and breathed in the clean air.

"I'm not yelling anything you guys don't know about me yet, about how much I hate the world and how I hate everything." she said.

She leaned back and took a deep breath.

"Aight- I'm done. JULES! YOUR TURN!!!" she shouted.

Jules turned to Jordan. He held onto the breaks and started speeding. Jordan sat up and got ready to slip into the driver's seat. It was risky. It seems unrealistic too, switching seats while driving. But it was us, we weren't realistic.

Jules crawled up quickly and then Jordan slid into the driver's seat at the speed of light. Jules kneeled on the middle compartment of the car.

"My sister's dead at 16." he sighed.

We all went silent. The only things we could hear was the loud blasting music and the car tires rolling.

"My sister *was murdered!* She was only 16! She was *so* excited to turn 17! She had a whole life ahead of her. I don't know if she'd end up in a *jail cell*, a *hospital room*, or a *high-class university* but, she would've done it. She always found a way." he yelled.

He sniffled. He wasn't crying but it clearly looked like he needed to.

"Enough, I don't want to focus on the negative stuff in my life." he mumbled.

He threw his head back and took a deep breath, "I hate everyone! I hate my parents! I hate Lily! I hate everyone at school, at work, the people, and how they treat me. I'm *SO* NICE to everyone and I get nothing back."

He lifted up his head and smacked the front window of the car, "Jordan! Jordan drive faster!!"

Jordan hit the pedal and Marina did the same to catch up. We went zooming down so fast it felt like a dream.

"WOO!" Jules screamed as he laughed at the feeling.

He stuck his tongue out and danced along to the music. A few seconds later, he jumped down back into the passenger's seat. It was Kai's turn. She kneeled on top of her seat and held onto Jules' seat to keep balance.

"Woah." she mumbled.

She threw her arms up and giggled. She almost fell over a couple times.

"My parents died when I was three! I escaped the orphanage five times throughout my childhood. Do you know what that makes me?" she

176

shouted, "I don't know! I don't know how I escaped when I'm this clumsy. Oh well, guess I'm immortal."

She smiled and adjusted her glasses. She climbed back down and Jordan stuck his head out of the car.

"WOAH YEAH THIS IS FU-"

"EYES ON THE ROAD OR YOU'LL CRASH US ALL!!" Jules shouted.

"I AM! I DRIVE BETTER THAN YOU SHUT UP!" Jordan replied.

Riah and Miles stood up and out of the car again.

"Marina, do you wanna have a go?" I asked.

She paused for a second.

"Sure." she replied.

She smirked and swung her head out of the window.

"BOOB--OO--LOO." she shouted.

"Huh?" everyone said.

She started cackling hysterically and I chuckled softly with her.

"It's an inside joke I still can't get over." she laughed.

19 years old and she still needs to get herself together. She always jokes but she knows when to

be serious. This wasn't a situation where we needed to be serious. We were having fun.

I looked over at Emily.

"Do you want to go up with me?" I asked.

She turned to me and thought for a second. She smiled lightly and nodded. We crawled up and stood out of the sun-roof as Marina zoomed the car down the tunnels.

She stood on my left smiling widely. The wind flew through her light blonde hair and her blue eyes glistened with happiness. Her shoulders didn't tense. Her hands weren't shaky. She was okay.

"Wow." she whispered in awe.

Riah and Miles were in the car next to us laughing their heads off screaming inside jokes only a few of us could understand. They were dancing along with the music like idiots aggressively.

I didn't need to scream the things I was angry about. I had too much to say. Emily didn't want to either. She only wanted to feel at ease that moment.

"WOO YEAH!!" she screamed with a huge smile on her face.

I smiled. I felt my lungs get clearer, my shoulders relax, and the wind crashing onto my face. Miles grabbed Riah's wrist and flew it up in the air. I leaned back and Riah and Miles gave me a look. They were trying to tell me to do something.

"Do it." Miles mouthed.

I raised an eyebrow then nodded. Emily was still next to me wiggling along with the music. She threw up her arms and stumbled for a second. She fell onto me slightly and clung onto my arm. I giggled and she caught her balance.

Okay. UH. Eye contact.

We held eye contact for the next three minutes laughing and saying everything that came into mind. I needed to make her think I was on good terms with her. I knew she thought I didn't like her like that, and *I don't*, but...

I needed her to doubt it.

9
two negatives, no positive
[JULY 11, 2019]

JUNE 1, 2019

"Erm, you said you and Mina were *dating* right?" the inspector asked me.

"Yes. Why?" I answered.

She sighed.

"People are informing me you guys weren't official."

I looked up at her then looked away for a second.

"I'm not good with labels, she wasn't either." I answered.

"What would you name you two if you *had* to label it." she asked.

I thought for a second.

"Complicated."

"Hm. Why?" she asked.

"I was *me*, she was *her*. We knew it wouldn't work but we still tried. We're like a strong tsunami and a lightning storm, together we destroy everything, *even ourselves.*"

JULY 11, 2019

"This case is confusing." Parker murmured.
She didn't mean to say that thought aloud.
We were at the beach sitting on the sand watching the waves crash. Breathing in the salty air as the sun's rays glowed over us. Most of us wore grey sweatpants or joggers with a random t-shirt. Emily was the only one with sweatpants and a swimsuit top. It was a blue one.

The night before, we finally drove past the tunnels and crashed at a random hotel. Jules paid for the majority of us.

"People are staring." Emily said.
She was sitting next to me in the sun while the parents were distracted with putting sunscreen on their kids. The little kids were too intrigued by the sand.

"Why would people stare?" I asked.
"We're all in joggers, at *a beach*." she answered, "The only one who's wearing shorts is Jordan."

I raised an eyebrow and looked around. She was right. People were raising eyebrows at us. I smirked lightly at each and every one of them to throw them off. I turned to her.

"Remember what Parker said?" I told her, "Who cares?"

She nodded and turned to Parker.

"You're right. This case *is* confusing. It's more complicated and deeper than what it seems." she explained.

"Then that means we have to start from the beginning." Parker explained as she gave us all a look.

Jules, Jordan, and Marina were in front of us goofing around. Riah and Miles were laying next to each other having a conversation that made no sense to anyone but them.

It was just Kai, Parker, Emily, and I sitting alongside each other looking into the waves. Kai was tired, she was trying not to fall asleep.

"*The beginning.* To be honest I have no idea where it starts." Emily said.

"It starts with Mina and Eden. We have to ask ourselves why her?" Kai yawned.

The three girls sat up and looked over at me. I turned my head to them.

"Hm." I answered.

"When and how did it all start?" Kai asked.

"When we started messing with each other or when we started *dating?*"

"The beginning of everything."

"Alright," I nodded as I stood up.

I walked over in front of the trio and sat down.

"I was 14, she was 13, we were just kids. She had a massive crush on me without actually knowing who or what the type of person I was." I explained.

I used to cry or feel terrible while talking about Mina after she died. Now I smile whenever I talk about her. I try to focus on the positive things and forget the negative for a moment. Kinda hard to do that since we were *both* negative.

Two negatives making a positive didn't count when it comes to Mina and I, did it?

"Where'd you guys meet?" Emily asked.

"7th grade science." I laughed.

The year Mina was boosted up a grade was 7th. We all knew the only reason why she passed was because Parker gave her all the answers and made her seem smart. The day she got boosted, I was sent to her classroom to tell her.

I remember the day I met her clearly. I walked into her science class. The teacher smiled at me then turned to Mina. Mina sat up in her seat in a heartbeat and her right leg started bouncing up and down.

"Mina...Willow?" I asked as I scanned the room.

I recognized the name. I was best friends with Jules at the time.

"I thought you guys met through Jules. I mean you were at his house 24/7, wouldn't you see her around?" Kai said.

"Nah, she was never home. She'd either be at my house, Arón's, Marina's, or-" Parker explained.

"Yeah, yeah we get it, Eden continue." Kai laughed.

Parker rolled her eyes playfully then slapped Kai's wrist.

"OWW!!!"

I narrowed my eyes as a judgy expression grew on my face. I shrugged it off and continued.

"Mina stood up and grabbed her stuff. I introduced myself but she interrupted me." I explained.

I remember it. She was standing in front of me with her books.

Mina was around 5'3 at the time, I was 5'4. Her natural hair was black but she dyed her hair a light blonde. She was skinny, she had the same body as a K-pop artist but you wouldn't see her on the cover of a magazine even though if she really wanted to be on one she'd figure out a way. She wasn't perfect but she was right for me. I wish I could've realized it sooner.

"I already know you." she interrupted.

I raised an eyebrow.

"How?"

"Jules talks about you and you're dating Alicia." she replied.

I scoffed, "You a stalker?"

She smiled, "No, Alicia is just popular. Which makes you popular too."

We continued walking down the hall. I had that intrigued look on my face.

"I'm... popular?" I asked.

"Meh. You're known as the *heartbreaker* or *the school player*." she explained confidently, "Not to double your ego or anything but all the girls in the grade have gone through an *Eden* phase, including the gays, and theys. They're just afraid to admit it sometimes."

She smiled as we continued to walk into the 8th grade hallway.

"You're not in my grade though. How would you know?" I asked.

"Well I am now aren't I?" she grinned.

We stopped at the door leading into the *math* classroom.

"So, you're *smart*." I said as I studied her.

"Nah." she chuckled, "I wanted to be in the same grade as Parker. She helped me cheat."

"You know Parker?"

"Course." she smiled as she swung open the classroom door.

"Wrong classroom." I laughed softly.

Mina stopped and watched the students turn and look at her. There was an awkward silence. She scanned the classroom. It looked nothing like a math class. She saw the spanish posters hanging and the spanish words and phrases on the whiteboard. She immediately knew.

"Lo siento." she smiled and shut the door.

`Translation: I'm sorry.`

She turned and smacked my arm.

"Why'd we stop here?!" she whispered as she tried not to laugh, "It made me think it was our math class!"

I laughed at her.

"You know spanish?" I asked.

"Yup, learned it from TV shows and google translate."

This is where I found out about her obsession with spanish TV shows and how she likes to switch languages back and forth to confuse people. Minutes later we walked into the *correct* math classroom. Parker was there, she turned to Mina and smiled eagerly.

"Hello Mina," the teacher greeted, "Eden, I moved your seat next to Parker's and.. Mina you'll be sitting *next* to him."

I looked at Mina and she gulped as casually as she could. She stood with her head high and her shoulders broad but I could tell she was nervous.

"Why'd you move my seat?" I asked.

The teacher forced a smile and gulped sharply.

"So you can show her around, help her out-"

"Alright." I interrupted.

"Plus, I switched your seat because *these* two wouldn't stop chatting during class and now they're fighting." she explained as she pointed to the two students.

The classroom was divided into rows of three. I sat in the middle, Parker on my left, Mina on my right.

That's how we met.

I looked at the trio and they were all smiling at me.

"You really miss her, don't you." Emily asked.

I nodded.

"O-*kay*, why were you guys so complicated?" Kai asked.

"Yeah, *why were* you guys?! I want to hear it from you." Parker said.

"It's a long story." I replied, "I can't even remember most of it."

Emily sat up.

"I remember it. She told me everything when we were friends."

I raised an eyebrow.

"And you're right," she shrugged, "it *is* a long story. Freshman year. You guys were friends, best friends throughout your relationship with *Alicia*, then when you and Alicia broke up during summer, you were stuck on her. Sophomore year, everything went to shit. Gia happened-"

I groaned and tiled my head back. I rubbed my eyes.

JUNE 1, 2019

"How are your past relationships? Would you say *you* and *your exes* are on good terms?" the inspector asked as she jotted down more notes.

"Why do we need to talk about my exes?" I asked.

188

"Why not?" the inspector shrugged, "People told me that's what you're known for, you're known as the *heartbreaker.*"

I paused.

"I mean, most of my exes are either psychotic or successful." I answered.

"Hm," she replied, "What was Mina? A psycho or successful?"

"Both. Depends on what your idea of success is."

"Who's your most recent ex other than Mina?"

To be honest, I forgot. I just answered the first ex that came to mind.

"Gia, but she isn't involved in this. She's been in Mexico visiting family for the past week. I left her during the beginning of sophomore year."

"How *do you* know she's on vacation?"

"Her instagram."

She nodded and wrote more notes.

"Okay, was she *a psycho* or *successful?*" she asked.

"Psycho. I don't really want to talk about her." I sighed.

"Who's your other ex, the one before Gia?"

I remember this one clearly.

"Alicia. She's not involved in this either. My exes have nothing to do with this, one goes from one boy-toy to another and the other has moved on." I explained.

"How's Alicia now? Have you checked up on her?" she asked.

I smiled lightly as I stared at the table.

"Yeah, she got a full scholarship to her dream school. She left school early to go pursue her soccer career." I explained.

Alicia and I were on good terms the last time I checked. I'm proud of her.

"Would you say.. you miss her?" the inspector asked.

I scoffed lightly.

"What are you saying?"

"I mean why'd you two break up? You seem like you still like her."

"No I don't. I don't miss her or anything like that. I still love her of course, she was my first love." I explained, "We broke it off during summer going into sophomore year because our futures didn't match up and she wasn't ready for a relationship full of commitment."

JULY 11, 2019

"You were secretly stuck on Alicia for a *LONG* time, Mina gave you advice but you took it wrong.

That's how sophomore year went, you went from mini douche to douche *bag* with Gia and all the other girls." Emily explained, "You pushed everyone away and went through a rampage. After a while, you and Mina kept driving each other crazy and giving mixed signals, you guys were living in each other's heads rent free, then *bloody hell*, finally, you stopped messing around!"

Mina and I were complicated because whenever she tried I pushed her away only to get closer to her again. Sometimes I did it on purpose because I tend to enjoy the adrenaline like she did.

We loved it.

"Driving each other crazy?" I asked.

"Hell yeah! She told me about the lunch thing." Emily exclaimed.

The lunch thing.

We were in the middle of an *argument*. It was sophomore year. To be honest I loved messing with her during that era but to be honest back then I only used the topic to distract myself from Alicia. One day Mina and Marina confronted me because Mina needed to tell me something.

They stepped onto the seats and jumped onto them in front of me swiftly and I lifted my head up casually. From their point of view, I looked like a psychopath.

I looked Marina in the eyes, she was about to kill me. She was a senior back then, she skipped her class to confront me with Mina. Without budging my head, I glanced over at Mina. She had that look on her face. She tried to act tough and act like she never cared, but she couldn't help but smile faintly.

I smirked lightly at her.

We kept eye contact. Her eyes widened a little. She didn't react much. Why didn't she react? She was good at acting, but I could tell it in her eyes, and the way she was breathing and quietly giggling with Marina. The way her cheeks turned red and she put her head down on the tables resting on her arms to keep it together.

She loved me.

She gets hooked on things, that's why we never let people give her things to smoke or snort, to love or hate, to buy or steal. If someone told her to do something she'd be tempted to do it, only to feel the consequences cave in later. Usually she's stronger than that.

That day people suggested her to flash me, offer her virginity, do something crazy and obnoxious only to get my attention because *she knew* I was mad at her. She never listened to those people, she just listened to the ideas then laughed them off.

She even confessed that she was hooked onto me, damn, she confessed.

"Um. So-" Mina smiled, "I really like you."

It's not like I already knew.

She loved me, so I drove her crazy.

"You know," Parker joined, "She called me the night you guys met and totally freaked out. She liked you from the start to finish. Four years."

"Damn." I replied.

"Anyway, we need a resource." Parker said as she called the rest of the gang over.

We all sat in a circle.

"The story of how they met or why they were so complicated isn't important, what is important is what the hell happened leading up to the death." Parker explained.

"Well jeez, what didn't happen?!" Miles sighed, "It was hell."

"Everyone has different points of view from what happened." Kai said.

"Then we need something to start with. Almost like a blueprint." Parker continued.

"Hm." Jules replied, "You mean the files?"

"Yeah, the files to the case. We need the whole story and evidence to piece it all together."

"Alright, how are we going to get the files?" Jordan asked.

"The police station?" Emily asked, "Or... we can check her old school locker for any clues."

"The school would've cleaned out all our lockers by now but we can check. But here's the important question, *how* are we going to get access to it in the first place? They won't give it to us if we ask." I explained.

Parker thought for a second then smirked.

"Miles," she said, "Call Cory."

10
the files
[JULY 12, 2019]

JUNE 1, 2019 [recorded tape]

"From these past three years, would you say Eden was a violent person?" the inspector asked.

"Eden?? It depends. Why do you ask?" Miles replied.

"During Mina's autopsy, bruises were found all over her body, do you think she could have been a victim of domestic violence?"

There were a few seconds of silence. You could only hear Miles breathing.

"No. *No* way. Eden would never." Miles explained, "Eden *may* not be a perfect person but he wouldn't pull a stunt like this. Mina wouldn't have let him."

"What about the Monday before she died?"

"Well.. that was normal for everyone."

JUNE 2, 2019 [recorded tape]

"How are things at home? Did you and Mina spend time together?" the inspector asked.

"Barely. Maybe when we were in junior high we hung out a lot but when we got into high school, she started to be distant." Jules explained.

"Really? When did you start to notice the distance?"

"Ever since she and Eden got together sophomore year."

"You said they were never official." she pointed out.

"Right." Jules paused, "They weren't. But, they weren't exactly *just friends* either."

JULY 12, 2019

We spent the last night running around Atlantic City wondering what we'll see next. Miles called Cory, Cory Valentine, number one prankster and class clown in our grade. Nobody hated him.

"Cory?" Miles asked.

"What's up Miles!" Cory replied when he answered the phone.

"Look I need you to help me with something, like the old days, we need to sneak into the school and get into Mina's locker." Miles explained.

We were in our hotel room. The walls were painted a pale yellow and the bedframes were brown and polished. Miles was on the phone pacing back and forth in the room. The rest of us were sitting on the two beds listening into the conversation.

"Well- why do you want to get into Mina's locker?" Cory asked.

Cory wasn't that fond of Mina, every class he had with her they got into screaming matches. They'd warm up to each other once and a while.

```
JUNE 3, 2019 [recorded tape]
```

"What was Mina like in school?" the inspector asked.

"I mean.." Riah answered, "Not really there."

"She skipped classes?"

"No. She just stopped talking once and a while."

"When did you notice?"

"Junior year."

"Who was she around the most?"

"Eden." Riah answered, "It's not really her fault though, well, it *kinda* is. She just hated everyone."

"But she didn't hate Eden?"

"Well sometimes, if you're talking about sophomore year then yeah, kinda, but junior year, no."

```
JUNE 3, 2019 [recorded tape]
```

"How was she?" the inspector asked, "How was Mina?"

"Everyone hated her." Evelyn answered, "Didn't matter to her because she hated them twice as hard."

"Did *you* hate her?"

Evelyn sighed.

"She was like a ticking time bomb, *helpless*, y'know." she explained in a rude sympathetic tone, "Every step she took, *something* got out of place, it was annoying."

"So.. you hated her."

"I wasn't the only one, trust me."

```
JULY 12, 2019
```

Miles scoffed and gave the phone to Parker. She was sitting right next to me.

"We think they have the wrong person. It wasn't Evelyn. We need to find clues." Parker explained.

There was a pause. Cory usually does it to process the sentence or for suspense. Sometimes both.

"Alright, meet me at the back of the school, 9:00PM sharp." Cory replied.

"We're in New Jersey right now, it's 5:30 in the afternoon." Miles whispered.

"Better get driving." Cory smiled as he hung up the phone.

So we did. We packed up all our stuff, checked out of our hotel rooms and left New Jersey. We settled the seating again, Parker drove Marina's car with Jules in the passenger seat and Riah and Miles in the back. Marina drove my car with me in the passenger seat and Emily, Jordan, and Kai in the back. We drove back to Maryland and reached the back of the school.

We got out of the car and stood there awkwardly.

"Where's Cory?" Kai whispered.

"He should be here somewhere." Parker whispered back.

Our heads turned swiftly over to the right as we heard the bushes rustle.

"Pow!" Cory shouted as he jumped out of them aggressively.

We all flinched.

Cory was tall, 6'2. He was a tall friendly black guy, had black eyes and short curly hair, he had glasses too. He's known as the *funny guy* in class. The guy who messes around all day but still manages to have straight A's. He got pissed off easily, he had his morals but sometimes he couldn't help but get mad and start a fight.

"You guys need to get into Mina's locker?"

"Yeah." Miles answered.

Cory was about to explain but Jules interrupted him.

"But, how are we even going to *get* in? What if we get caught or they catch us on camera?" Jules asked.

"Well if you'd let me explain," Cory rolled his eyes, "I called my friend, Aníbal, he temporarily shut off the cameras for.."

He lifted up his wrist and checked his navy blue watch.

"About 20 minutes." Cory continued.

Cory told the majority of us to stay outside as he, Parker, and Miles snuck inside the school. We watched Cory carefully open the window to climb in. Mina had a top locker, locker #101. Our school colours were maroon and grey, Mina had a maroon locker. Around 15 minutes later Miles hopped out of the window.

"Nothing. They cleared it out." he said.

Parker hopped out of the window after him.

"Let's go to the station." she suggested, "We'll definitely find something there."

We all drove to the station. We were at the back and Cory slid open one of the windows.

"Marina, Jordan, you guys stay in the cars. You guys will be our getaway drivers just in case something happens." Cory explained, "The rest of you, stay with me."

Cory climbed through the window silently and looked around. He turned back around to us swiftly.

"Sh! Silent!" he whispered.

I climbed through next. I stood up and looked around. White and blue bricks aligning the walls, black chairs and coffee tables, and random items on each shelf.

Kai climbed in, she tripped on the rim and fell on her face.

"oW-"

"Sh!" Cory interrupted.

Kai stood up and gained back her balance.

Parker, Jules, Miles, Riah, and Emily climbed in carefully one after another. We all walked down the wide hallway silently and slowly. We knew that if we got caught, we're screwed.

I looked over at each office to check if anyone was there. It would've been rare though, it was 11:00PM at night. I looked over at the office on the left at the end of the hallway.

Lamp on.

I lightly hit the arm of the person next to me. I turned. It was Emily.

Oh.

I decided to play along with it.

"What is that detective doing here at almost midnight?!" I whispered.

The detective from that room coughed loudly. Kai flinched and her leg hit one of the coffee tables. It made a noise louder than my own screaming thoughts.

"¡Joder!" Cory exclaimed quietly.

```
Translation: Damn it!
```

He started panicking silently. We all scattered out at the speed of light and hid. We hid behind the couches, bookshelves, walls, anything that could keep us invisible.

The detective walked out and stood at the end of the hallway. I moved my head a little. I was hiding behind the arm of a blue couch. The couch was on the right wall of the hallway. There was another couch on the opposite side of the hallway. Emily was hiding behind the arm of it too.

"Who's there?" the detective asked loudly.

I turned my head slightly, not enough for the detective to see me. It was Detective Max. I had to whisper every time I needed to communicate.

"Emily!" I whispered, "It's your Step-dad!"

Emily turned her head to me and raised an eyebrow.

"What's your Step-dad doing here?!" I asked.

"He's probably working on a case! He loves this job to death and he takes it very seriously!" she replied.

"Well obviously not enough since he arrested his own step-daughter!"

"¡Cállate!" Cory whispered.

```
Translation: Shut up!
```

Emily and I turned our heads forward quickly. Cory was hiding behind the side of a dark wooden bookshelf.

Detective Max sighed and rubbed the back of his neck.

He walked back into his office mumbling, "Man, I think I'm going crazy!"

"Alright, the storage room is on my right. Parker, Jules, you're going with me to find the files." Cory explained.

I turned my head, Parker and Jules were hiding in an office, they slowly lifted their heads up in sync as they heard Cory.

"Emily, you go distract your Step-dad so he won't suspect anything!" Cory whispered.

"He's a *detective!* I'm not good at lying!" she whispered back.

"Oh c'mon!" Cory replied, "You pretended to enjoy Evelyn's existence for 17 years! You got this."

Kai snorted. It wasn't loud but we could all hear it.

"You should've eaten her in the womb." Kai giggled sarcastically.

Emily giggled faintly, "That's not funny!"

She quickly covered her mouth to cancel out the noise. She stood up and walked into Detective Max's office promptly.

"Hi Max!" she said casually.

"Bloody hell! Emily, you startled me!" he sighed.

"Sorry,"

"What are you doing here? How'd you get in?"

Cory swung his hands around like a maniac signaling everyone to get to their places. He sorta looked like a ceiling fan.

"Eden! You take Riah, Kai, and Miles with you and try to get out of here without getting caught! Parker, Jules, and I will go get the files!" he explained quietly.

I sat there to process it.

"Damn it! The security cameras!" I said quietly, "The cameras!"

"Don't worry Aníbal hacked these too! We have 14 minutes left!" Cory said as he, Parker, and Jules ran into the storage room.

Riah and Miles lifted their heads up from under a desk. Their faces were bright red and they were silently snickering. They quietly walked out of the office. Kai jumped up from behind the vending machine. I stood up and looked around.

"Down the hallway! If we take a right there's an exit door!" I explained.

They all nodded and followed me. We walked down the hallway slowly and I turned around and walked backwards to see if all three people were still behind me.

Until I bumped into someone.

I stood there frozen. I felt the panic flow through my head. The chills flying down my spine.

Damn it!

I turned around as casually as I could. It was Detective Toby. I hesitated for a second.

"Ahh! There you are, I've been looking for you everywhere!" I said.

There was a girl next to him. She had tan skin, black shoulder-length curly hair, brown eyes and she was 5'6. She was standing next to him with her eyes widened.

Detective Toby raised an eyebrow.

"I found something. Something...*important.*" I said.

"It's 11:20 at night."

"You know how much Mina was important to me."

"Mmm.." Kai remarked.

I turned around back to Kai.

"Do you have something to tell me?"

She shook her head.

We followed Toby and the girl into his office. Light grey walls, dark oak furniture, and a beige file cabinet. There were mugs with pens and pencils and papers scattered around the desk. There were framed pictures and accomplishments all around the walls.

"Hold on, I left my coffee in the break room." Toby said as he walked back outside of the office.

There was a table. It was grey and had high-chairs. Miles, Kai, Riah, and I sat down awkwardly. They were as confused as I was. I was trying to figure out how to make up a story and have them play along. I was also trying to figure out a way to lie without having a *detective* notice.

"Who are you?" I asked the girl.

She was sitting in Detective Toby's spinny chair spinning it in circles like there was no tomorrow.

"I'm Aisha, Aisha Abboud." she replied.

She stopped spinning in the chair and wobbled her head back and forth.

"I'm Detective Toby's sidekick!" she replied happily.

"How old are you?" Riah asked.

"Fifteen."

"Uh-"

"Detective Toby's my adoptive older brother. Even though he's a *grown adult* and *I'm* a teenager, he let me help out with his job early!" Aisha explained, "His parents adopted me from Egypt fourteen years ago."

Toby walked back into the office with a mug in his hand. It was dead silent in the room. It was awkward too. Detective Toby tried lighting up the moment.

"Alright, *chatty cathys,* what do you want to tell me?"

We all stood up.

I looked over at Miles. He was eyeing my pocket. I had the letter in it. I kept the letter with me at all times so no one could take it.

"Well- we just needed to ask how the case was going?" Riah asked.

I reached down to my pocket and Miles tapped the table. I looked up.

He looked me dead in the eye and shook his head.

My hand drifted away from my pocket.

"Well we're still investigating." Toby replied, "Did you guys really come all out here at almost *midnight* to ask how's the case going?"

I looked down at my phone. I got a text from Emily.

Say I was visiting Max and you guys drove me. Then say since you were already here you wanted to check on how the case was going.

"We-" Riah said.

"No." I interrupted.

There was a short silence. They all turned their heads and looked at me waiting for an explanation.

"Emily wanted to visit her Step-dad so we drove her. We just thought it'd be convenient to ask you now since we're already here." I explained carefully.

"Huh." Toby replied, "When you bumped into me you said it was something important."

"It *is* important. I mean, we think Evelyn wasn't the killer."

"Leave it to us."

"We *have* been leaving it to you guys. And look where it got us." Miles pointed out.

"Don't worry Detective Max and I, we won't disappoint you. Inspector Alex has been working hard on this case too. We have your backs." Toby comforted.

He turned to Aisha.

"I see you've met my little sister." he smiled.

"I- uh-" Kai replied.

"We better get going. Emily needs a ride home." I said as we all eyed each other.

We walked out of the office casually until we heard a loud-

"HEY! HEY! WHO'S RUNNING OUTSIDE WITH FILES?" a worker yelled.

It sounded like Inspector Alex.

I felt panic shoot down my spine. Riah and Miles turned to each other as their eyes widened. Kai was confused.

"Aren't you...going to go..check that out?" Kai asked Toby.

Riah quickly slapped her wrist. Not enough for Detective Toby to notice.

"Huh?" Detective Toby replied.

"Someone just yelled that someone was stealing files."

"No- Inspector Alex is just watching a TV show." Toby answered.

The four of us sighed in relief without making it noticeable. The panic and confusion faded away.

He turned towards her office.

"WHICH IS VERY LOUD BY THE WAY." he shouted sarcastically.

"Alright uh- I'm going to go get Emily." I said.

We walked out, grabbed Emily from Max's office and once we got out of the station. We ran. We ran into Marina's and my car and drove away. Cory, Parker, and Jules managed to escape with the files. The file box was in the backseat. Detective Toby and Aisha were looking out the window. My concern was if they saw the box in the car.

"Miles, why didn't you let me show Detective Toby the letter?" I asked.

We were on the way to Cory's house to drop him off.

"He would've taken it and went to the storage room, therefore he would've caught Parker, Jules, and Cory." Miles explained.

I raised my eyebrows, "Oh.."

We drove to Marina's house after dropping Cory off. We all gathered around and sat in the basement on the couches. Jules brought over the box and opened it. Parker walked over too. Parker was holding a black notebook.

"Mina's autopsy results." Jules sighed.

He lifted up the papers and read them.

"Two arrow wounds, one through her left lung and one through her right thigh." he explained, "She had bruises all over her shoulders and torso."

"Bruises?" Parker gasped, "Hold up- what do you mean bruises?"

"Bruises." Jules repeated, "Purple ones."

Mina got into a lot of fights. She either won all of them or laughed at the opponent for how stupid they are.

JUNE 1, 2019

"Did you get along with your classmates?" the inspector asked.

"Yeah. I usually stay out of stuff unless I find it amusing." I replied.

"Did *Mina* get along with her classmates?"

I scoffed quietly.

"Meh, 50/50. One half hated her guts, y'know, wanted her dead or wanted to see her embarrass herself over and over again. It entertained them." I explained, "The other half either didn't know or care who she was or only talked to her because they needed something."

The inspector looked up at me slowly. Her eyes showed me she felt sorry for Mina. But she didn't need to.

"Well, what about her friends? Or you?" she asked.

"I mean... Parker *was* close with her, but she hung out with Kai and Jules. Miles used to be close with her when they were kids but he was distant after he got with Riah. Marina? She's two years older and she used to baby her and sometimes the things she said out of anger hurt." I told her, "Mina avoided Jordan. She knew he had a little crush on her and Mina and Emily haven't spoken in a long time."

"And what about you?"

"To be honest I can be a shitty person."

JULY 12, 2019

"How'd she get the bruises?" Riah asked.

Riah asked the question but deep down we all knew the answer.

This wasn't new. It's been going on for years. Jules and Mina would show up to school with random bruises sometimes. It was their parents.

"Jules," Parker said softly.

"No. It wasn't my parents, Parker. They hit me but they never tried hitting Mina ever since she hit them back freshman year. Ever since then they made her life hell." Jules explained.

"What do you mean made her life hell?" Emily asked.

"They verbally and emotionally abused her. She just stopped reacting to it after years because she didn't have energy to care." Jules explained gently, "They hit us every once and a while but it was mostly me."

Why didn't we help their situation? Jules wouldn't let us.

"We need to tell the inspector! They thought it was Eden at first!" Miles said.

Jules scoffed, "Eden? Seriously? If he pulled something like that Mina would've made *his* life hell."

"Then why didn't she?" Parker asked, "Look I'm *totally* sorry Eden but you can be *such a* bitch it's literally painful to defend you."

I widened my eyes and looked up at Parker.

Parker, the girl who didn't care. Why is she making a comment about me?

I guess I know why we drifted apart now.

"I don't know." I answered.

Emily scoffed.

She didn't make a comment. Which is surprising for *her* because she always had something to say. She always had an opinion on everything. But, she didn't say anything when Parker was shouting at me, she just looked at me like I was some monster. I could tell she wanted to tell me off as much as Parker did.

"Eden, you treated her like shit." Parker snapped as she stormed upstairs to calm down.

She was talking about sophomore year.

At least I think she was.

I was sitting there not being able to look anyone in the eye. They were all mad at me but they had done stuff to Mina too. We were all hypocrites.

"Let's not get sidetracked." Jordan spoke up.

The whole time Jordan was just giggling along quietly with Parker's remarks. He hated me as much as she did.

"You can't report my parents. All our money will be gone, what is my sister going to use for college!? How's Lily going to feel about this!? My house and all my stuff will be thrown down a drain!" Jules explained.

"Is this really what you're worried about right now?" I snapped.

They all turned to me.

"Well who else would it be? It wouldn't have been Jules' parents if they rarely beat her." Jordan asked.

There was a pause.

"Gia." we all said.

"*Gia?* Your ex-girlfriend?" Riah scoffed.

"She's not an ex if she and I never dated." I replied, "It was just a fling."

"Yeah. A *few* flings." Riah mocked.

"Gia and Mina fighting? Oh please." Miles laughed.

"No. I know both of the-"

"No you didn't." Marina interrupted.

I looked up at her.

Is everyone mad at me now? What?

"You *thought* you knew Mina, but *ya* didn't." Marina snapped.

I tried not to snap. Of course I knew Mina, I knew her better than anyone, but Marina knew her better.

"Well I knew Gia. She'd never fight Mina herself, she'd get her college friends to jump her." I replied.

"Huh- and *did* that happen?"

"No, because Mina would've brought *her* college friends to help her."

"Arón?" Riah asked.

I nodded.

Parker came back downstairs. She was still angry.

"Alright." I said as I stood up from the couch, "Why is everyone pissed at me?"

"They found Mina's diary and read it on the way home." Marina answered.

"Who's they?"

"I was driving, Parker, Riah, and Emily were in the car." Marina explained, "They sure were not happy with the entries."

"Let me guess, it's the diary from 8th grade?" I snapped.

"No. Diary from sophomore year. Mina had a bad memory and she also didn't have enough patience to write about her and her serious problems." Parker answered sternly, "There were barely any entries but we sure found a few *interesting* ones."

"That still doesn't explain why *all* of you are mad at me." I said.

"Because the rest of us already know what was in Mina's diary. She told us herself before .. y'know.. she died!" Jordan said.

I scoffed.

"What did the diary say? Let me see it." I sighed.

Parker turned to grab the notebook out of Jordan's hands. Jordan was sitting on the single couch reading it. Parker snatched it and gave it to me.

```
diary entry #7?

Dear diary,
Eden's ego just shot through the
roof. He's being an asshole.
```

I looked up from the diary and sighed.

```
He's only pulling these stunts to
impress Alicia. He acts like I don't
know. He only does this shit to look
```

cool in front of his friends. He asked me out. As a joke. He told me if I ever thought he'd ever date me then I must be high on drugs.

He says it wasn't his idea. I'm pretty sure he only told me that so I won't beat the shit out of him.

Sometimes my anger gets the best of me. I confronted him at his locker the next day. I wanted to slap him but I couldn't bring myself to, I only shoved him to watch him tumble over a little. At least that made me feel better.

I should really let go. If he had the balls to do this then he's not worth it. But I can't, I can't let him go. He's not doing okay, he's going crazy. And for a girl? Oh please.

I mean… at least his day was ruined too. I saw Alicia and Ethan make out in the janitor's closet. LOL.

I shut the notebook and clenched my jaw.

"Is this really why you guys are mad at me?" I snapped.

"Did you read the part about Alicia and Ethan?" Jordan snickered.

Ethan was my best friend. We were almost identical, people always told us the only way they told us apart was the freckles. I had freckles, he didn't.

We were super close but in junior year we split apart. I trusted him with my life. He made out with my ex? Damn.

"No, I don't give a shit about that." I answered.

Miles widened his eyes and jumped up. Riah followed. Seconds later they came trotting back to the couches snickering with two bags of..

Popcorn.

"You couldn't even make it past one entry did you? Well there were seven entries, they're all about you screwing up." Parker snapped, "I used to stay up at night worrying *my ass off* because I thought she was going to do *something stupid* or *something she'd regret* FOR YOU! She was stuck on you and now she's dead."

"So you're telling me it's *my* fault she's dead?!" I snapped back.

We all went at it. Fighting, to be honest if Mina saw us tonight she would've been surprised.

"I remember everything Eden! This was only *one* story. Imagine the countless times you hurt her!" Parker said, "Kai, remember the screenshot story?"

"Mhm." Kai replied, "She spilled out her mind to you then you screenshotted it and sent it to *her brother* laughing!!"

She giggled as her eyes teared up in anger.

"I mean are you really that stupid?"

Anger. It's not my best emotion.

"We were 15 years old!" I shouted.

"WE WERE IN SOPHMORE YEAR!!" Parker shouted back.

Whenever someone in the group is mad it's better to leave them alone unless you want to see a side you have never met yet.

"I--WAS---BORN--IN--MARCH!" I shouted angrily.

Marina started cackling, mumbling the stuff we said under her breath. It's what she usually does.

"I--WAS--*BORN*--IN---*MARCH!!*" she mocked as she cackled.

It caused me to start laughing too, I started tearing up in anger.

"Look if I got to go back to those days and fix it I would." I sighed.

"Yeah. Right." Parker mumbled.

The files were scattered out everywhere on the coffee table. It was overwhelming to look at all the different sides and views of the case.

"Damn guys look, it's Evelyn's mugshot see?" Miles chuckled as he held it up.

Evelyn looked fierce and tough in the photo. Her eyes were sharp and she was clenching her jaw. She was clutching onto the placard and her nails were scratching on it. Her blonde hair was up in a ponytail, it was messy and a little frizzy. Her mascara was smeared all around the edge of her eyes.

"Woah! That's like straight out of a movie!" Kai gasped.

"Guys. I think Inspector Alex saw Cory, Parker, and I with the files." Jules said.

"Huh-" Kai replied, "Detective Toby said it was from the TV playing down the hallway."

"Well they're going to realize the files are missing anyway!" Parker said, "And Toby and Max knew we were there that night, it'd be obvious. So what?"

"Alright, I guess." Jules replied.

We needed to drive somewhere to stay. Detective Toby and Max and Inspector Alex were going to search for us when they found out. We couldn't go to any of our houses, especially Jules. Jules' house reeked of memories I didn't want to relive.

"Alright get all the papers, we're going to Arón's house." Marina said.

11
arón, grab the booze
[JULY 14, 2019]

"Oh wait, what if he's not home?" Emily asked, "I mean it's a Friday afternoon, what if he has work?"

"Doesn't matter." Marina replied, "He lets me hang out at his house all the time, I even have my own key."

We drove to Arón's house. He was in the kitchen standing behind a counter trying to figure out how to make a smoothie.

Marina unlocked the door and walked in. Arón didn't even look up from the direction sheet. He didn't even make a face or question everything.

"¿Cómo--hago--yo-----eh?" he mumbled.

```
Translation: How--do--I-----huh?
```

He got frustrated. He turned and grabbed a red apple and chucked it at the wall and grunted. He shut his eyes and took a deep breath, he opened one eye.

"Hola Marina."

"Hola." Marina replied.

The rest of us followed her in. His house was small-ish but big enough for nine people to stay for a little while.

Riah and Miles have been arguing about who knows what for the past two days. They seemed fine but they started fighting out of the blue. They're usually the happy couple with the backstories. They were always laughing, throwing items at each other, smiling and blushing. They're straight out of a movie.

They're what Mina had always wanted.

But they've been angry at each other. Scoffing and mumbling rude remarks under their breath when an argument didn't go their way.

Arón looked up. Marina was standing on the opposite side of the counter.

"¿Qué estás haciendo?" she asked.

"Tratando de averiguar la hoja de instrucciones." he replied.

`Translation:`

"What are you doing?" she asked.
"Trying to figure out the instruction sheet," he replied.

Marina shrugged and picked up the manual. "There's a translated version on the back." Marina giggled.
"I know!" Arón replied, "I'm.. trying to learn more English!"
Marina laughed and helped him read the instructions. The rest of us went to the living room. Riah and Miles were going at it... again. They paced into the room throwing their arms around.
"Why do you want to know *so bad!?*" Miles shouted.
Arón looked up cluelessly and raised an eyebrow.
"Don't worry about it." Marina whispered.
"¿Qué?"
"They're just fighting over... I don't know." Marina replied.
The living room was large. There were maroon couches and rugs. The walls were white and had grey accents. The warm white lights made the room look beige.

"It says on your report you refused to tell them where you were!!" Riah replied, "Can't you see it makes you look suspicious!?"

Miles stood there staring at the floor as Riah stood there patiently beside him. She turned towards him preparing for what Miles was going to say.

Miles sighed deeply and rubbed his eye. He turned to Riah and looked directly into her eyes.

"I was with Evelyn," he said softly.

The room went silent. All our eyes widened and we gave each other looks.

What. Just. Happened.

Riah stood there frozen. Her eyes wide and her mouth open. Her eyes were red and teary.

"Well." she gasped softly, "I hooked up with Jordan."

The whole room gasped quietly.

"So I guess we're even." Riah snapped gently.

Miles stood there clenching his jaw and teary eyed.

"I know," he whispered.

He broke the eye contact and looked up at the ceiling. He took a shaky deep breath.

Riah sniffled sharply and walked out of the living room. We all looked at each other nervously.

Miles was just blankly staring at the floor trying not to cry.

Emily looked over at Miles then slowly paced out of the room and followed Riah. I slowly stood up from the couch.

"Miles." I said softly.

"What?" he snapped, "Are you going to ask why I did it?"

"No. Why Evelyn? Out of all girls." Parker asked.

Parker was sitting on the couch facing the left wall next to me. I was kind of surprised she didn't try to murder me yet but she's Parker, she doesn't stay mad at people over petty reasons.

"I skipped 7th period to meet up at the sunflower field for the films. On the way I saw Evelyn crying in the hallway." Miles explained.

He slowly walked over and around to the couch facing the TV and sat down. He wouldn't look anyone else in the eye.

"She was sitting on the floor leaning against the wall. Crying. I felt bad. I didn't want to walk past her bawling her eyes out." he continued.

"It was *Evelyn*. Maybe she deserved whatever happened to her." Kai said.

"But she didn't!" Miles snapped, "She didn't deserve it! I stopped walking and asked what was wrong. It was her Dad."

The room went silent again.

"Her Dad left her and Emily when they were seven. She was upset because she found out her Dad reached out to Emily and didn't reach out to her." Miles continued, "When Emily found out, she blocked him on everything. He was only going to reach out, give them hope, then leave again. It's been happening for years."

"To spark jealousy?" Jules asked.

"Yeah."

"That still doesn't explain why you hooked up with her." Jordan said.

Miles turned his head to Jordan. He looked angry. His eyes were fired up and he was clenching his fist. He raised an eyebrow.

He knew this entire time didn't he?

"Why'd *you* hook up with Riah?" he snapped.

Bloody. Hell.

Jordan went silent. He smiled lightly.

"How did you find out?"

Jordan looked like he was proud of it. Riah was pretty. Miles was attractive. Jordan was satisfied he got a chance to steal Riah right below Miles' nose.

"Kai." Miles replied.

Jordan's head swiftly turned to Kai. His tongue was in his cheek, he looked annoyed.

"What? Someone had to tell him." Kai shrugged.

Miles was always like Kai's older brother. Kai always told him everything. It would look like a hard decision for her, she was close to both Jordan and Miles.

"That still doesn't explain how it even happened." Jules said.

"ALRIGHT!" Miles shouted.

We all flinched.

"I was *comforting* her alright! I felt bad. If *my* Dad left at seven and reached out to Anna just to give her hope I'd be upset too! Evelyn's Dad did that and left her with unanswered questions." Miles explained, "I wanted to cheer her up! We were *goofing* around running and laughing in the halls, then she kissed me. We just got caught up in the moment."

We heard footsteps. Loud, angry footsteps. All our heads turned to the living room door on the left. Miles was the only one staring straight forward.

"WHEN EMILY SAID EVELYN WAS WITH ONE OF US I DIDN'T EXPECT IT WAS YOU!!" Riah shouted in tears.

Emily chased her into the room and gasped. Riah was crawling over the couch shouting while trying to rip Miles apart.

"Fucking hell." Jules sighed as he rolled his eyes.

"What's wrong with her?!" I asked.

"She asked Arón for some booze." Emily shouted as she grabbed Riah's shoulders.

"WHY?!" Jules shouted.

"To cope?! *I don't know!*"

"*Did* he give her booze?" Jordan asked.

"Yeah!"

"WHY?!" Jules and Jordan shouted at the same time.

"The--ouch-Riah--*legal*--age---of--drinking--in---Spain---is--16!" Emily panted as she tried pulling Riah away.

"It's 18!" Marina shouted from the kitchen.

"UGh! I don't know but the booze got to her quickly! She's drunk! Angry drunk!"

Riah crawled on top of Miles and he fell onto his back on the couch. Riah slapped him.

"REALLY? EVELYN? OUT OF ALL GIRLS!" she cried.

"THAT'S WHAT I SAID!!" Parker cackled.

Marina rushed into the room to pry Riah off of Miles. We were all scattered across the room

230

panicking, swinging our arms around like idiots, and trying to pull Riah and Miles away from each other.

Kai and Parker were laughing.

"GO RIAH!" Parker laughed.

"GO MILES!" Kai giggled.

Riah was on top of Miles slapping his face, smacking his chest and shoulders, while screaming. Miles would never hit her back. He wouldn't dare. He knew she was drunk. He was laying on his back trying to pry her off of him while shouting.

"You *hooked up* with some *OCEAN OBSESSED* junkie!" Miles shouted.

"WHAT DID YOU CALL ME?!" Jordan shouted.

"You're the one to talk! You hooked up with someone who's hooked up with half the grade!" Riah screamed.

"It was just a kiss! I told her I had a girlfriend! She didn't know!"

"Yeah right, Evelyn knows everything. We've been dating since we were 13! She did that on purpose."

"Enough!" Marina laughed.

Arón ran into the room, once he saw the fight he tried not to giggle.

"Jo--der." he mumbled, "Don't...don't.. *break* anything!"

He walked out of the room awkwardly and figured out how to use the blender. Throughout the whole entire fight we heard fruit being blended and Arón singing a spanish song.

"This is so petty!" Parker giggled.

Kai stood up to mess around. She started spinning around aggressively with her arms out. She looked like a ceiling fan.

Once Parker saw it she started cackling. She stood up to spin with her but Kai lost her balance from spinning too fast.

WACK!

Kai's left arm hit Parker's chest. She flew back with her arms in the air and her left arm hit my head. I went crashing down the carpeted floor. The room went silent.

There we were. Laying on the ground like idiots because we crashed into each other like dominos.

Riah, Miles, and everyone else stopped shouting and turned to us. It was painfully awkwardly silent. They stood there breathing heavily, raising their eyebrows looking at the three of us on the ground.

5 SECONDS LATER

They all started shouting at each other like maniacs again. Miles managed to sit up. He pushed Riah off of him and stood up. Jules held him back as Emily and Marina held Riah back. Riah was kicking and shouting. Jules didn't need to use a lot of power to hold Miles back. Miles was just standing there trying to catch his breath.

What did Kai and Parker do? They were sitting on the couch next to me laughing their heads off cheering on the fight. What was Jordan doing? Giggling angrily trying not to get up and beat up Miles himself.

What was I doing? I was frozen watching the fight debating whether I should involve myself.

"SO WHAT? DID *YOU* KISS HER? OR DID YOU GUYS-"

"NO. IT WAS NOTHING OKAY? I JUST TOLD HER I HAD A GIRLFRIEND AND SHE LEFT." Miles shouted.

"IF IT WAS NOTHING WHY DID YOU KEEP IT A SECRET FOR THIS LONG??"

"BECAUSE-"

Jordan lost his temper. He stood up swiftly and ran into Miles. He slammed and pushed him. Miles fell over the couch.

Jules let go of Miles and sighed angrily and turned to me.

"The hell are you doing?!" I scoffed as I ran over to Jordan to pry him off.

Jordan punched Miles. Right where his original bruise from the night he went missing. Jules and I pulled Jordan off before Miles could do anything. He was so upset he was capable of breaking Jordan's skull. Jules grabbed Jordan's shoulders and threw him off. I grabbed Miles and pulled him away.

"What are you even mad about? You just want to get involved so you can have Riah!" Miles shouted.

"Shut up! Don't talk to me like that!" Jordan replied.

"You think you're so much better than me, hm? Always hating me since the start."

"Alright, ENOUGH!" Marina shouted.

When Marina gets mad and shouts it's scarier than a zombie apocalypse and a back to school commercial combined. The room went silent.

"Emily, get Riah out of here, Jordan you're going outside, Miles you stay here." Marina said sternly.

Riah was still sobbing.

"Arón?!!!!" Marina yelled.

"¿Qué?" Arón screamed back.
"¡Conseguir el alcohol!"
"¡Vale!" Arón giggled.

```
Translation:
"Arón?!!!!" Marina yelled.
"What?" Arón screamed back.
"Get the booze!"
"Okay!" Arón giggled.
```

Jules followed Jordan outside and tried to calm him down. Jordan's face had marks and his knuckles were scratched. Miles sat down on the couch and winced. His knuckles were bright red. He also had huge marks on his cheek and neck from Riah as well.

"That fight was stupid." I mumbled.

"She's just angry. I don't blame her." Miles defended.

"But *she* hooked up with someone too!" Kai said, "You have a right to be upset as well."

"I'm sure what happened with me and Evelyn is the same thing that happened to her and Jordan." Miles sighed.

He laid back on the back rest of the couch and rubbed his eye.

Parker was staring into space. She spoke her mind.

"Has anyone noticed Jules has been way nicer than before?" she said.

"Huh?" I replied.

"I mean, he's been insanely nice to all of us since Mina died."

"He's *always* overly nice." Miles mumbled.

"He's been touchy and doing favours. It's like he's guilty of something."

"Puberty?" I giggled.

"He's 17! Turning 18 in five months!" Kai giggled.

"I think he's just guilty of not being there for Mina or something. I don't know! The boy's always guilty about *something*. Maybe he's just trying to be an older brother to all of us instead of Mina now." Miles explained.

Parker nodded and looked at the door. She sat up and walked out of the living room.

"I'm going to the bathroom." she mumbled.

I raised an eyebrow. I suspected something, I saw that suspicious, guilty look on her face.. I waited a few seconds. Then followed her. She walked down a hallway and into the bathroom. I didn't go in.

11.2
frozen peas

I heard two voices in the bathroom. It sounded like something important.

"You need to tell him, Emily." Parker whispered.

I stood there beside the door listening to their conversation.

"He's going to hate me. He's going to *really* hate me." Emily sighed, "You tell him! Tell him it was a mistake and you should've told him from the start!"

"Why are *YOU* telling *ME* that?" Parker argued, "You should be the one telling him! Tell him why you did what you did at the party!"

"Well at least tell him what *you did* and what *you know!*"

"Mmmmm, you should too. You know more than me. You did *much more* too."

They started speaking quieter. I turned my body closer and closer to the door. But that was my mistake, I accidentally knocked a picture frame down.

CRAP!

Parker and Emily stopped talking. I heard the doorknob rustle.

Run.

I paced into the kitchen down the hallway. Arón was humming while chugging his purple berry smoothie.

"Hola." I panted.

Arón turned and gulped. He spoke slowly. He's been forcing himself to speak pure English for the past two weeks.

"Want some?"

"Sure,"

He snatched a clear glass cup from the drawers and poured me a cup. I tried to act natural. I didn't want them to know I was eavesdropping. Especially when I knew.

I knew one of them was the murderer.

Emily.

It was Emily.

Parker? No way. Why would Parker kill Mina? Why would Emily kill Mina?

None of them had huge motives but if you had to choose between who is capable of killing a person like Mina..

Emily.

I knew I had to get closer with Emily now. I had no choice. She knows. She walked down the hallway and eyed me and Arón.

Arón turned around while making a *different* type of smoothie. I turned and raised an eyebrow.

"How many smoothies are you going to make?" I chuckled as Arón plopped cubes of mangos into the blender.

"Eh.... when my uh-" Arón replied.

He turned around and pointed to the freezer.

"Freezer?" I asked.

"Yes." Arón smiled, "When my freezer.. runs out of fruits."

I turned to Emily.

"Hey." I smiled.

I needed to. I really needed to. She either knew who killed Mina or did it herself. It felt like I already knew the answer to my question. I needed to make sure.

"Hey." she replied, "How's Miles doing?"

She turned her head and eyed the living room for a second. Parker was already back in the living room with Kai and Miles. They were all laughing about who knows what.

"I don't know I've been in here with Arón for..."

I turned to Arón. He looked up at me cluelessly.

"Fiv-"

"Fifteen." I interrupted, "Fifteen minutes."

I turned to Arón and gave him a signal look. He raised his eyebrows and then shrugged. He turned to Emily.

"Do you.. want a smoothie *Emma?*"

"Emily."

"Oops," he giggled.

"Eh, no thanks." she replied.

Arón walked into the living room with three mango smoothies. Emily walked over to me and sat on the counter.

Okay. Start a deep conversation. Easy!

"Can you believe we're actually doing this?" I chuckled softly.

"Hm?" Emily replied.

Bloody hell this would be way easier if it was Mina.

"I mean, running away, figuring out this case on our own." I said.

I sat up from leaning on the counter and walked over to her. I dragged my finger across the counter as I walked.

"Yeah." Emily chuckled, "My Mom called me 66 times. I haven't answered once. I figured Max would've told her something."

"Hm."

"Have *your* parents called?"

I felt my lungs grow hollow. I stood there frozen not knowing what to tell her.

"My parents are in London." I smiled lightly.

"Oh! You're british too!"

"Yeah." I said awkwardly, "But I have a faint accent, I've been here for years."

"Me too! I sound more American than British."

Crap. The conversation isn't deep. It just sounds like small talk. What would Mina say?

"If your life was a movie who would the villain be?" I asked.

Mina asked me the question once. It was 1AM on a school night. She couldn't sleep.

"I don't know. Probably my Dad or Evelyn." Emily answered, "What about you?"

"The villain... probably me."

Emily scoffed.

"Why would you say that?"

"I always fuck things up." I sighed.

I turned to her. My face was only a few inches from hers.

"With everyone. I always disappoint."

"What do you mean?" Emily asked, "Your friends? Parents?"

"No." I scoffed, "I don't need validation from others. I couldn't care less about my parents' opinion on me."

"I can't feel that way."

I don't know what to reply.

"Hm. You're 17, almost an adult, who cares if your parents don't like you? Your Mom only nags you for your family image right? She doesn't care if you're hurt or in trouble does she?" I explained.

"No." she sighed, "You're right."

She smiled lightly and looked me in the eye.

Okay. Totally not going to regret this.

"We're pretty lonely right? Do you ever feel alone in a room full of people? Our friends have mindsets we wish we could have while on the other hand they wish they could have ours. They never care, *careless, carefree.* While me and you, we care too much. So maybe... we could be lonely together."

I paused and she didn't say anything. I leaned in and cupped her face with my hand.

I kissed her.

242

She was sort of startled. I knew she felt something, she felt the electricity. While me on the other hand, I felt nothing.

She pulled away from the kiss and smiled. I couldn't bring myself to smile back, I just gazed into her eyes and hoped that did the trick.

"Meet ya back in the living room, yeah?" she asked softly.

I nodded and watched her hand leave my shoulder. As soon as she left the room my smile faded completely. I covered my eyes with one hand and my lips quivered.

I sniffled, "What the hell am I doing, man?"

I had to cry quietly.

I was so tired. The type of tired sleep couldn't fix. I hardly recognize myself anymore and knowing what I just did made me realize it.

I knew I had to do it, she hasn't opened up to anyone unless they already knew the truth or because she's catching feelings for them.

1 HOUR LATER

We were in the living room again.

"Eden, go get Parker and everyone else who isn't in here." Miles said.

I walked down the hallway past the kitchen.

"Parker?" I asked.

"In the bathroom! I'll be out in a minute!" she answered.

I walked back down the hallway. Riah and Jordan were in the guest room discussing something. They spoke quietly even though it sounded like they wanted to shout at each other.

"Why are you making it such a big deal?!" Riah whispered angrily.

"What do you mean?" Jordan asked.

"It was *just* a kiss! You're making it look like we went on a honeymoon together!" Riah argued, "*YOU* kissed *me* and *I* told you I had a *boyfriend*. Then you *got upset and threw a fit-*"

Jordan scoffed.

"You got upset over it so I stayed to comfort you." Riah explained, "Nothing. Happened. Between. Us."

"I knew you had a boyfriend, Riah. Can't you see I like you?" Jordan confessed.

Riah scoffed.

I knocked on the door before it could get worse.

"Yes?" Riah asked.

I opened the door.

"We're meeting up in the living room." I said.

Riah nodded and turned to Jordan.

"It was a mistake." she finished.

We walked into the living room, Jordan was walking in front of us, he looked pissed. He looked even more pissed when Riah went and sat next to Miles. Miles turned to her and Riah turned to me.

"Thank you." she mouthed.

I was confused for a second, it finally clicked that she was thanking me for getting her out of the guest room situation.

"It's my specialty." I grinned quietly.

Riah turned to Miles and smiled.

"It was just a kiss. Nothing happened." Miles explained.

"I know. It was just a kiss for me too."

They smiled at each other and Miles wrapped an arm around her shoulder.

Parker walked in and narrowed her eyes.

"So.. they just magically made up?" she asked.

"Mhm." Miles chuckled.

We decided to look for more clues in the files. We found something. We found a recording of a conversation between Mina and..

Alicia?

It was a video tape from the school security cameras. Jules picked it up.

"What is this? Vintage?" he giggled.

"It looks ancient." Miles mumbled sarcastically.

We played it on the TV, all sitting on the couches watching the tape. Arón was in his room upstairs working on a project.

The tape was recorded six months after Alicia and I broke up. It was sophomore year, I was angry at Mina but don't remember why. Mina was sitting on the ground with her arms resting on her knees. I couldn't tell if she was angry or crying. She just had that look on her face. Alicia walked by and saw her. She sat down.

It was a free period. They were sitting next to each other looking forward.

Alicia was around 5'4. She had shoulder length dark brown hair and brown eyes. She had freckles, pale skin, a tall button nose, and a pretty big smile.

"What's up!" she asked Mina.

Mina glared at her.

"The ceiling." she replied.

Alicia scoffed playfully.

"No really, what's bothering you? Don't tell me you're fine. We both know the real answer."

Mina sighed and rubbed her eyes.

"It's... Eden."

"Oh no." Alicia giggled.

Mina scoffed and smiled, "I know I shouldn't care 'bout him and his *stupid* ego but I do."

"I've been there."

246

Alicia stood up and started pacing back and forth in the halls.

"Let me tell you something," Alicia smiled.

"Go for it."

"That boy, is *one* in a million, correct?" Alicia asked.

Mina nodded.

"That doesn't mean he's worth it." Alicia explained, "*That* boy will *mess*-you--up. He's a tornado that will destroy everything in his path to get what he wants. And if he wants a girl, he'll do anything. Even if it means he has to hurt people to find someone who'll heal him."

"Damn. He hurt you too didn't he?" Mina asked.

Mina already knew the answer to that question, she only asked it to see if Alicia would confess.

Alicia stopped pacing and rubbed her eye.

"No." she replied "I hurt him. In response he hurt you. I've learned a lot about him."

"No shit, I'm the one who told you the-"

Alicia started talking before Mina could finish.

"He does whatever it takes. Hell, he talks like he's narrating a *teenage coming* of age movie! He *doesn't* care who he hurts even when he says he does. When he says he didn't do something because he didn't want to hurt you, he only did you a favor, that doesn't show that he cared." Alicia explained.

She was giving out the explanation. She had to talk in a way for Mina to remember it.

"What he does is he makes *you think* you're important to him but in his point of view you're just *a bus-stop* or *a short vacation*. After a while he leaves you with *unanswered questions.*" Alicia ranted, *"He always fucks things up.* He's the boy with attachment AND commitment issues. It's exhausting."

"I can't give up on him now!" Mina sighed.

"Oh please. You gave up on *everyone but* him. He's no different. He's just a boy with issues, didn't he warn you? He told you he had sides, Mina. You just got used to the pretty ones."

Mina took a deep breath.

"Yeah, Ali, he's got sides, NO SHIT! He warned me about them before I could figure them out myself! *I* signed up for this! *I* wanted to *figure him out* and *check* on him to *make sure* he's okay." Mina ranted, "We both know that this whole *rampage* of his was caused by *you.* I know it wasn't your fault or intention but it wasn't his either."

Mina knew the things Alicia was saying were true. The things she replied back were also true as well, she understood me better compared to her. The way she said things made it seem like she's always wanted to say that to her face.

    Alicia sighed.

    "The thing is, he has nothing to lose. That's why he's such a fucking bitch." she snapped, "Look, I know the reason why he turned into one was because of me but he'll heal if he finds and chooses a healthy way. If he has the balls to do all this shit then he's not worth it Mina, he's not."

    Mina sighed.

    "Do you understand?"

    "What? That he's a douche with issues or he's an asshole with an ego." Mina scoffed.

    "No. He only gives a shit when you're gone." Alicia finished.

    Abandonment issues.

    Everyone in the living room looked over to me. I was frozen staring at the TV. My stomach felt hollow. My mind went crazy. I felt horrible.

    "Before you guys get mad at me just remember I was 15 years old." I sighed.

    Everyone heard about the rampage I went through during sophomore year but now everyone knew the whole story behind it. Not everyone understood how my mind worked. I'm always thinking.

Mina told me I seemed emotionless or emotionally unstable. No in-between.

"Is it true?" Parker asked.

"What?"

"Is it true that you only care when they're gone?"

I knew that answering Parker's question wouldn't change her opinion on me. I just want to redeem myself.

"No. I *do* care. I just *don't* know *how* to express it."

"Kinda like Mina." Jules joined.

I picked Mina's diary from the coffee table. I opened it and looked through the pages.

Protect her.

"Uhhh guys?" I spoke up.

"What?" Riah said.

I showed them the page. It said nothing but "*Protect her.*"

"Hold on, what page is that?" Marina asked.

"66." I answered.

"Bloody hell." Emily gasped softly, "That's my sports number."

"Does that mean anything?" Jordan asked.

We all looked over at him. He still had that pissed off look on his face.

"Yeah Mina was an idealist. She paid attention to details." Marina explained.

Emily started getting anxious. We all knew what Mina wrote was for Emily. The question was why do we need to protect her? Who do we need to protect her from?

She stood up slowly and walked out of the room. She walked back into the bathroom again. Everyone in the living room looked at each other awkwardly. I stood up and followed her to comfort.

I wanted to get out of the room too. I just heard Alicia destroy the crap out of me.

I followed Emily into the bathroom. Emily was in there running the faucet.

"Em, you okay?" I asked as I opened the door slowly, "Can I come in?"

"Yeah." she replied softly.

I walked in slowly. Emily was looking at me through the mirror. Her heart was pacing and she looked extra anxious. I put my hand on her right shoulder lightly.

"Ow!" she hissed softly.

I widened my eyes at her. Why'd she flinch?

"What's wrong?" I asked.

"It's fine it's not your fault, m-my shoulders are j-just s-sore."

"Hey, you okay? Don't tell me yeah, I know the correct answer."

"I-" Emily stuttered, "I'm just nervous."

"About the notebook?"

She nodded and covered her face with her hands.

"This case is deeper than it seems. I know you've been hearing that for days, or weeks, even months but, it's even deeper. Below the surface. The answer might be right below your nose and you wouldn't see it." she explained as she gazed into the mirror.

"Eden! Emily! Dinner!" Marina called.

"I'm not hungry." Emily sniffled.

I nodded and walked out of the bathroom. Arón was handing out plates and cups of food. The dining table was small. It could only fit three people. The rest of us had to eat in the living room.

"Eden, go bring this plate to Emily." Miles told me as he lifted up a plate of food.

I grabbed the plate and raised an eyebrow.

"What is this?" I asked.

"Chicken, potatoes that weren't supposed to be mashed, and peas."

I picked up the fork and poked the peas a little bit.

MARCH 30, 2016

The waiters served us our food. He thanked the waiter and looked at the plate. Chicken, mashed potatoes, peas and carrots.

I picked up the fork and started eating. He looked at me and raised an eyebrow.

"When was the last time you ate?"

That's when I realized I was eating as if I hadn't eaten in days.

"I haven't eaten in weeks." I answered him, "Only a few scraps per day."

He scoffed, "No wonder why you're so skinny."

I shrugged lightly then continued eating.

"Careful you might choke on the peas!" he said as he lowered my hand from my mouth.

He called the waiter. She paced over.

"The peas are frozen," he explained.

The waiter apologized.

"You should be." he said proudly, "You could've made the child choke."

"No, no, no, it's fine!" I said gently.

He turned to me and smiled.

"You're so polite now!" he gasped.

He turned back to the waiter.

"Who do you think we are? Some low-lives?" he snarked, "Low-lives that eat frozen food?"

The waiter apologized, grabbed the plates, and hurried away.

"What happened to not saying anything that doesn't hurt more than getting shot?" I asked.

"Ehh, that rule is still there, but you also have to stand up and say something once and a while. So then people don't walk all over you." he explained, "Do I look like a door-mat to you? Do *you* look like a door-mat?"

We started quietly chuckling at each other.

JULY 14, 2019

"The peas are frozen." I told Miles.

Miles and Arón looked over at me. Miles walked over to me.

"Oops, Arón!"

Arón paced over. They started grabbing all the plates from everyone giggling and replacing the frozen peas with carrots. When they finished I grabbed the plate quickly and walked to the bathroom.

"Hey Emi-"

I forgot to knock. Emily gasped quickly. She had bruises. She was standing in front of the mirror in a sports bra trying to cover them up with makeup. I stood there frozen with the plate of food in my left hand.

11.3
this isn't a coming of age movie

"Sorry." I said as I put the plate on the counter.

She was standing there with that shocked look on her face. I shut the door and locked it.

"What happened to you? There's bruises all over you."

"I don't know how to explain." she whispered, "He'll hurt me again."

"Who?"

She sniffled as she glanced up at me.

"Why did that person do that to you?" I asked.

"To make sure I don't talk."

I stood there trying to process it.

"Can you tell me *one* detail? I won't say anything." I said gently.

"Why?"

"I want to help you."

She sighed and shut her eyes.

"What is it?" I asked.

"Mi-"

"Mina?"

"Yeah. Mina, she wasn't actually pregnant."

"HUh?" I gasped.

I felt a sense of panic rush to my head. It felt like the world just flipped upside down.

"It was a lie, I told him she was so he could leave her alone but he got mad." she sniffled, "I made it worse."

Her eyes started tearing up.

"I don't believe you." I said.

"Think about it Eden! Use your *head* for once! Mina hated children so why would she have one? Why would she have one at 16!?"

She was crying. Does she really think I'm this stupid?

"Okay.. then who was the person you told?" I asked carefully.

"J-Jul"

"No." I interrupted, "That's bullshit."

I walked out of the door. I didn't believe her. I didn't want to believe her either.

I had no one to talk to, I kept overthinking. Miles and Riah had their own problems, Jordan's pissed, Parker and Kai don't take me seriously.

Parker would probably look at me like I'm stupid. She's best friends with Jules.

Marina.

I walked down the hallway nervously. Marina was in the kitchen wiping the counters. She knew something was wrong. She knew immediately.

"Get outside." she said.

We walked out to the front yard and sat on the curb next to each other. She looked over at me.

"What's wrong?"

"Nothing." I mumbled.

She scoffed.

"C'mon now, I know you, you're that type to be nice to people and be friends with everyone, but you secretly hate them. You hate everyone."

"What are you saying?"

"Do you even like anyone in that house right now?" she said as she pointed her thumb behind her, "Or do you just tolerate them?"

I shrugged.

"*Miles* is okay but I don't really know anything right now. 'Bout me, 'bout life, 'bout anythi-"

"Ay! You better stop talking like you're narrating a romance movie before I can't take you seriously anymore!" she snickered, "This isn't a coming of age movie."

"Sorry." I smiled.

"Look I care about you alright, you're a little brother. You have to be careful with the world. You're lucky I didn't kill you when I found out you were smoking. *Smoking, drugs, all* that crap, it fucks you up bro! Stay away from that! I told Miles to make you quit, did you do it?"

"Yeah." I chuckled, "Well, you beat my ass every time I do something wrong."

"Well, someone's gotta take care of yah." she sighed as she looked at me in empathy.

I sighed. I gave in. I told her everything. Everything Emily told me. Usually I couldn't talk to Marina about these things, she barely takes me or *anyone* seriously. Sometimes she *does* take you seriously but she's not afraid to share her pure opinion even if it's extremely harsh. She's not the ideal person you'd want to talk to about personal issues or being soft. But she's been changing, trying to listen and understand, she changed after Mina died.

"Hm. So Emily's accusing Jules?" she asked.

"Yeah! It's obviously not true, right?"

"I don't know, think about it. Where was Jules the night it happened?"

"I-" I replied, "I never asked, I assumed he was at school."

"Well, he doesn't have a big motive, the motive Emily gave him made no sense. Why would Jules get mad over that?"

"I don't know. Emily has the biggest motive out of the group, maybe she's just screwing with us."

"Yeah," Marina sighed, "But I've always had a bad feeling about Jules, even from the start."

I scoffed lightly and a small smile grew on my face.

"Oh c'mon, you have a bad feeling about *everyone!* Even me!"

Marina always had bad feelings for people. She usually was never wrong about them either. It's from experience. Sometimes she'd be blinded and think the bad people are the good ones.

"Meh, you're right." Marina replied.

She stood up and started thinking.

"Anyway, I mean think about it! Why didn't Jules have a colour at the funeral? And Mina knew she was going to die right? Why didn't she give us a sign?"

"Don't be stupid," I sighed, "You know Mina, she always liked to test us to make sure we care, she acted like she didn't need us but keeping us around *did* help her cope."

"Yeah I guess you're right, so here's the real question, now how the hell did Emily get those bruises?"

12
burn // poison
[JULY 14, 2019]

"Really? A sci-fi movie Eden?" Miles chuckled, "Let's watch a horror movie."

It was nighttime, 11:00PM. Marina and I went back inside to check the files so we'd know where Jules was that evening. But by the time we got inside, they already put the files away and cleaned up the space. So we all finished eating and wanted to hang around and stay for the night. Emily was in the kitchen washing the dishes and Arón was mopping the floor in the dining area.

Riah and Miles were picking out a movie.

"I thought you weren't allowed to watch R-rated movies until you're 18." Riah giggled.

"That rule was placed *years* ago, I'm *17!* Close enough!" he laughed.

Jules was in the other room talking to Jordan because he noticed Jordan was getting pissed by the second.

Jules came back to the room, he asked if anyone wanted a soda. Most of us said no because of the caffeine or because they aren't in the mood.

"Eden, do you want one?" he asked.

I turned to him. I was sitting on the couch next to Riah and Miles.

"Yeah, sure!" I replied.

He went to the kitchen and a few minutes later he came back and passed them out. Mine was already open, I didn't think much of it so I gulped down half the can. He walked out of the room again.

The rest of us were sitting in the living room watching the movie until we heard a few coughs.

"Shh... SHHH... it's going to be a jumpscare." Kai whispered.

Suspense music started creeping in. We were all scared to death but so interested in the movie.

"Noo.. NOOO!! Why is she going in there?!" Miles asked.

"It's *always* the blonde girl." Marina sighed.

BAM!

"AH- Jesus!" Parker screamed.

Riah and Miles jumped and clung onto each other. Marina and I started hysterically laughing because she saw me flinch in my seat and yelp. We all sighed in relief and chuckled at each other. It's been a while since we had moments like that.

"Hey, do you guys smell that?" she asked.

"Smell what?" Miles replied.

Gasoline?

We heard something in the kitchen. It was Emily. She hissed in pain sharply and a few glass plates were clattering against each other.

"You good?" Riah asked.

"Yeah, just accidentally cut my finger." Emily answered, "I'm going to the bathroom for a band-aid!"

Most of the room shrugged and didn't think much about that. Kai was still wondering where that smell came from.

"Tsk-"

I looked over. It was Marina. She was motioning her head towards the door. She wanted me to go after her.

"Seriously though, do you guys *not* smell that?" Kai repeated.

"Yeah I smell it," Miles answered.

"I'll go check it out." I said.

I walked down the hallways slowly. I looked to my right at the bathroom door, Emily wasn't in there.

I heard fire crackling.

Smoke coming out of the guest room.

Oh crap.

I shifted closer to the right wall as I continued walking down. There was a guest room at the end of the hallway. I looked inside slowly.

Oh my-

"HEY!" I shouted as I started pacing closer and closer into the room, "The hell are you doing?!"

Emily swung around swiftly. I couldn't see anything because of the smoke. It filled the room. The fire alarm was ripped off the ceiling and thrown onto the floor.

Emily tried rushing me out of the room. I resisted and looked behind her. *The case files.* The files were burning into crisps on the ground as we inhaled the smoke. Every bit of evidence was burned. Every interrogation tape, every important conversation, everything. Even Mina's diary.

The fire spread quickly. It spread throughout the walls and to the other rooms.

"What did you do?!" I shouted.

"Eden! What's going on back there!" Miles shouted as I heard his voice echo down the hallway.

I rushed into the room. Jules was there. He turned around with a shocked look on his face trying to process it. Emily grabbed my arm and pulled me out of the room. I turned and she was pinned against the wall.

"What did you do?" I asked sternly.

She was whispering. She looked scared.

"He made-"

"No, NO! Don't give me any of that, we know that's not the truth! Jules would never!" I interrupted her.

"Sh!"

She started crying softly.

"You burned the files, Jules came in and tried taking it out but it was too late, correct?" I argued.

"No! I don't *care* if you don't believe me, *you're* the one who wanted to know in the first place!" she whispered.

"Do you really think I'm fucking stupid?" I scolded, "If Mina being pregnant was a rumour *started by you* then why'd the inspector tell me different?"

"I- I told her to-"

Jules ran out of the room. He eyed Emily.

"What did you tell him?" he asked sternly.

They started arguing, arguing over whose story was the truth and the other was fake. Both sides sounded genuine. I didn't know who to believe.

Them arguing cost us time. The hallways and ceiling were glowing red and orange flames. We needed to get out of the house. We didn't have time to argue.

"Arón! The house is on fire! Arón!!" Marina shouted down the basement door.

"¿Cómo?" Arón answered in panic.

Jules and Emily were still arguing. I didn't know what to do. I just grabbed each of their wrists and dragged them down the hallway before we were burnt into crisps.

"I can see it from the living room!" Riah gasped.

We were out in the main hallway. In between the kitchen, the living room, dining area, the hallways to the bathroom and bedrooms. We could barely see because of the fog growing around us. I started to get dizzy but I figured it was from the smoke.

Miles paced up to me and tapped my shoulder.

"Did you get the files??" he panicked.

I sighed.

"Don't even start!" I mumbled as Emily and Jules started screaming at each other and to the whole room.

Arón ran up the stairs and almost tripped over the bags aligned on the floor. Something fell out of a backpack. It landed right between Emily's and Jules' bag.

Arón bent over and picked up the small packet.

Rohypnol.

A drug used to treat severe insomnia and assist with anesthesia.

Arón and Marina saw the pills and their jaws dropped as they slowly raised their eyes up at Jules and Emily. Both of their arms lifted up slowly trying to process what was in Arón's hand.

Riah quickly ran out of the living room.

"What are you guys waiting for?! Get out of here!" she shouted.

We couldn't. The fire was growing rapidly through the floors and ceilings. The front door was on fire. We were all standing there as everyone started screaming at each other. We couldn't get the fire extinguisher out of the cabinets because the whole kitchen was on fire.

"It fell out of the bag!" Marina shouted, "I know that drug! I know it well! It-"

I started losing my balance.

"Guys, what's wrong with Eden?" Miles asked with concern.

I was dizzy and my head started spinning.

"Eden!" Marina shouted to grasp my attention.

I couldn't process a thing. My muscles started weakening. I passed out blank and woke up outside of the house. By then the whole building was on fire and people around me were yelling. My ears started ringing. My head was pounding.

"Guys! Eden's awake!" Riah gasped.

"How?! The drug can last up to twelve hours." Marina exclaimed.

"Whoever drugged him might've given him a little piece." Miles explained.

I sat up and rested myself on the ground with my elbows supporting myself.

"Where's Kai?! Guys?!" Parker panicked.

I turned to my right. The windows were foggy and all you could see was flames.

I turned to my left again. Everyone was pacing around panicking while Emily was calling 911.

"Kai's still stuck inside! Guys!" Parker panicked again.

Parker was pacing around debating on running into the house to find Kai knowing she's most likely dead. She knew Riah and Miles would stop her. She was softly crying but the anger started caving in. She knew the fire was started on purpose.

"Parker! Jordan's already inside looking for Kai! We can't have any more people, we might lose you guys!" Riah argued as she held Parker back.

"I don't care!" Parker screamed in anger.

This is where she broke. She lost Mina and she couldn't lose Kai either. She went crazy. She started kicking and shouting. She shoved Riah and Miles off of her and ran into the house again.

Everyone started panicking. I was still confused.

"Guys, they're sending help in about 10-15 minutes." Emily sighed as she lifted the phone away from her ear.

"What's going on?" I asked softly.

"Jules started a fire." Marina and Miles said at the same time.

"No, are you guys sure it wasn't Emily?" Riah argued.

Arón was there. He was panicking because he just lost everything. His house, his earnings, Marina was comforting him telling him it's going to all work out but she got busy arguing about who started the fire.

"Well, *one* of them started the fire ON PURPOSE and drugged Eden!" Miles scoffed.

"It was Jules, I *swear* I saw the rohypnol fall out of HIS backpack." Marina argued.

Jules started taking that to offense.

"W-What?!" he shouted, "You swear a lot of things!"

"I've always had a bad feeling about you!" she shouted back, "It never faded away!"

She was angry.

"You have *a bad* feeling about *everyone*, even Eden! But *now* he's like a little brother to you and you *always* defend him like your life depends on it!"

"What does *this* have to do with *me?*" I asked.

I was still on the sidewalk. I didn't feel like getting up. I didn't know if I had enough energy to.

"It was Emily. I've known her since primary school. She's always hated Mina, she's always hated us." Riah said, "She always pulls a stunt like this and blames it on others!"

They all started fighting. Especially over things that weren't even close to the whole point. They were all under pressure and scared, they fought like they've been holding it in for years. Miles and Marina targeted Jules for always bringing me up in arguments. They said he always tried to turn them against me. They weren't wrong.

"Guys... this *isn't* our biggest *issue* right now!" I told them.

Marina was standing there arguing with Jules. She was sick of it. We were all caught off guard because of how off topic it went.

"You always start *shit* you can't finish!!" Marina shouted angrily, "Then you *twist* things around and make *Eden* look like the bad guy!"

"This is getting off topic." Miles sighed.

"No, I'm being serious! Now what is he gonna say now? That Eden *drugged himself?*"

"*Probably.* Maybe he did!" Jules mumbled.

"SEE?!" Marina shouted as we all flinched.

Riah and Emily were fighting. They were shouting and accusing each other of things.

I looked over at Arón. He was annoyed. He looked tired too. He was sick of it, sick of all the fighting. He was also pissed at the fact a bunch of teens just invaded his house and let it catch on fire. He sighed and took a deep breath in.

"¡Cállate!" he shouted loudly.

By now everyone knew what it meant. We all went dead silent. All we heard was flames crackling and faint fire truck sirens.

"Enough!" he shouted.

Suddenly Parker and Jordan ran out of the house. All our attention shifted over to them. They were covered in smoke marks coughing and bits of their clothes were burnt. They were dragging Kai out of the house. She looked worse than the two combined but it didn't look permanent.

"We got her!" Parker shouted, "She passed out cold in the dining room!"

The fire trucks and ambulances came. They put out the fire and sent Kai, Parker, and Jordan to the hospital to check if anything serious happened to them. They sent me along too, I still had the drugs in my system, I kept going in and out of consciousness. Obviously that wasn't normal.

I woke up in a hospital bed in a separate room. Blue and white walls and light oak furniture. There was a small TV playing silently on my top left. Marina was sitting next to me, looking at me with that look on her face. She felt bad.

"What happened?" I asked.

"Apparently.. Kai was asleep when it all happened. Riah tried to wake her up but she was in deep sleep. When she eventually woke up, she said she tripped over an apple and hit her head on the table. She got knocked out again." Marina explained.

"An apple?!" Arón gasped.

I turned to my right. It was Arón. He was standing there nervously.

"Yeah, that's what she told us." Marina replied.

"I think I threw that apple." he giggled awkwardly with his eyes widened.

Marina and Arón started giggling at each other softly. They would've laughed louder but it was 3:00AM in the morning.

Marina stopped laughing when her phone started ringing. She raised her eyebrow. She had that look on her face. The why is this person calling *me* face, the why is this person calling me at *3:00AM* face.

"The inspector's calling me." she spoke up.

13
you can't fake footage
[JULY 15, 2019]

"Um, hello?!" Marina answered in a funny voice as she picked up the call.

"Put me on speaker. *I know* you're with some of your *friends* right now." the inspector said sternly.

"Alright." Marina mumbled as she put Inspector Alex on speaker.

"Am I on? Good." Inspector Alex said, "We know you took the files."

You could hear a muffled argument in the background. Detective Max and Toby were fighting about who should've been more cautious.

Marina and I felt a rush of panic shoot down our spines. We knew they were going to notice but it still caught us up in the moment.

"Go to the police station. Now." the inspector ordered.

Marina was about to answer but Inspector Alex hung up on her. Marina sighed.

"We're busted."

Arón and I both had convertibles, he just had a black one instead of a white one. We all split up into three cars this time. Miles, Riah, and I went with Arón, Kai and Parker went with Marina, and Emily and Jules went with Jordan as he rode in my car.

Parker rolled her eyes.

"Make sure these two don't fight." Parker reminded Jordan as she pointed at Emily and Jules.

On the way Arón looked upset. We all felt bad.

"Miles." he spoke up.

"Yeah." Miles answered.

He was in the passenger's seat looking over at him.

"Te dejaré y luego conduciré a la casa de un amigo, ¿vale?"

"Vale."

```
Translation: "I'll drop you off
then drive to a friend's house,
okay?"
```

"Okay."

"I'm sorry." Riah worried.

"Lo siento." Miles translated.

"We didn't mean to, we didn't know that was going to happen." I explained.

"I know." Arón sighed.

He dropped us off at the station and drove away. We met the rest of the group inside.

Parker and Jordan barely had any injuries. They recovered quickly, they just had a few patches around their bodies. Kai had a few burns on her shins. She was knocked out cold at the hospital but woke up a few hours later. We were all done being treated even though we still felt off. The station gave off weird unsettling energy, we didn't know if it was us or what was going to happen.

We were all sitting on the soft beige couches in the main lobby.

Inspector Alex walked in. She looked angry but she tried to keep it cool. Detective Toby was already in the room, he looked nervous. Detective Max paced into the room, he was emotionless, he looked like he was about to explode.

"We found footage of the day Mina died." Inspector Alex announced, "It was caught on the cameras on the traffic lights near the area."

The whole room sat up with an alert look on their faces.

"We wer-"

"We *were* going to go get *the files* to *piece* the case together but *SOMEONE* stole them." Detective Max exclaimed sternly as he interrupted Inspector Alex.

He was angry.

"Why'd you guys steal them?" Detective Toby sighed.

We all started talking at once. Talking over each other and arguing. We were surprised at how much energy we still had. That made Detective Max become angrier.

"Alright ENOUGH!" he shouted.

We all jumped. Detective Max eyed Emily, he looked angry but not as angry with Emily. Instead, he looked disappointed. He looked like he was wondering how his daughter got caught up in this shit.

"You, explain." he said sternly as he pointed at me.

"We wanted to take things our way, finish the case ourselves, because obviously Evelyn *wasn't* the murderer, correct?" I explained.

The inspector sighed.

"It's not that big, you two!" she said as she turned around to the two detectives slightly.

Detective Max scoffed, he started mocking her under his breath. Inspector Alex rolled her eyes and continued talking.

"They can just give *ALL* the files back untouched, they've learned their lesson. I *can* understand why they did that, it was a *very* bad idea but I understand." she explained.

"Problem!" Kai spoke up.

All our heads turned to her.

"The files caught on fire, all the evidence is gone." she admitted, "*Completely* gone."

We watched the inspector's heart drop down to her feet, the two detectives groan and rub their eyes. We felt bad. It was our fault.

"How'd that even happen?!" Detective Toby asked.

Surprisingly Detective Toby was the calmest out of the trio in the moment, usually he's the most eager and jumpy one.

"Don't--even--start." Miles grunted.

Riah's head lifted from Miles' shoulder.

"The fire was caught on purpose." she explained.

Detective Max almost went through a rampage. It's like he knew something like that

279

would happen. Detective Toby walked him out of the room before he could say something he'd regret.

"What are we going to do now?" Jordan asked.

"Start from the beginning." Parker replied.

She was sitting on the couch resting an arm on a knee, looking forward staring off into space. Her eyebrows raised as more thoughts rushed into her head.

"Now what footage are you guys talking about?! Why haven't we heard about this?!"

"It was leaked to us last night." the inspector replied, "It was sent to us anonymously."

She turned on the tv, we figured she was about to show us. We all had that look on our faces waiting for what we were about to see.

The footage played.

There was a black car sitting in the parking lot.

Right next to the sunflower field.

Someone opened the car door. The person walked around the car and opened the passenger's seat. They picked up the quiver of arrows.

Black with neon green stripes and pink feathers.

The arrows.

The person turned and started pacing into the field like they needed to do something.

Something like killing.
They were wearing all black. Head to toe.
The footage stopped.
We were all silent in the lobby. Riah finally spoke up after a few seconds.
"C- Can't you just figure out who it was by the license plate?" Riah asked.
"It was a stolen car. The person who originally owned the car had nothing to do with the murder."
"How would you be sure of that?" Jules asked.
"The original owner hasn't drove in decades, he's a paralzyed old man." Detective Toby sighed as he walked back into the lobby.
Inspector Alex rewinded the video and zoomed into the killer.
Brown hair. Poking out of his hood.
All of our hearts dropped.
The inspector zoomed out. The killer was tall. Taller than the car.
At least 6'0.
We all had our mouths open slightly. Our hearts racing and our heads spinning. Everyone was nervous, I was scared out of my mind. I knew who tried to kill me a couple months ago. I knew it well. I knew who just killed Mina. The ruthless girl who was so excited to turn 17.

We looked over at Miles and Jules. The only two boys who were tall and had brown hair.

We were all breathing heavily, Inspector Alex and Detective Toby gave us a moment of silence to process what we just saw.

A tall boy with brown hair just stole a car and ran into the forests aligning the sunflower fields on May 31st, 2019.

And Miles..

Miles knew it wasn't him.

14
who is eden
[JULY 15, 2019]

"So,"

We all started arguing, picking sides knowing who it really was. Marina? Marina started hyperventilating angrily. She was firing up. She sniffled and shot up from the couch and started going for Jules' neck. Riah and Parker jumped up and held her back as she kicked and swung her arms around while screaming at Jules.

"WHY WOULD YOU DO THAT?" Marina screamed in pain, "She was your SISTER!! *SISTER!!*"

Jules raised an eyebrow and his jaw dropped dramatically.

"*WHY* would you think it was ME?!" he shouted back at her as he stood up from the couch,

"You're right, she *was* my sister, which is precisely why it *WASN'T* me!"

The whole room started shouting at each other. I was sitting there silently trying to process everything.

"It was OBVIOUSLY Miles!" Jules argued as he pointed fingers at him, "HE has the bigger motive! What motive do *I* have?!"

Miles' jaw dropped slightly and he shot up from the couch.

"What *motive* do I *possibly* have?!" Miles questioned.

He was angry. Everyone was angry. Jules was pissed people were targeting him, Miles was pissed because Jules was targeting him, everyone else?

They just figured out who killed Mina.

Of course they were angry, but they were scared too.

One wrong move and they'll be next.

"You've *always* been rude to her, Miles!" Jules shouted, "People think you guys were *Mina and Miles,* the *childhood iconic duo!* But you didn't even consider her as a friend! You always dissed her when she was alive!"

"Okay well, we all know *childhood duos* never work out in this little group of ours." Parker snapped and she looked at me.

Miles stood there silently with his head up, his eyes red and a little teary.

"It was you." he whispered under his breath.

Parker and Riah managed to get Marina under control. Kai was sitting there in shock, she was still shaken up from the night before. Emily? Emily was sitting there quietly nervously fidgeting with her fingers. I stood up slowly to get a better look at her.

That's when it hit me. It was her. Emily leaked the footage.

Now Jordan and I were standing up looking at the fight going down debating on whether we should say anything. I kept eyeing him. He obviously sided with Jules.

"NO IT WASN'T! WHY WOULD *I* DO IT!" Jules screamed.

It echoed throughout the lobby and the inspector made a face. She was judging us. Detective Toby was standing there, eyebrows lifted and eyes wide.

"This is one.. wild.. group!" he murmured.

Detective Max walked in.

"Alright ENOUGH!" he shouted as the room went silent, "Bloody hell."

We all looked over at him. The only thing we heard was our heavy breathing.

"We have an extra copy of files in the back of the storage room." he sighed.

Inspector Alex and Detective Toby sighed in relief.

"Why didn't you tell us that??!" Riah exclaimed.

She was so tired she could barely catch her own breath.

"Well we're going to continue the investigation. Every single one of you, stay in the area, no vacations, nothing. If we need to interrogate you we need to know where you are located." Detective Max ordered.

At this point just put us on house arrest.

"We're going to start interrogating tomorrow." Detective Toby explained.

"How much stuff do we have?" Inspector Alex asked.

"Pretty much everything besides Mina's journal." Detective Max answered, "Didn't find much on there when we did have it."

"Did you check page 66?" I asked as they all turned to me.

"Why?" Inspector Alex asked.

"It said nothing but to protect her."

"We'll take care of it." Detective Toby sighed.

"Where's your sidekick? Aisha?" Kai finally spoke up.

She was trying her best not to fall asleep.

"She's at home sleeping, I mean, it's 4:00AM." Detective Toby replied.

They finally sent us out of the lobby. We were able to go home but none of us knew what *home* truly felt like anymore. We formed a circle in the parking lot. We were down to two suspects.

"So.. who do you think it is?" Jules asked.

Marina rolled her eyes.

"Are you really trying to start a world war in the middle of a parking lot right now?" she snapped.

"I don't want to fucking hear it Jules, it's four o' clock in the damn morning. NONE of us have enough patience for this shit." I snapped.

Marina turned and looked at me quickly, she looked proud.

"It's just a question!" Jules argued, "Plus, I'm *curious*."

He took a look at each and every one of us and raised an eyebrow.

"Parker?" Jules asked.

Parker looked up from zoning out. She nodded. She didn't like getting involved in things, but she always did.

"Jules. It can't be Jules. Mina was his sister!" she explained genuinely, "But I don't know, you *and* Miles are both capable of pulling a stunt like this."

We sort of expected that answer coming out of Parker, she was close to both of them. But she knew who really did, she was always closer to one than the other.

Miles gasped quietly.

"She was my sister's best friend. MY best friend also."

"Oh? So you're admitting it now?" Jules snapped, "Well you're too late, she's six feet under because of what YOU DID!"

"Well I don't know!" Kai joined, "Both of you guys *are* capable but none of you have big motives!"

Kai was only trying to break up the fight.

"Bullshit!" Marina scoffed.

"You're right! I mean if... *Eden* was one of the suspects you guys would think it was him! He's more capable of doing shit like that than me and Miles combined!" Jules argued.

Riah narrowed her eyes and made a face. She was grumpy, she just wanted to be dozing off in bed.

"Why are you bringing up Eden?" Riah asked.

"It's *just* an example!"

"Well it's a bad example."

I felt a dose of anger shoot down my spine. I was tired. I just wanted everything to end. It was so annoying.

"Mina knew she was going to die, right? Well why didn't you have a colour at the funeral?! Why is Emily targeting you?!" I exclaimed.

Everyone turned to me. They knew that when I genuinely shouted in anger I get scary. My face turns red and my eyes vibrate.

I start sounding like a lunatic.

Some crazy lunatic.

As soon as I brought up Emily she inhaled sharply and turned away slightly from the circle. I knew I shouldn't have pointed that out. Marina made it worse.

"Yeah, how the hell did she get those bruises?!" she asked.

The whole group gasped and looked over at Emily. She sighed.

"So you think it's me." Jules sighed.

"Who else would it be?!" I argued.

I stayed confident while arguing. I had that look on my face, full of pride and amusement.

"You got the nerve, the---fucking--nerve to accuse ME of killing *my own* sister." Jules snapped angrily, "*Bullshit.* You think you're the shit, right Elliot?"

My face expression went blank.

I felt the world collapse onto me in seconds. I remained in eye contact with Jules. The rush of panic shot up and down my spine. I felt the group stare me down. I gulped fiercely.

"Elliot?" Parker scoffed as she tried not to laugh.

"ELLIOT?!" Jordan scoffed.

The whole group went silent after that.

"You thought I didn't know?" Jules chuckled sarcastically, "When were you gonna tell them?"

"Tell us *what.*" Miles asked angrily as he glanced over to me.

"That he's a fucking liar." Jules scoffed.

I broke eye contact.

"But I'm confused," Kai said as she raised an eyebrow, "Why'd you call him Elliot?"

"Well his name isn't Eden." Jules explained, "He's not from the UK, his parents aren't in London, he's literally German!"

"I'm not surprised." Parker scoffed.

"And *why* does that matter?" Riah rolled her eyes.

They said those remarks at the same time.

"BECAUSE HE LITERALLY *CHANGED HIS IDENTITY* AND LIED TO US *FOR YEARS!* WE KNOW NOTHING ABOUT THIS DUDE!" Jules shouted, "WE DON'T KNOW HIS *INTENTIONS*, WHERE HE'S FROM, WE DON'T KNOW IF HIS STORY ABOUT MINA IS TRUE IF HE CAN'T EVEN TELL US HIS REAL NAME! ¡COÑO!"

I exhaled slowly. I looked over at Marina. She was looking at me with concern, she was alert, she kept eyeing me.

"Is your sister even real?" Jordan asked me, "Explain how she suddenly *abandoned* you after Mina died."

"Ede- Elli- Eden?, is that true?" Miles asked as he looked at me with that look in his eye.

He was in disbelief.

"Yeah. My real name's Elliot." I admitted, "Elliot Baker."

Kai and Parker started laughing. I raised an eyebrow. Their coping method to everything is to make jokes. I pretended they were in shock instead of making fun of me.

"Imagine being named Elliot." Parker laughed as she wiped away her tears of laughter.

Kai started giggling.

"Not the time guys." Emily giggled softly.

Jordan started attacking me like crazy.

"So y-your name's Elliot?" Jordan scoffed, "So what else did you lie about?"

I sighed and I looked him dead in the eyes.

"You probably lied about Mina. You prolly killed her yourself and that's why you always target Jules!" he yelled at me.

I raised my eyebrows, "Huh?! Excuse me? Did that footage we just saw slip your damn mind?!"

"We've all had a bad feeling about you! Now you made it worse! Your little secret isn't a big secret anymore isn't it?"

"Dude-" I scoffed in amusement.

He raised an eyebrow.

I've been waiting to say this for years.

"You're just mad at me. You've *always* been mad at me! And for what?! Because I *stole* your *girlfriend?!*" I scoffed, "She never even looked at you, let alone dated you."

The rest of the groups' eyebrows raised and their eyes widened. They knew this was coming. I was just saying what everyone was thinking.

"You're just mad Mina liked me. You KNEW she would never like you like that and *you still* tried, you knew *damn* well she liked me better." I laughed, "Now Riah too? See? You're a homewrecker who somehow always *fails* to homewreck. Riah let you down easily but Mina didn't, she told you to piss off because you wouldn't leave her alone, now that's why you're so pissed at me."

Riah and Miles chuckled slightly but quickly covered their mouths.

"The only reason why you're targeting me is because you liked Mina too." I finished.

The group slowly shifted away from me, they wanted to stop arguing. We awkwardly went into the cars and drove everyone back to Marina's house. No one made eye contact with me during the ride home, when we walked inside, that's where reality hit us like a slap to the face. All our stuff was gone. All our stuff was burnt up in Arón's house.

We were tired, most of us immediately went to sleep. I needed to explain myself. I just didn't know how.

"Marina?" I asked.

She was in the kitchen drinking whiskey. She barely slept.

"What should I do?" I asked her as I walked over.

"Just let it be, telling them will only risk it."

"No, I don't care if I risk myself." I sighed, "We're already dealing with a lot and for me to be seen as a shitty person, it's not fun, Marina."

Marina scoffed. She probably wondered since when did I care about their opinion of me. I know I only tolerate them but they're all I've got left.

"Then... tell them. Tell them everything. 'Cause right now *everyone* is against you. You need to come forward." she explained carefully.

"When?"

"*WHEN?*"

"When should I confess?"

"Not tonight, tomorrow morning. Everyone's sleeping right now, we had a long night." she sighed.

"But they'll think I made it up! They'll think I used the time to make up the story."

"Shit, then do it now." Marina chuckled softly.

We went to each room and woke everyone up. 5:37AM in the morning, no sleep last night, they were all already irritated at me anyway, why not make it worse?

We made everyone meet up in Kai's room. Her room had beige walls and her bedsheets were light blue and coral orange. They all sat down in their pajamas rubbing their eyes, yawning, and complaining why they didn't get any sleep because of me.

"Yeah, *yeah,* keep complaining, Eden's gotta tell you something." Marina giggled confidently.

294

"What now? More lies?" Jules scoffed.

"What's the point of calling him Eden?" Jordan sighed.

"Yeah, why would *we* want to talk to you?" Riah asked as she glared at me.

"No. I need to explain. I don't like it when you guys look at me like this."

They all had that surprised look on their faces, they didn't expect me to confess to something like that. Parker however, she did.

"No you're right, you don't. You *act* like you don't care but I've known you longer than everyone in this room, you have always been a narcissistic asshole from day one." Parker snapped, "You-"

"Hey! Hey! ¡Oye! ¡Oye! Let him finish!" Marina defended me.

She turned and gave me the signal look.

"My parents weren't in London." I explained,

I'm telling the truth this time. My parents aren't in London, they're in Berlin with my little sister Heidi. She's 13 years old.

13 years old.

And she doesn't know she has an older brother.

I haven't seen my parents in three years.

"Why?" Riah asked.

I paused.

"They left me." I finally answered.

The room went silent. All their facial expressions were the same, they all felt bad because they all went through something similar. Marina? Marina looked proud of me.

"How'd that happen?" Miles asked.

"It was my 14th birthday." I explained.

My father and I weren't close growing up. He had expectations, he hated how I was, he always reminded me he wanted a different son. I really tried but it was no use, I gave up after a while.

He wanted to make it up to me on my 14th birthday.

"Surprise! A trip to America!" he cheered as he woke me up one day.

"Bullshit!" Jules exclaimed as he listened to my story.

"Yeah! How does your family know English that well if y'all were from German?" Jordan argued.

"You mean *Germany??*" Miles giggled.

"Shut up! This hooligan woke us up at 5:30 in the morning, give me a break!"

"I got kicked out of every school in the area so they sent me to a boarding school in London." I admitted, "I learned English quickly."

"And your parents?" Parker asked as she stared me down, chewing her gum slowly.

"My parents grew up in London but they moved back to Berlin and had me, they know both languages." I explained.

My Dad woke me up and made me pack what I needed. I wasn't sure at first, he's never nice to me.

"Why'd you get kicked out of schools?" Miles scoffed.

"I was a troublemaker." I answered.

"How so?" Kai yawned.

"I did everything Mina has done, some things were worse, the only difference is, I got caught."

My Dad drove me to the airport. I wouldn't stop asking questions.

Where exactly are we going, Dad?

Why are you being so nice to me, Dad?

Is Mom going?

"I should've known." I said as my eyes teared up a little, I quickly wiped them, "I was smart, just too naive."

I had my suitcase, I was excited. I turned to my Dad, I noticed he didn't have his suitcase.

"Dad, where's your suitcase?" I asked.

"I already gave it to them, they're putting it in the plane for us." he explained, "Want me to give them your suitcase?"

I nodded.

We continued walking. My eyes kept exploring the airport. I have never been to an airport that fancy before. I started to wish I had eight eyes, I kept almost running into poles or tables because I wasn't looking forward.

We heard a lady announce that our plane is leaving in ten minutes. My Dad and I quickly went over to the area to get ready. I wasn't smiling, I had that curious, intrigued look on my face because my Dad didn't like how I smiled. He said it made me look like I was up to something stupid.

The lady announced that our plane was leaving in 5. My Dad quickly shot up from his seat in the waiting room.

"I have to go to the bathroom." he said, "Board the plane and wait for me, you know your seat right?"

I nodded as I held up my plane ticket. I tried not to be as eager but I was excited. I thought he changed.

"Our suitcases are already on the plane, just wait for me." he ordered as he walked away.

So I did. I boarded the plane and waited patiently for him. I had a window seat. I was looking out the window smiling lightly. I was facing the airport looking at the large windows trying to find my Dad. I saw him, he quickly boarded the plane and sat beside me.

The plane ride was simple, I slept the entire time and my Dad just eyed me. When the plane landed, we had to go through the procedures in order to be allowed in the country. I don't remember most of it because of how boring it was. Finally, they let us out of the airport, we had our suitcases and all I did was try not to smile.

We drove to the city, we were in Virginia. I didn't speak much to him on the plane, I was afraid I'd start an argument. I finally had the courage to ask him.

"Why are you being so nice to me?" I asked.

We were walking down a sidewalk. Barely anyone was around.

"I'm not," he replied.

I raised an eyebrow.

We reached an alley.

"I don't remember much from here." I said.

"Why?" Jordan asked.

"Cause... I woke up hours later on the ground in the alley alone." I explained.

I woke up and rubbed my eyes lightly. There were shards of glass below me. I looked down at my clothes.

Shit.

I was covered in alcohol.

And drugs. Illegal Drugs.

My head hurt. I sat up and looked in front of me.

My suitcase.

I opened it.

Nothing. Absolutely nothing.

All my clothes, all my belongings, gone.

There was a note.

```
Don't bother looking for me, by
the time you see this I'll be flying
back to Berlin. You terrorize our
family, you are no longer my son.
```

I sat there with the note in my hand. I couldn't even keep it still. My whole body was sore, my chest was aching and my left eye hurt like hell. There were cuts and shards of glass all over my face and arms.

I closed my eyes.

This is a dream.

This is a dream.

This is a dream.
This is a dream.
This is a dream.
This is a dream.
This is a dream.

I'll wait up in my dorm and they'll make me do that stupid geometry assignment again.

Dammit they know I suck at geometry. Why can't they give me an algebra assignment?

Wake me up.
Wake me up!
WAKE ME UP!

I opened my eyes. I was still sitting in the alley.

"My Dad left me in a dark alley." I said.

The room was silent listening. I couldn't tell if they cared. Only Riah had that look on her face, she felt like crying for me.

I was 14, barely a teenager. I cried to the point where I couldn't breathe out of my nose because of how stuffy it was. I got the small hiccups while crying, my eyes stung whenever I tapped them.

I stood up and crumbled the note into my pocket. I started walking down out of the alley but I was limping. I never limp, I don't care how sore my legs get but I never limp.

"Hey!" someone yelled.

I quickly turned around.

Shit. Police.

"Who are you?"

I stood there stupidly and paused for a moment.

"Elliot Baker!" I replied back.

Shit. I shouldn't have told them that.

My eyes widened and I started sprinting. They chased after me because I was covered in cocaine and smelt like a fruity cocktail. I knew that once they realized I was a person under 18 in America they'll have to send me back to Germany. That's the last thing I needed.

I ran even though my legs hurt. My whole body felt like hell. They were yelling and screaming at me, I was afraid they were going to shoot or tase me. I ran into a crowd of people. I needed to blend in.

I looked down at my shoes as I ran.

Neon coral.

Fuck.

Of course. They'll point me out in seconds.

I had to be smart for once, I took off my sweater cuz I was covered in drugs.

Oh shit.

Well they'll point me out easier if I had no shirt on.

I threw on the black t-shirt I had *under* my sweater while running for my life. I had black sweatpants on. The only description they'd have of me is neon shoes and a black outfit.

They were still after me. I jumped through the crowd, over benches and trash bins, through streets and across blocks.

"Out of the way!" I shouted as the ladies around me yelped and flinched.

I jumped over a fence and continued running. The feeling of stress and adrenaline was oddly comforting.

"OUT OF THE FUCKING WAY!" I shouted louder.

I ran and ran. I turned around, the cops were even closer this time.

Shit! Shit!! SHIT!!!

I was running through a parking lot. I jumped over a red car and heard the person inside yell.

HONK!!

I bent over and ran through the cars and reached the other side. The parking lot had a fence aligning it. I jumped over and turned around. The cops were nowhere close to catching up to me. I chuckled in relief and flicked them off and continued running into the city.

"That's what I thought!!" I cackled.

I finally lost them. I was exhausted. I was afraid I'd pass out and have them catch me but the adrenaline distracted me.

I saw a man. He was tall, 5'11, he looked young but he seemed like he was in his early 40s. He had black curly hair and brown eyes and a long, well defined, pointed face. He was dressed elegantly, *too* elegant for the city we were in. He had a fancy black suit and a bow-tie. He was talking to another man until his eye caught onto me. He walked over to me slowly with that curious look on his face.

"What's your name?" he asked me.

I stood there awkwardly. I didn't know what to answer.

I looked up and I saw a sign. It was big and red with gold accents.

EDEN CENTER.

A Vietnamese American strip mall.

"I'm Eden." I answered.

The man raised his eyebrow.

"Eden... Brooks."

"Look into my eyes," he said, sounding rather intimidating, "I'm like a human lie detector. Don't lie to me."

I sighed. He sounded like a psychopath. I sorta *gave in.*

"Elliot Baker."

Shit. I shouldn't have told him that, shouldn't I?

"Well, my name is Axel, Axel Fabian." he smiled.

"Axel!" the other man said.

"It's *fine!* He told me his real name so I can tell him mine." he replied to him, "I'm sure *my* reason to hide it is just as big as *his* reason."

The other man sighed.

"Forgive my little brother, Salvador," Axel smiled.

"Salva." he corrected.

"He's just really... cautious." Axel continued.

"Why are you guys so cautious?" I asked.

They both looked at me then eyed each other, they looked back down at me again.

"Forget *that*, why are you covered in drugs?" Salva asked.

"And you smell like alcohol." Axel pointed out.

"There's glass all over you!"

Salva was a little taller than Axel. He had wavy fluffy black hair and brown blank eyes. He looked like he was in his late 30s. He had a mustache and beard and a round charming face and black round-ish vintage glasses. He wore button up shirts and beige pants. He dressed like his Aunt Gertrude shopped for him.

"And why are you covered in bruises?" Axel asked as he raised an eyebrow.

I looked down at my chest and lifted my shirt up slowly, bruises, I turned my head to the closest reflective thing I saw near me. I looked at myself, I had a black eye and my bottom lip had a cut. There was a shard of glass in the area between my eyebrows.

"So that's how you got that scar?" Riah asked.

My scar. It looked like a lightning bolt between my eyebrows and above my nose. It was deep and extremely visible.

I turned back to Axel and Salva.

I told them what happened, I tried not to cry. Everytime I cried in front of my Dad, he'd make fun of me and say my face looked like a dried up prune. I didn't know if I could trust them, they seemed suspicious but they weren't dressed like they were going around jumping people. For an odd reason I felt safe around them.

"So, y-your Dad? He just left you?" Axel asked.

"A- And you're telling me he jumped you *first*, then left you?" Salva continued.

"Well I don't know! Who else would it have been!?" I shrugged, "He left me a note. That's where I knew he left me for good, covered in drugs and alcohol to get me in a bigger mess than before."

Axel and Salva took a look at each other and Salva sighed.

"Don't you dar-"

"We need to help him!" Axel pleaded softly, "I mean look at the poor boy!"

Salva sighed, "Fine. You help him. Just be careful."

"Be careful of what?" I asked.

They both turned to me, that's when I figured I should just shut up.

"You ask a lot of questions." Axel smiled.

He put his right hand behind my back and brought me to a local thrift store. Salva walked away and got into a small red ibiza.

"Awh man! I wouldn't be caught dead in this place!" Axel said as he compared his suit to the clothes on the rack.

"Then.. why are we here?"

"Cuz you're covered in... *questionable* substances and you need to get them off of you immediately." Axel explained proudly, "Also the *neon coral* shoes are weird. You look like the highlighters on Salva's desks."

He started giggling at them.

He bought me a clean black t-shirt and grey ripped jeans that were a little baggy on me. He also made me change my shoes.

"I can't stand looking at those horrid shoes!" he giggled, "Here, what about these black ones?"

Black converse.

"Okay!" I shrugged.

"So you're saying, your Dad just left you here?" Kai asked.

"Yeah." I replied.

"So *that's* why you randomly showed up at the end of eighth grade!" Jules exclaimed.

"Yeah but... his birthday is March 29! He showed up in the beginning of April." Riah pointed out.

"What did you do during that week?" Miles asked.

"Axel helped me throughout that week, he taught me everything I know."

He brought me to the diner, to the field, he helped me get my life in order.

"What happened to him?" Parker asked, "Can we meet him?"

I sighed and shut my eyes. I haven't talked about what happened to him in years. I looked up at Marina. She looked over at me then nodded.

14.2
expect the unexpected

"Wait, Marina knows?!" Jules gasped.

I didn't know if I should answer. I sat there awkwardly silent.

"Yeah, I did know, what about it?" Marina defended us, "He told me because he trusted me and I didn't judge him!"

They all glanced at Marina then at me.

"Anyway, continued, *Eden.*" Marina said.

"April 4th, 2016." I sighed.

Axel and I were giggling at a tropical bar near the beach knowing I wasn't allowed to drink anything. This was the first time I've seen him without a suit on, he was wearing a red hawaiian blouse with yellow flowers and beige shorts. He was telling me about all his past adventures with Salva, he told me he had to go back to Spain soon.

"Really?!" I exclaimed, "Can I come with? Spain sounds amazing!"

Axel chuckled then sighed.

"Well, you see, my *adventures* with Salva aren't technically... legal." he explained.

I sat there with my eyes wide open.

"You guys are murderers?!" I gasped quietly.

"Tsk- no! Salva would never. His first rule is always *no deaths*. We're robbers!"

"Heists?"

"Heists."

I sat there in amazement.

"Can I join?" I suggested.

"No, you're too young, little one." he smiled.

"Oh c'mon! I've had *experience* before!"

Axel chuckled then sipped his black coffee.

"Your experience is intense shoplifting and pranking and scamming strangers on the internet. I taught you how to use a gun but that's not enough."

"Well... technically, it took loads of skill to pull that off! I went on the run too! The only reason I got caught was my stupid friends ratted me out." I sighed.

"Well, I'm sorry little one, I'll have to go soon. You don't need me that much."

I frowned. He was the closest thing to a father I've ever had.

"I told Salva the plan, he's picking us up then giving you a house and then we'll practice your backstory," he explained.

Suddenly we saw Salva walk in from the back of the bar. He told us to follow him through the back in 15-17 minutes. Axel nodded. He stood up promptly and pushed in his chair.

"Alright little one, are you seeing the beginning of our end yet?"

"I don't want to." I frowned.

"Well, let's stay positive, c'mon it's our last moments together!"

He patted my head then we heard a noise.

Police sirens.

We heard people yelling, telling everyone to freeze.

Axel and I quickly took a look at each other, we couldn't figure out if the police were there for him or for me.

"¡Vamos!" he shouted as he grabbed my wrist and dragged me out of the bar.

The police already saw us by then.

"Don't let them see your face!" Axel shouted to me as we ran.

We ran, surprisingly we felt more at ease than before. Ironically we were running away to get our freedom but we already felt so free, the adrenaline made us run faster. We couldn't stop giggling from the feeling. Running from cops, the best thing you can ever feel.

We heard gunshots.

"C'mon! Run, little one!"

"I'm not running without you!" I yelled.

He started shifting behind me.

"What are you doing?!" I shouted.

"I can't let them shoot you!"

The police started throwing smoke-bombs into the streets, we couldn't see anything.

Boom.

"No, no, no!" I screamed, "He didn't do anything!"

He was laying there on the ground covered in blood with bullets through his chest.

"¡Mierda!" I shouted as I ran over to him.

"You pronounced it wrong." he chuckled.

My head was pacing. I didn't know what to do. I didn't know what was next.

I was more angry than before. They killed him. Why him? It could've been me and I wouldn't have cared. Axel was a role-model, a mentor, a brother, a father figure. Now he's gone.

I was only 14.

"Run," he muttered.

I had tears streaming down my face. I kept tapping him repeatedly to keep him awake but there was no use.

"Meet up with Salva and he'll take care of you, tell him his older brother loves him." Axel sighed, "Meet you in the afterlife, little one."

He did the salute thing. When you curl your hand and leave the pointer and middle finger up but not completely stiff and straight.

Then you salute but your hand isn't on your forehead. It's near the height of your nose. You do a messy salute, a sloppy but neat one. No stiffness but you're also not flopping your hand.

"Oh, is that why you always do that now? To remember Axel?" Kai asked.

"Yeah, I never want to forget him, he saved me."

I remember kneeling down next to Axel, I really didn't want him to go.

"I'm sorry." I cried.

I couldn't even see anything because of my tears and the smoke.

"It's alright little one, I've been a narcissist my whole life, a bit of an asshole, y'know? Now I will die with dignity because I helped you, little one." he smiled.

I heard the police shouting and I shot up.

"You remind me a lot of my daughter, Payton. Now I get to see her again." he sighed, "Take care, little one."

I ran. I ran all my anger out and they didn't follow me. I heard them shout.

"Where's the little blonde boy that was with him?!"

I didn't turn around. I just kept running. I ran around the bar and found Salva. I jumped into the front seat and started sobbing. I covered my face immediately.

"What?! ¿Qué pasa?" he asked.

I couldn't even speak one word correctly. The hiccups I get when I cry makes me sound stupid.

"Axel's dead." I sobbed.

Salva's face went blank. He turned forward slowly and took a shaky deep breath. His eyes started tearing up and he was hesitating to say anything.

We started crying at the same time, he started driving. We drove through highways and I saw the WELCOME TO MARYLAND sign.

"I told him to be careful." Salva muttered, "To just surrender and I'll get him out of prison afterwards."

We drove to a small pretty neighbourhood. We got out of the car and he gave me the key.

I opened the front door, inside it looked like an ordinary house with couches and lamps. He sat me down on a blue couch and he kneeled down in front of me then sighed. I wiped all the tears off my face.

"Repeat after me," he said.

I nodded.

"My name is Eden Brooks." he introduced sternly.

"My name is Eden Brooks."

"My parents are in London, England."

"My parents are in London."

"England."

"England." I corrected myself.

"I came over here years ago to live with my sister," he explained.

"I came over here years ago to live with my sister,"

"Okay good." he sighed, "Now say it again, don't forget."

"My name is Ell-"

He cleared his throat.

"My name is Eden Brooks." I introduced myself, "My parents are in London, England. I came over here years ago to live with my sister."

Salva nodded, "Good. Never, EVER, mention your real backstory to anyone again. Remember

315

what Axel taught you? He made you talk in a british accent, now do that so you match your backstory."

"I don't need to!" I exclaimed.

He raised an eyebrow.

"Can I come with you?" I pleaded, "Please just let me go with you!"

He sighed.

"I don't want you to go! Please just stay." I whispered.

"I can't! You have to stay here, start a new life, this could be good for you!" he explained.

No, it wasn't. But participating in heists wasn't good for me either.

I took a shaky deep breath, "You can't just leave me here, I'm just a kid."

My pass was going to expire in six months, after that I'd be illegal.

He sighed deeper then rubbed his eyes.

"Promise you'll be back some day?" I asked.

"Promise." he replied.

"I enrolled you into a school, now I'm your legal guardian, Salvador Fabian, but if anyone asks you answer Salva Brooks and nothing else." he explained, "If you ever need to call your *sister, do* it, say whatever you need to say and she'll play along."

"Who's *she*?"

"A colleague of mine, she's willing to help you, we'll call her... Maddie Brooks, got it?"

I nodded.

"Remember, be smart, use your head," he reminded me, "and *stay* out of trouble."

He stood up and started walking towards the door.

"Wait!" I said.

He turned around.

"Do I have to lay low or anything?" I asked.

"Huh?"

"Like- how do I make friends? *Correct* friends, friends that won't rat me out."

"Easy," he replied, "Just don't tell anyone then they have nothing to rat out."

I sighed. This was a serious matter. It was hard to accept that this is my new reality at first.

"Well, here, follow me," he said.

We walked outside to the front porch. He looked around then pointed to the right.

"There's a girl on her porch... obnoxiously throwing pebbles at squirrels," he observed.

I looked over. It was Kai giggling loudly while watching the squirrels scurry away.

"And there's a girl on the porch eating cherry licorice and smoking cigarettes," he continued.

It was Parker. She was laughing at Kai chasing after the squirrels.

"Oh. So, that's how you met us?" Kai asked, "When I was hanging out with Parker?"

"Mhm." I replied.

Salva looked over at me and put his hand on my shoulder, "Go introduce yourself to them!"

"Meh..." I replied.

"Well I have to go, Eden." Salva said as he started to walk forward to his car, "Goodby-"

"Don't say goodbye, please, it makes me think you'll be gone forever." I said.

"Okay," he replied as he adjusted his glasses, "See you later, *Eden.*"

He walked around the red small ibiza and opened his car door.

"Wait!" I called.

Salva looked up.

I ran up to him and hugged him tightly. I was going to miss him. He patted my head then I let go.

"Cya Salva." I murmured.

He drove away and I didn't take my eyes off of his car once. I sighed.

I spent the rest of the day messing around in my house like a normal 14 year old. I had the best time of my life. Watching TV, eating until I threw up, sleeping peacefully, hot showers, blasting loud music, I loved it. I loved being free.

I suddenly remembered I had to go to a new school. I needed a friend, I paced over to the window in my room, I saw Parker riding her bike down the street.

I had an idea.

I ran down to the garage hoping Salva left something in there for me, I found a black bike. I smiled, opened the garage, and hopped onto the bike swiftly. I zoomed the bike after her.

"Watch out! Watch out!" I shouted.

"Then.. you crashed the bike into mine." Parker said as she listened to my story.

"Mhm." I giggled as the rest of the group stared me down.

I remember the day clearly. We were on the ground in the middle of the street laughing at what happened.

"Sorry!" I said.

"Sorry?" she yelled sarcastically, "You crashed your bike into me!!"

She was giggling like a maniac. I stood up and adjusted my bike.

"Where the hell- the hell did *you* come from?" Parker asked as she laughed louder.

"I just moved here!" I answered happily, "I'm Eden,"

"Eden who?"

"Brooks." I answered.

"Well." she replied as she picked up her blue bike, "I'm Parker Smith, since you're new, hang around me!"

"Why?"

That was a stupid question.

"Cause you seem like a troublemaker." she giggled.

I raised an eyebrow.

"I can be too but my Mom's strict as hell, lay low with me will ya?"

I shrugged, "Okay!"

"When Eden crashed his bike into Parker's... what an introduction." Kai giggled.

I paused, long enough to make them know the story was over.

"Did Mina know?" Riah asked.

"Of course she did," I replied.

"Alright," Jordan scoffed, "Who else in this room knew?!"

"Marina and Mina were the only two," I replied, "I don't know how Jules found out."

Jules sat up in his seat and raised his eyebrow, "I figured it out."

"How did Mina and Marina find out?" Miles asked.

"Mina figured it out during freshman year, she told Marina then Marina got on my ass about it." I chuckled softly, "They kept it a secret when they found out the real story."

There was another pause in the room. Everyone was zoning out.

"Alright, I'm exhausted, can we go to sleep now?" Riah asked softly.

"Yeah, yeah." Marina replied as everyone left the room.

Riah watched everyone leave and stopped in front of me. We were standing in front of each other as she stared into my eyes.

"I- I'm so sorry Eden." she said.

She had her arms crossed and her cheeks were red. She hesitated for a second then uncrossed her arms. I raised an eyebrow and waited. She hugged me and dug the side of her face into my chest. I narrowed my eyes and wrapped an arm around her and my other hand on her head.

"I'm just glad you're here and safe." she sighed.

Miles and Marina were still in the room. They were watching the moment with their eyes widened.

"That was unexpected-" Miles chuckled quietly as Marina giggled at his remark.

"So you're an illegal immigrant." Riah scoffed sympathetically, "How could you be so stupid? Telling us?"

She lifted up her head and let go.

"You guys all hated me an hour ago." I said.

"What difference does it make?" Riah replied.

I shrugged. She was right.

"Once the police figures out they'll send you back to Germany in minutes. I'm surprised you even made it this far since you're not registered." Riah sighed, "None of us will rat you out... I- I hope."

I was kind of surprised. Riah and I were barely close but we were almost like siblings when we talked or hung out with the group. She was like a younger sister to me even though she was twelve days older. Almost like a sister in-law since Miles and I were so close. She sighed and walked out of the room.

Miles and Marina stayed for a minute.

"I'm going to use the bathroom." Kai said as she left the room.

"So, Elliot- uh-" Miles said.

"Hm,"

"Do I call you... Elliot or Eden?"

Marina looked up at us and raised an eyebrow. She was sitting on the bed watching the conversation with her eyes narrowed.

"Elliot's long dead, it's Eden now, I've always been this way." I explained.

"I'm sorry that happened to you, you could've told us man!" Miles apologized.

"It's okay," I replied, "and no, I couldn't, it was too risky."

"How'd you pay the bills at the house?"

"Carla." I explained.

Maddie Brooks.

My fake sister was a 5'5, 19 year old, blue eyed blonde. She didn't look related to me at all but she held the image well, skinny and bold. She would come and visit to make sure no one would suspect anything and I wouldn't get wrapped in the foster care system.

She also came to give me money from Salva for the bills.

The first time I met her was during July 2017, I was 15. She just walked through the door and gazed around like the house was a museum.

"Um- PARKER??? IS THAT YOU?!!" I yelled, "MILES?! MARINA??? MINA!!!!"

"I'm in your room." Mina replied, "Dummy."

Mina was with me when I met my fake sister for the first time.

"Who the hell just walked into the house?" I panicked.

I was in the shower. I quickly jumped out and threw on my pajama pants and ran out of the room. Mina was downstairs with the lady waiting in the living room.

"Who is it?" I asked as I walked up to her.

Mina turned to me and scoffed, "Jeez Eden put on a shirt!"

I chuckled and threw on my black t-shirt in my hand.

"Some spanish lady is here for you, she's hot." Mina grinned quietly.

I snorted as we turned to the lady.

"I'm Maddie Brooks."

"HUH?!" Mina and I reacted as our eyes widened and our jaws dropped slightly.

Maddie's real name was Carla. She only spoke in an American accent when she needed to. She gave me a look and after a few seconds I figured out what it meant. I was supposed to play along.

"Oh yeah," I said, "She knows."

I nodded my head over to Mina. Carla sighed.

"Didn't Salva tell you not to tell anyone?" she asked, "Can she be trusted?"

She walked up to Mina and observed her. Mina just stood there nervously blushing.

"Who are you?"

Mina narrowed her eyes.

"Mina Willow?"

Carla didn't really feel like a sister. She just showed up a few times after a while to make sure I was eating well and paying the bills correctly. I wanted to get to know her better but she was never there.

Salva kept a safe full of cash inside my closet just in case I really needed it. Carla gave me the code to it before she left.

"Damn, so you have an... interesting life!" Miles chuckled as he listened to my story.

"Yeah." Marina laughed, "You turned out to be a weird kid all these years."

"It causes great times to be made." I sighed happily.

"Alright, now... you know it wasn't me... right?" Miles asked.

Marina and I looked at him. The conversation took a turn.

"I didn't kill Mina. You guys know that!"

We didn't know what to say to him.

"I was with Evelyn," he admitted.

"We know." Marina said, "So what are we going to do about Jules?"

"Well, I know him, he's strong, mentally and physically, so.. what do we fight a murderer with? What do we use?" I asked.

There was a short pause. We all looked at each other with that look on our faces, we softly smiled to lighten up the moment, it's like we could read each other's minds.

"Guilt." we said.

15
the whiteboard
[JULY 16, 2019]

"Look, I know it was Miles. You would never kill your sister like that, I know how much you cared about her." I said.

Jules stood there looking at me carefully, he nodded.

"So what do we do now?" he asked.

I thought for a moment.

"About Miles?" I paused, "Lock him up."

7 HOURS EARLIER

"Look! I found your old costume!" Miles whispered.

"Do you guys still have the arrows?" Marina asked.

9:00AM, we were looking through Kai's closet. Kai was back from the bathroom the night before, she noticed we were talking about something serious.

She walked into the room with an orange in her hand.

Miles, Marina, and I were in a circle discussing the plan. Kai threw up the orange, smacked it, and watched it fly to the opposite side of the room.

Bonk.

"AH! Oh-" I yelped.

The orange hit me right on the head. We were going to ask who it was but we already knew.

"Kai." Miles giggled as Marina started cackling.

"Alright, whatchu guys up to??" Kai asked as she hopped onto her bed.

We continued discussing the plan together.

"The arrows??" Miles asked.

"No, they took all of them." I replied.

"Then make new ones," Marina suggested, "Make sure they're exactly the same."

We nodded.

"Should we get the rest of the group in on this?" Miles asked.

"I don't see why not." Marina sighed as she stood up.

We didn't know how to talk to the group without looking suspicious to Jules. We were still at Marina's house, everyone else was scattered around in the basement laughing around like usual. We went down there. I immediately scanned the room for Jules, he wasn't there.

"Hey Parker?" I asked.

She was laying on the long couch watching TV chewing mint gum.

"¿Qué?"

"Where's Jules?"

"He's being interrogated at the station right now."

Miles, Marina, Kai, and I took a look at each other.

"Okay, gather everyone up, we need to talk to everyone." I said.

"Wait." Kai interrupted as she tugged my arm tightly, she talked quietly and guided us back upstairs, "What if someone snitches?"

"Why would they snitch?" Marina asked.

"Because they can be *involved* with the murder, covering things up, we can't trust anyone."

Miles and I took a look at each other.

"Technically *we* can't even trust each other, I mean the four of us." Miles pointed out.

"Well, we have to try!" I sighed, "What are your motives and alibis?"

We sat down together in the living room upstairs near the kitchen.

"I don't have a motive to kill Mina." Miles said.

"Wait-" Marina said.

She had to pause and make sure the sentence that was about to come out made sense.

"Mina knew she was going to die."

"Yeah we know." Miles said.

"Sh!" Marina replied, "Listen, she knew, she brought Eden to the sunflower field, and Jules tried shooting both of them, correct?"

"Yeah." we all replied.

"That means we have to collect *two* sets of motives from each one of us, one motive for Mina, one motive for Eden."

We all paused and looked at each other.

"That's so weird though, if she knew that, why would she even bring you to the field in the first place?" Miles asked.

I shrugged. We all knew we couldn't answer that question. Mina was confusing.

Marina stood up and walked over to the huge whiteboard placed on the wall next to the TV.

There were already drawings and doodles on it, she quickly took the eraser and wiped the whole thing clean. She wrote Mina, big and green on the top. She turned back around to us, we were facing her wondering what she was doing.

"Mina, the victim, but Eden's *also* one of the victims but he survived." she said as she wrote my name down in purple under Mina's.

She proceeded to move over to the left of the whiteboard, she wrote each and every person that had access to the arrows.

Eden Brooks
Jules Willow
Parker Smith
Kai Murphy
Riah Jones
Miles Cooper
Emily Clarins
Evelyn Clarins
Marina Murillo
Jordan Covey

"Did I miss anyone?" she asked.
"Don't think so." Kai replied.
Marina sighed.
"Eden, what's your motive, or *possible* motive?"
"How is this going to work? What if one of us lies or makes it up?" Miles asked.
"You're right." Marina replied, "But we have to at least give it a shot."

"Well we know he was with Mina, he most likely doesn't have a motive unless it has something to do with Alicia." Kai said.

"I haven't spoken to Alicia in years, she's all the way in New York City right now!" I said.

"Well she's the whole reason why you went on a rampage!!" Kai scoffed.

"What about Kaiden?" Miles asked.

"Nope, haven't heard from her since sophomore year." I answered.

"Gia?" Marina asked.

"Hell no."

"... Katie?" Kai asked.

"Fucking hell Eden why do you have so many exes?!" Miles scoffed as he held in his laughter.

"Heartbreaker." Marina teased.

She turned around towards the whiteboard and started writing with a bright red marker.

Eden Brooks- no motive, alibi- Mina

"Alright, Jules is next."

"He never told us where he was that day." I said, "I mean I just assumed he was at school because people were talking in the background."

Marina nodded then turned around.

"What would his motive be?" she asked.

"It could be anything, Mina could've found out one of his secrets, or-" Kai explained.

"No wait-" Marina interrupted, "Miles, go get Emily."

"Why?" Miles asked.

"Because she knows the real story."

"And what if she's lying?" Kai asked.

"That's what Eden was supposed to figure out, pretend to fall in love then she'll start slipping, right?" Miles asked.

He looked over at me as Kai and Marina eyed me.

"Well... did you?"

"Kinda... I felt bad though." I admitted.

"Did you feel bad ghosting Kaiden or... Eva the blonde from the UK?" Marina snickered.

"No..."

"Thought so."

"Hold on Eden, don't tell me you actually give a damn about Emily do you?" Miles scoffed.

I paused.

"Like... none of us like her, NONE."

"Then why'd you let her in the films?" I asked.

"I didn't. It was Mina, I just pretended it was me so then everyone wouldn't get mad at Mina when she's dead and can't defend herself." he admitted, "The group would've been pissed and confused if they found out *she* let her in."

He looked down at the ground.

"You fell for her, didn't you?"

"No, I just care about her. She's a person too. You guys know how *SHE* gets when she gets her heart broken! Remember what happened with Finn?" I defended, "Or EJ? Or Ethan?"

"Ethan?" Miles asked as he lifted his head up and his eyes widened.

"I haven't spoken to him in a long time." I explained.

"No, I meant did Ethan actually break her heart?!"

"Oh yeah, he really liked her then he got bored." Kai snickered.

"Didn't he date Evelyn.. for five months..." Miles muttered awkwardly.

"No, five years. They started dating when they were 11 and broke up sophomore year."

"Yeah then he liked Emily," I giggled.

"And now Emily likes you? Right?" Marina asked.

"Yeah, she fell for me. What have I done?! I can't break her heart! She'll go crazy again!"

Marina sighed.

"Congratulations Eden, the fiesta, the tunnels, then the kitchen moment at Arón's house, now she thinks you're hot." she said sarcastically.

Kai and Miles giggled.

"Oh well stop stalling and get Emily in here!"

Miles stood up and moments later he came back with Emily following him.

She sat down, "What?"

"Look y'know what you told me? At Arón's house?" I asked.

"Yeah…" she replied softly, "but you didn't believe me."

"Well now he believes you so spill." Miles said quickly.

There was a tiny pause, Emily took a deep breath as we all stared her down.

"Mina wasn't actually pregnant." she admitted.

"WHAT?!" Kai and Miles both shouted at the same time.

"¿QUÉ?" Marina shouted as she flung her arms around obnoxiously.

Marina was funny like that, even in serious situations she'd always goof around. Sometimes it was her coping method.

"Yeah. I told Jules thinking it would give him a sign to leave her alone."

I groaned as soon as I heard that sentence enter my ears.

"Why would you think THAT would make him leave her alone?" Miles asked.

"I don't know! I thought that would make him give up!" Emily replied.

"If Mina actually had a child what were you guys going to do?! She was 16!" Kai asked.

"I don't know, she hates children and I grew up without a father, we wouldn't know how to parent." I sighed, "We always joked about it before, we said we'd want them to turn out just like us, but better, we agreed on naming them Toni or Payton."

Emily and Kai smiled at me.

"Toni?" Miles giggled.

Our conversation was interrupted by a phone call. It was coming from Miles' phone. He picked up.

"Hello."

He was silent for a few minutes listening to the person behind the call. He hung up.

"I have to go to the station, they're going to ask me a few questions or two." he sighed, "Mind if I take your car, Marina?"

Marina shook her head.

A couple long moments later we finished piecing the board together, we even ran out of space on the left side. We wrote the possible motives everyone had to kill *Mina*.

Eden Brooks- no motive, alibi- Mina
Jules Willow- no motive, alibi- none
Parker Smith- motive: issues/psycho, alibi- Kai
Kai Murphy- motive: prank gone wrong, alibi- Parker
Riah Jones- motive: jealousy?, alibi- Jordan
Miles Cooper- motive: forced to prove love?, alibi- Evelyn
Emily Clarins- motive: freshman homecoming, alibi- none
Evelyn Clarins- motive: hatred, alibi- Miles
Marina Murilo- no motive, alibi-

"Wait, where *were* you and Jordan?" I asked.

"We were at a frat party with Arón." Marina explained.

She pulled out her phone from her pocket and scrolled. She found a video and showed us.

It was a colourful party, Jordan was in a red hawaiian shirt and funky sunglasses obnoxiously laughing, Arón was twirling around spontaneously with a drink in his hand, Marina was recording as she laughed with them. There were two strangers beside them, one girl with shoulder-length dark brown hair, bangs, and brown eyes, one boy with short black hair and blue eyes. They were giggling and dancing around Arón happily.

"Arón also recorded some clips for his insta story." Marina explained as she put her phone back in her pocket.

The board continued.

Marina Murillo- no motive, alibi- Arón
Jordan Covey- no motive, alibi- Arón

"Okay, we wrote the motives for Mina, now we need to write the motives for Eden." Marina said as she walked over to the right side of the whiteboard.

Jules Willow- motive: jealousy? <u>crushing on Mina?!</u>
Parker Smith- motive: <u>hatred.</u>
Kai Murphy- no motive
Riah Jones- motive: revenge?
Miles Cooper- no motive
Emily Clarins- motive: forced?
Evelyn Clarins- motive: hatred
Marina Murillo- motive: revenge?!
Jordan Covey- motive: jealousy?

The whiteboard was finished. Motives for Mina on the left, alibis in the middle, and motives for me on the right.

Emily and Kai were talking while observing the whiteboard.

"Dang, this is confusing." Emily said.

"No shi-"

"Kai and Miles have no motive?" Marina interrupted.

"Yeah Kai's never clumsy around Eden," Emily explained.

"Sometimes you scare me Eden." Kai admitted as she tried not to giggle.

"I do?" I said.

"You scare everyone." Emily said as she wrote more on the whiteboard.

"Okay wait, what's the point of this? We already know who the murderer is, why are we listing everyone's motives?"

"Because again, people might be involved in it along with the murderer." Kai said.

"I am." Emily admitted.

We all turned to her immediately.

I raised an eyebrow.

"I can't escape, if I tell anyone I die, if I leave him I die, there's no way out." she pleaded, "Guys, you have to help me!"

We all looked at her silently.

"Did Mina know?" I asked.

"What?"

"Did Mina know you needed help?"

"Yeah she knew everything that was going on."

I sighed and shut my eyes, "Shit."

"That explains the diary and why Jules and Mina were starting to get distant." Marina said.

I sighed.

"We need another whiteboard." I said.

"We don't have one." Kai and Marina said at the same time.

I turned to Emily, she was standing there caressing her elbow. It's like the more time passed the more anxious she got. She sighed and rubbed her forehead as she continued scanning the board.

"Emily, who else is involved?" I asked carefully.

She looked up at me as she bit her nails nervously.

"Two other people."

"TWO?!" the three of us gasped as Emily stood there awkwardly.

"They're in the same situation as me, they're being forced." Emily admitted.

The three of us sighed in relief.

"Okay gather everyone here, we're going to plan." Marina sighed.

I started walking.

"What about Jordan? He's like... Jules' best friend!" Kai worried.

"He liked Mina more than Jules. He'll be fine." I echoed as I paced down to the basement.

"Wait, why'd the inspector tell us she was pregnant?" Kai asked Emily.

"As soon as I was interrogated I told her everything, she got it out of me quick."

There was a moment of silence as Marina and Kai narrowed their eyes down at Emily.

"Bad liar." Emily shrugged, "I'm guessing she asked you guys about it to see if I was lying."

"So she was in on this?" Marina asked.

"I don't know. Maybe she was trying to help me at first... but got the wrong idea then arrested Evelyn."

We gathered everyone up to the living room, Jules and Miles were still at the station being interrogated. We went over the plan, it was simple.

Surprisingly Jordan agreed to it. He looked down at his phone.

"Jules just texted me." he spoke up.

We all looked at him.

"He's coming back here in ten, Miles is still being interrogated."

"How's he not arrested yet?!" Parker murmured.

"Whatever, when he comes back you guys all know what to do, correct?" Marina reassured.

We all looked at each and every one of us in the room, signaling our agreement. We waited, we had to make sure we did it correctly, because if the plan goes to shit so do we.

15.2
damn stickers

Moments later, 3:00PM, Jules came walking through the front door. Most of us had to resist the urge to give him a good beating and let him fall in a ditch. There was a lot of tension in the house, nobody could ignore it. We all paced throughout the house, it looked like we were in a rush but Jules didn't notice. Riah quickly jumped onto the couch and covered her face.

"Marina!" Kai whispered.

"¡Mierda!" she replied as she hurried over to wipe the whiteboard.

Jordan ran over quickly to help. Parker and Emily were in the kitchen trying to act normal.

"How'd it go?" I asked as I walked over to Jules.

His shoulders immediately tensed up and his arms flew up in the air.

"Why would *you* want to know?" Jules snapped, "You still think it's me!"

"Look, I know it was Miles. You would never kill your sister like that, I know how much you cared about her." I whispered.

Jules stood there looking at me carefully, he looked at my hand, placed subtly on his shoulder, he nodded.

"So what do we do now?" he asked.

I thought for a moment I was about to answer but Parker interrupted.

"Jules, when are they going to arrest Miles?" she asked casually.

He turned to Parker, then glanced at Emily beside her, she was opening a juice carton and pouring it into cups. Jules shrugged. He looked over at the living room.

"I can't believe it was him, this whole time." Riah sighed as she rubbed her eyes, "How's Anna going to react when she finds out?!"

"She'd be crushed." Kai sighed.

Riah looked up and then looked at me, "What are we going to do?"

"About Miles?" I paused, "Lock him up."

Jules looked at me then at Riah, then at the whole room. I eyed Parker, we made eye contact as she gave me that clueless look she always has. I gave her a signal look by smiling slightly and winking.

Just like the old days.

Jules didn't notice because he always thought it was my ego. Parker got the signal.

"Guys, we should have a memorial for Mina." Parker suggested.

"Yeah we should, *after* the *murderer* is locked up." Marina said sternly.

Riah groaned.

"Won't be long, Miles will be behind a jail cell soon, he might even share one with Evelyn." Kai giggled as she walked into the kitchen area, "Only joking Emily!"

Emily snickered softly. We all had to pretend we were unsettled at the fact that someone so close to us killed Mina. Well to be honest we *didn't* have to pretend. We just had to pretend with a different person.

Jules was a close friend but he was sort of a loner. We all knew that the whole reason why he was friends with us in the first place was because of Mina.

But I always had *some* faith in him. I guess I proved their point.

"Where should we host the memorial?" Jordan asked, "Who are we going to invite?"

"Mina's favourite teachers, her spanish friends, then us, make sure no one like Evelyn shows up." I said as I walked through the living room while Jules followed, "Make sure no one she hated shows up."

"That'll be one *small* memorial." Parker snickered.

"Make it in the sunflower field." Emily suggested.

We all turned to her then everyone turned to me.

"I mean if it's okay with you, Eden." Emily reassured, "I don't want you to get any flashbacks or PTSD..."

I thought for a second, maybe that's not a bad idea.

"That's not a *bad* idea, let's do it there." I said.

So we planned it. 7:00PM was the time of the memorial, we didn't want it to be huge. I walked over to Marina's room and knocked on her door.

"Jordan, I *said* I didn't *steal* your *fruit* snacks!" she shouted.

"It's Eden." I said.

She started cackling obnoxiously.

"Come in!" she said out of breath.

I walked into her room, white walls, red LED lights, black furniture and sheets, and fruit snack wrappers in the trash bin.

"Do you have it?" I asked quietly.

"Have what?"

"The gun!"

She sat up from her bed and paused the TV. Her eyes were wide open.

"Yeah I do, I'm not sure if it still works though." she answered.

"Can't really go on a test run when everyone's here." I sighed.

Marina rolled off her bed and walked over to her dresser. She opened the drawer and pulled out the pistol. It was a small handgun, the top half was black, the bottom half was a pale yellow.

"You know how to use it?" she asked.

"Of course I do," I replied, "... it's yellow."

"I don't know!" Marina giggled, "I didn't buy this! I stole it."

I chuckled softly, "How am I supposed to look intimidating with a yellow gun?!"

"How are you supposed to look intimidating *at all* with a *pastel yellow* phone case?"

There was a tiny pause of silence until we broke into laughter.

"Salva bought the case for me!!" I giggled.

"Really? Have you heard from him?"

She and I leaned against her dresser as the conversation continued.

"Yeah last year he sent me a new phone and case," I smiled, "but I haven't seen him in person since 2016."

Marina turned her body towards me and looked me dead in the eye.

"O-kay, ready?" Marina said.

She held up the gun as I took a deep breath.

"Ready."

7:00PM we were told to meet at the sunflower field. We all drove ourselves. I was walking down into the field with Jules, he wouldn't shut up.

"I still can't believe you thought it was me."

I didn't respond.

"Like *seriously!* She was my sister!"

I didn't respond.

"Oh so now you're ignoring me."

"It's resolved." I finally said.

I made sure that made him shut up.

We continued to walk down the field, and I started to regret making the memorial take place there. I kept getting visions of the night it happened. I knew we had to because the more guilty we could make Jules feel, the better.

We reached the hill. Exactly where Mina died. My stomach started to feel hollow and my heart felt heavy.

This is where Jules' heart started to drop.

Tripods for film cameras.

"What is this?" he asked as he looked at me.

I looked him dead in the eye and shrugged innocently. Me trying to be innocent is like Mina trying not to get attached to things. No matter how hard I tried, people knew the innocent look didn't suit me. I couldn't pull it off.

Everyone started gathering around. They were in their costumes.

THE costumes.

Emily stepped out of the field, she had her costume on, it was a long puffy teal blue dress. It looked elegant, like in the movies, it had a few rhinestones and a few ruffled white accent pieces, it was long sleeved and was tight around her waist up but below it was almost like a gown. She had a black quiver on her right shoulder and the arrow in her left hand.

The arrow.

The black arrow with neon green stripes. In her quiver, it had the same arrows, black with neon pink feathers. She walked towards us without breaking eye contact with Jules. I liked this side of her. She looked tough and intimidating, I was proud of her.

She took a look at me and tried not to smile, I nodded slightly, not enough for Jules to notice, and winked at her.

Next was Riah, she had the same dress on but it was green and showed her shoulders. She *also* had a quiver of arrows. She looked tough as well, she wasn't all smiley anymore.

Miles was back from being interrogated, that's what shocked Jules the most. He was in character too. He had a white ruffled long sleeved shirt with a black vest and bow-tie. Jeans, belt, combat boots, and the bow and arrows. He stepped out from the field and held Riah's hand. They started walking down together. They kept eye contact with us. Miles looked angry, not infuriating but he looked determined.

"Eden," Jules said.

Before he could say anything Parker and Kai walked out of the fields. Parker wore baggy vintage jeans and combat boots. The upper half of her was more masculine, she had a navy vest under a white long sleeved shirt that was ruffled at the sleeves. Her hair was held up in a messy bun with a wooden stick.

Kai had the same type of dress Riah and Emily had. It was orange but it didn't have any sleeves. It was almost like a corset. She had gold jewelry around her neck and wrists and on her ears.

Both of them had the arrow and quivers.

"Eden, what is this?" he repeated.

I ignored him.

"Are we missing anyone?" I asked the crowd.

Marina and Jordan stepped out from the field, they were holding cameras and microphones for the set.

"Okay everyone ready?" Parker asked.

Jules walked over slowly and picked up a quiver of arrows and the bow. He walked forward a little bit as he put the quiver on.

I paced over to Parker quickly.

"How'd you get the new arrows?" I whispered.

"The same way we did before." she whispered back, "Now get ready!"

I turned to Jules, he was squatting down at the water bottles, I saw him spiking one. He stood up and walked away from the pile. I walked over to the bottles, I realized each one was labeled with our names, Jules drugged mine.

I bent down and carefully peeled off the sticker with my name on it then placed it on Jules' bottle, I put Jules' sticker on my original bottle. I picked up my new bottle then walked back over to Jules, I even took a sip to not look suspicious. He watched me drink a quarter of it.

The group was scattered around as Jules observed everyone closely. He tried to act as clueless as possible. The group was moving around cautiously trying to look as casual as possible. Marina and Jordan were circling around the others while filming them.

Parker shot an arrow into the open field as Marina caught it on camera. Parker turned around.

"Did Mina want a black convertible or Jeep?" she asked.

"Huh-" Jules asked.

That question caught him off guard. I slowly shifted back to Jules. I made sure to stay a little behind him.

"She wanted a convertible." Miles answered.

"I thought she wanted a Jeep!" Riah replied.

"She couldn't really decide," Kai explained, "but she knew she wanted the car Eden has, y'know, the vintage convertibles."

Kai shot another arrow into the field as Jordan filmed it.

"She really loved our 7th grade math class. Don't know why though." Parker sighed.

"Yeah I remember that, it was me, Riah, Parker, Emily, Mina, and Cory." Miles said, "Now remember her first track meet?"

They all brought up old stuff about Mina. All the stuff she loved or looked forward to. It went through Jules' head and stayed there.

"She was good at hurdles, she just couldn't sprint and jump over them without hesitating." Emily smiled, "I was there for every one of her track meets."

They all turned to her with a confusing look on their faces.

"I went for Evelyn," she explained, "but it gave me an excuse to watch Mina compete too."

"She was an angry person." Marina sighed, "We all knew that, she ran her anger out everytime the coaches put her in the 4x4 relay event."

"Who was her comfort person?" Jordan asked.

They all sighed happily at the same time.

"We all know the answer to that." Emily said as they all looked at me.

Jules thought they were looking at him at first, once he realized he turned around to me and narrowed his eyes.

"Did she ever tell you that?" Jordan asked me.

"Of course she did, 8th grade." I answered.

During the constant questions and confrontation Jules' face turned more and more pale and his eyes started to grow dead.

Sugar-coating was the best option here. Most of the things they said was to make Jules guilty and make them *less* guilty.

"Who do you think knew her the best?" Kai asked.

"Marina and Eden." Emily said.

"Who understood her the best?" Miles asked.

"Parker." Kai giggled, "But I understood her humour the most."

The whole time I tried not to make faces, it was no use.

Riah and Miles started asking more questions. They took turns answering them.

"Favourite people?" Miles asked.

"Her track coaches." Riah answered, "She said she felt safe around them."

"Favourite colours?"

"Brown, black, and green."

Miles turned to me.

"Where did she want to visit? Eden?"

"Spain." I answered proudly, "Obviously."

"She was excited to turn 17, her favourite number." Marina said, "Y'know what she wanted to do this summer?"

"Eden, you explain." Parker said.

"She wanted to run away together in July and come back in October." I said, "She didn't even know where we'd go, she just wanted to live without knowing where she'd end up the next day."

"Y'know she hated everyone at school, she said they're all too worried about themselves and the stuff that didn't matter." Parker said.

"She told me about this stuff." I said.

Mina relied on the fictional world, right? At first she tolerated *some* students then eventually she couldn't tolerate any. She hated everyone, everyone and everything pissed her off. People hated her back as well, she just didn't have enough energy to even acknowledge it.

"People don't like you because of how annoying you are." Ethan told her when he made fun of her once.

I wished I defended her but he was my friend at the time and she wasn't.

"Literally no one likes you." he said, "People just think you're a cold hearted bitch."

Mina never cared. She took the word bitch and cold as a compliment, she loved being called that because it fed her ego. The real insults that affected her were being called dramatic or sensitive.

Odd.

She knew she had us, all nine of us, but she even told me she felt lonely around us. She always felt like we secretly hated her, she'd overthink it sometimes but once junior year came around she didn't care anymore.

"If they hate me, too bad, it's not my problem." she said, "I prolly hate them too, no biggie."

"So she hated all of us?" Jordan asked.

"No. She tolerated most of you guys, her favourite people were-" Marina explained.

"No, don't finish that sentence." I winked.

Mina hung out with Marina most of the time, she talked to me and Emily the most, she talked to Riah and Miles about relationship advice because they were trusting.

To be honest she hung out with her spanish friends the most, they understood her better then all of us combined. But she never truly relied on us, she was afraid we might leave her.

"Why don't you hate me?" I asked her during sophomore year, "I did a lot of shitty things and you knew, you knew this whole time."

I'm not really the type to admit something like that but with her, I couldn't help it.

Mina and I were like a blueprint.. the perfect blueprint of a fucking disaster.

Like I said, Mina and I together were like a lightning storm and a tsunami, but we had our moments once and a while. We were crazy, everyone figured at least one of us was going to end up dead if we won't stay away from each other, they were right.

When you talk about Mina you'd have to remember what side of her you're talking about. She had personality sides like I did. It was exciting for both of us, wondering which side we'd talk to today then the next. Although both of our sides seemed like the same thing..

Unpredictable ticking time bombs.

"I defended and protected you because I wanted to." she explained, "You remind me a lot of myself, that's why I can't hate you."

"What--a-shame." Kai said sadly, "She's dead now."

They all started taunting Jules.

"One arrow through her chest, one through her thigh."

"She could've lived."

"She loved track."

"She loved adventures."

"She couldn't find any happiness inside so she had to make her own."

"She wanted the movie life, the life like the romance novels."

"Then one day she gave up and said fuck novels, I have my own story to follow."

"But she's dead." I finished.

They all quickly pointed an arrow at Jules, Jules did the same knowing if he actually shot anyone he'd have the same end.

"Do you ever feel bad? Jules?"

Jules' face was bright pale by now, the only colour was from his eyes. His lips were quivering. The rest of the group was trying not to break down as well.

"We miss her like crazy!" Kai said softly, "Why would you do that?!"

Sometimes we don't notice how important things are until we lose them.

"Y'know Anna couldn't sleep for a week straight after the funeral?" Miles said.

Jules was about to run. He turned slightly and took a step backwards. He stopped as he heard it.

I cocked the gun and pointed it directly at his head. I made sure everyone heard it.

Marina smirked. She always believed in me deep down.

"Really." Jules said, "A gun? Eden? You're too much of a pussy to actually shoot me anyway. Do you even know how to use it?"

I clenched my jaw, pointed the gun up at the sky swiftly, and pulled the trigger. It made a loud noise and Jules flinched.

"A pussy, yeah?" I smirked.

"YEAHHH!!!!" Marina laughed and cheered as she raised her finger up in the air.

The rest of the group tried to stay serious. They all really wanted to release the arrow from the bow and hit Jules. They couldn't.

I needed to taunt him more, it was working, he felt more and more guilty. I was shaking, I wanted to pull the trigger but I couldn't, not yet, I needed to make him admit something, something that could make him sound mad.

"Mina would-"

"I didn't mean to hit her," he admitted.

The group's faces dropped and their eyes widened. My face went blank and my heart felt heavy.

"I didn't mean to kill her," he said softly.

His voice started breaking and a tear fell.

"Then who were you trying to kill?!" Miles scoffed.

I heard his voice grow angrier.

"Eden. Fucking. Brooks."

I started to feel heavy again, like what happened at Aron's house. This is when I realized me switching the stickers on the bottles did nothing. He spiked both of them.

Those damn stickers.

16
they're cat fighting again
[JULY 17, 2019]

"Okay, what were you doing on July 16, 2019?" the inspector asked me.

"Seriously, this again? You already know who did it this time! You're wasting your time."

I woke up from that dream, I was laying in Marina's car. My head was pounding, it felt worse than that time at Arón's house. I sat up slowly, we were zooming down the streets, we were in a rush. It was 3:00AM in the morning.

"Eden?"

I turned to my right, it was Miles. I looked up forward, it was Parker and Kai. Parker was driving while panicking and Kai was telling her to keep her damn eyes on the road.

"What's going on?" I asked.

"Jules drugged you," Parker sighed, "Again."

"Well I know *that*."

"Shit started to go down as soon as you passed out cold."

I looked over at Miles, he had that look on his face, all anxious and frightened.

"So... what happened?" I asked.

"A lot." Parker panicked, "Now we need to go save Emily."

"Save Emily?!" Miles and I both gasped.

"YES! DO YOU TWO BUTTCHEEKS PAY ATTENTION AT ALL?!!"

Kai started giggling loudly.

"In *Eden's* defense he *fainted* so that's why he's clueless."

"Hey! I didn't *faint*! I was drugged."

"*Yeah, yeah, blah, blah,* it's the same thing." Miles teased.

"O-kay who invited the christian?!" Kai shouted.

She swung around in her seat and glared at Miles. She was using the tone to tell us she was just joking around. At first I thought they were drunk but then I realized this is how they usually act.

"Huh-" Miles replied.

"I'm an atheist." she said sarcastically while she waved her hands around.

"Okay."

"Yeah she's right who invited you?!" Parker joked.

"Riah, Marina, and Jordan took the other car!" Miles defended himself.

They all started yelling at each other aggressively under the pressure. To be honest I was too drugged to tell if they were being serious or not. I know they weren't genuinely angry at each other.

"EVERYONE SHUT UP I'M TRYING TO DRIVE!" Parker screamed.

"WHY ARE WE *SUCH* IN A RUSH?!" Miles asked.

"BECAUSE WE *NEED* TO *SAVE* EMILY!!"

"Save Emily from *what!?*" I asked.

They ignored me, or did they? I don't think they heard me through the screaming.

"Emily can take care of herself!" Miles shrugged.

"Not if she's going to be killed if someone finds her!"

"WHAT!" I shouted.

There was a short silence, they started shouting again.

"I WILL CRASH THIS CAR RIGHT NOW IF Y'ALL DON'T LET ME DRIVE!" Parker shouted.

"DON'T YOU DARE PARKER!" Kai replied.

"SHUT UP KAI!" Miles shouted.

"SHUT UP MILES!"

"WHERE'S EMILY!" Parker yelled, "I WILL SHOVE A SHOT-PUT UP YOUR NOSTRIL."

"YOU SOUND LIKE MINA!!" Miles gasped.

"SHUT UP ABOUT MINA!!"

"I'M PANICKING!" Kai screamed.

"IS THAT THE COPS?!"

"OH SHIII-"

"O-M-G" Parker gasped sarcastically, "MILES THE *CHRISTIAN BOY* CUSSED!!!"

Parker and Kai started giggling and celebrating. Kai was dancing in her seat waving her arms around.

"YEAHHH YEAHHHHHHHHH!!!!" Parker yelled.

"PARKER! PARKER! *WATCH* OUT!" I shouted.

She wasn't paying attention and we were about to crash into a tree. A big, lumpy, fat tree. We all started screaming obnoxiously as she quickly swung towards the right and Miles and I crashed into each other. We all quickly caught our balance and we were all breathing heavily with our hair in our faces. The car continued driving.

"Can--SOMEONE---*TELL*----*ME* what the *FUCK* is going on!?!?" I shouted.

They all kept silent and turned to me.

"You passed out cold and we all started fighting. Jules took your gun and made a run for it." Kai explained.

"We all split up into cars to go after him but then we realized Emily was missing." Parker continued, "We guessed she made a run for it as well."

"Why didn't you guys just shoot him?" I asked.

"He was running into the fields, we couldn't see him well enough to aim." Miles said, "We also had to make sure you weren't dead."

I scoffed.

"I don't understand, why would he do this? Why would he want to kill *me?!* We've been *friends* since 8th grade!" I asked.

That sounded like a stupid question.

"He's always been against you and you knew that." Miles said.

"What possessed you to become friends with that *THING!*" Parker shouted.

"SAYS YOU! You were *besties* with him too!!" I said.

"Ok Dr. Seuss." Kai giggled.

Parker sighed.

"Okay, I'm going to explain it, listen carefully so you actually understand this shit."

Jules was supposed to kill me. Mina knew so she wrote the letter for me. She knew he was planning to kill me on the last day of junior year so she brought me to the sunflower field to make sure Jules couldn't catch me alone.

I understand the day more clearly now.

"Eden," she whispered.

We were in science class, the teacher was really kind, he let us watch a movie on the last day.

"Eden, do you want to get out of here?" she whispered to me.

We sat next to each other in science, I turned to her.

"Yeah, where do you want to go?" I asked.

"The sunflower field! For the films."

"We're filming today?"

"Yeah, that's what Miles told us."

"Mkay." I smiled.

I had no idea. She brought me to the sunflower field and we ran through it blasting music and being stupid like usual. We sat down on the hill, then she turned to me. She turned her whole body towards me.

Now.

She got shot.

"She knew she was going to die, she set herself up so *you* could still live!" Parker explained.

"Holy shit." I murmured.

I had a million questions.

"Why couldn't she just ask for help? Go to the police?" I asked.

"One, she hated cops. Two, it's been happening for years. Don't you notice Jules was always against you?" Parker explained, "Making fun of you, spreading rumours, embarrassing her when she's in front of you."

He was crazy for her. Well in general the guy was crazy but for her... 10x worse.

Day after day, every damn time she was near me he'd say something to embarrass her. He'd always tell her *things* I did to turn her against me but the image she had of me in her head never changed. At first it was the little things like grudges and rumours or sketchy things I *did* but it never worked. The last solution he had was to kill me.

Mina hated that.

Mina hated almost everyone but one.

"He shot Mina, then he tried shooting you but hit Mina again." Parker explained.

"Does this not make sense to you?" Miles asked me.

"It's so stupid but it could be true." I answered.

"COULD!?" they all gasped.

"Look, Emily knew everything!" Parker explained.

Emily told Jules that Mina was pregnant. Bad idea. He obviously didn't take it well. When she got interrogated she told the inspector her side of the story but it wasn't enough. The inspector was helping at first but got the wrong idea after interrogating more people.

Like Jules, the pathological liar.

"Do you not remember what happened *before* she died?" Miles asked.

Yeah. I do now.

MAY 27, 2019

Jules told the group Mina was pregnant but one catch, he told them I was sleeping around. Mina obviously didn't believe him, to be honest, it was confusing.

Mina, Miles, and obviously Emily didn't believe him. Mina can tell if people lied, she confronted me over and over again to make sure.

"Is it true? Are you *actually* sleeping around? Is that why I keep seeing you with Kaiden?" she asked.

She sounded mean and intimidating, I knew she was hurt. I turned to her and looked her directly in the eye.

"No." I answered, "I was with Kaiden to tell her off."

"*Why* do you need to tell her off?"

Kaiden cheated on me last year with some *wanker,* she didn't know I found out.

"I haven't seen her in a long time after I ghosted her. She wouldn't stop *fucking* calling me so when I *did* see her in person, I took the opportunity." I explained.

"Oh!"

Her shoulders rested and she wasn't tense anymore. She smiled.

"Damn." she snickered, "You could've let me be there! I would've brought popcorn."

I laughed.

"Well, you gotta tell Marina the truth about this whole.. *mess...* she'll kill you." she explained.

I raised an eyebrow.

"She tackled a boy down and beat the shit out of him last week."

"Really?!" I gasped.

I wasn't surprised, it sounded exactly like something Marina would do. Mina knew how intrigued I looked. She always said I looked like I was a little scared of Marina but also looked up to her.

"Well I'm not sleeping around, I know better." I said, "Why would I do that?!"

"I don't know." she replied, "What are you going to do about this?!"

"Confront him."

"Can Marina and I come??!" she asked.

She always had that bright look on her face. She loved talking to me.

"Why?"

"We're betting on it, duh. $150. Obviously I'm getting the money after today."

"Huh- um- okay."

I confronted Jules that day. It didn't exactly go as planned.

Last Monday of the year. We were outside in front of the high school. Jules was there, he was leaning against one of the poles confidently.

I walked out of the school with Mina and Marina on each side of me. We looked tough, exactly like the movies. There were people around to watch as well, everyone knew Mina and Jules and everyone knew Marina and I. We were all popular for different reasons.

"Ah! There's the man-whor-"

"Watch your mouth Julian." Marina scoffed.

Jules stood up straight and walked over to me.

Marina and Mina were being the usual, they were watching every move and giggling and gasping. They even brought a bag of popcorn and soda. The teachers were surprised to see Marina again. Most of them hoped they'd never see her in their sight after she graduated, some of them were even surprised that she graduated at all. She was a funny troublemaker. It was more of a problem to them than to her.

Jules walked up to me and we remained eye contact. I lifted my head up slowly and eyed the crowd, by now everyone had the same opinion of me.

"The hell is your problem?" I asked.

"Hey, hey, *I'm* not the one sleeping around." he shouted obnoxiously.

I rolled my eyes. He acted like he didn't move one day past middle school. He wasn't even angry either, only cocky and full of himself.

"Alright." I chuckled as I began to walk away.

I didn't want to deal with him.

"Ah yes, the usual." he taunted.

I stopped walking. I didn't bother turning around. My smile faded with my tongue in my cheek.

"You're too much of a pussy to do anything." he scoffed.

The crowd was dead silent. We only heard Marina and Mina chewing on popcorn.

"Don't do it." Marina whispered.

"Shut up Marina, I want to see this." Mina snickered.

Everything happened so fast.

I swiftly turned around. Jules was standing there grinning proudly. I charged towards him and tackled him to the ground.

"YOOOO!!!!" Marina gasped.

"YEAHHHH!!!!!" Mina exclaimed.

We started fist fighting. I threw the first few punches.

"¡COÑO!" Jules shouted.

He kicked me off of him and pinned me to the ground. He laid his hands on my throat. I heard Kai and Parker watching.

"Ah jeez," Parker sighed.

"They're cat-fighting again." Kai remarked.

Parker slapped Kai's arm and they both started cackling.

"Stay away from Mina." Jules ordered.

"Who's going to make me?" I grinned.

Jules scoffed as he watched my face turn red. I shoved him off of me and stood up. I was breathing heavily.

"You sound more like Marina every day." he winced.

I chuckled as I watched him stand up and stagger over to me. Riah was in the crowd as well, once she noticed the blood on my knuckles she rolled her eyes.

"I'll go get Miles." she sighed as she ran away to find him.

"Ready for round two?" I grinned.

"Not the first time you've said that to someone other than Mina right?" Jules mocked.

My facial expression went from amused to annoyed. I wanted to bash his face in more than anything. I snatched his neck, yanked him down, and kneed him right in the stomach. He winced and got ready to punch me back.

I quickly swung to the side and watched him miss the punch. I chuckled proudly then punched him right across the face and watched him tumble over, swinging around his arms and breathing heavily.

I wiped the blood off my nose and sighed in relief. I lifted my head up to the ceiling and smiled. I staggered over to him and got onto top of him quickly. I punched him across the face and couldn't even see his nose from how hard it's bleeding.

This is where I simply couldn't control it anymore. I used my left hand to pin him down and my right to repeatedly punch him over and over again. He didn't have enough strength to fight back.

"EDEN!" Miles yelled.

The crowd was reacting like usual. To be honest I couldn't hear them, my ears started ringing and all I could see was me punching him.

"Is someone going to stop him?!"

"Shoot! He's going to kill him!"

"EDEN STOP!"

"EDEN THAT'S ENOUGH."

There was only one thing that could bring me back to reality, her voice.

"SHIT! EDEN THE COPS!" Mina shouted.

I swung around and saw the cop cars driving right over to the fight. The sirens started caving in as the crowd faded away. I got off of Jules as Mina ran over to us. She didn't even bother looking at her brother.

I wrapped my arm around her shoulder to piss him off even more. Jules stood up slowly and scoffed as he eyed her.

"Dad's not going to like this." he scoffed.

He was out of breath and his left eye was swollen shut.

"Alright, it looks like I won't be home tonight, like usual." Mina grinned.

"That *one:* you got knocked up, and *two:* that the guy that knocked you up got in a-"

"Ma'am were you involved in this fight?" the cop asked.

There were a few cops approaching us. Mina was about to answer but I answered for her. I knew what she was going to say, she was going to say something to protect me.

"No, she wasn't." I smiled.

"Well you have to go." the cop ordered, he looked over at Jules and I, "You two are going to the station."

"Alright." I sighed as I hugged her and kissed her forehead.

The day after the fight I showed up to school. At that point I was famous. Everyone gave me looks and girls' jaws dropped as I walked down the hallway. Once Mina saw me she went over to check on me. She already knew what happened, she just wanted an excuse to talk to me. I knew.

Marina and Mina scurried over to my locker with an intrigued look on their faces.

"Hey shawty." Marina said.

"What happened?!" Mina asked excitedly.

"It's resolved." I smiled.

Miles was there. To be honest he had no idea what was going on.

"Ayee!!!!!!" he said all smiley as he walked over to us, he turned to Mina, "Why is Jules telling people that *you're* saying Eden's *sleeping around?*"

"¿Cómo?" she gasped.

"He's just mad he lost." I said, "That's an easy fix, I'll just tell everyone she's not saying that."

"People already hate me." she shrugged, she seemed like she didn't care, "They'll believe him over me."

I still felt the need to make her feel better.

"Who has more friends, me or Jules?" I asked, "Me. He had us but now we're gone, no one will believe him."

Miles and Marina eyed each other then shrugged. Mina and I started giggling at each other, we do that everytime we get each other in trouble.

JULY 17, 2019

"So that's why Jules killed Eden!?" Kai asked, "That's stupid."

"He was crazy." Parker said.

"For real!! I called him a psychopath once and he got *sooo* mad." Miles giggled.

"You guys knew about this right?" I asked, "All the drama that went down that Monday?"

"I knew about the drama but I didn't get involved." Parker said.

"Why?"

"Because it's not my problem."

Kai giggled. She knew about the drama as well, she just couldn't take it seriously.

"This was so obvious. Why didn't anyone point this out before?" I asked.

"It was too normal of you two, you guys always fought." Parker sighed, "People didn't really think much of it."

"I remember being questioned about the fight," Miles said.

"We all were questioned, we all said the same thing as well, we said it probably didn't mean anything because it was so normal to us."

"Did Mina ever confirm she was pregnant?" Miles asked, "Even though we know she wasn't."

"She never answered." I responded, "Everytime Jules would yell it in the hallways or cafeterias, she'd take her smoothie Arón makes for her every day and pour it down his shirt."

"Damn." Parker replied.

"Alright enough about Jules' motive, why do we need to save Emily?"

16.2
deja vu

Parker sighed.

Emily knew everything. She and Jules hooked up a few times and she tried leaving him but he kept manipulating her into staying.

She thought hooking up with me would give her a chance to cry for help.

"That explains the bruises." I murmured, "They *were* actually from Jules."

I still had questions.

"Parker, how do you know all of this?"

I was wondering how she knew the entire story.

"I knew everything too, that conversation you heard at Arón's house was... yeah." she admitted, "I didn't get hurt though, if Jules touched me I'd beat the shit out of him."

"Then why didn't you tell anyone?" I asked.

"He blackmailed me. He was going to tell my mother I was bisexual and you know my mother, bat-shit crazy, she wouldn't have taken that well. Plus, if I did beat him up he'd hurt Emily." Parker explained, "Trust me Eden, if I could do anything I would've done it by now."

We all sighed.

"Shit." I sighed, "Then how did Evelyn get arrested?"

"It was my fault." Miles muttered.

```
JUNE 11, 2019 [recorded tape]
```

"You weren't fond of Mina, you hated her." the inspector said.

"I tried making it up to her!!" Evelyn exclaimed, "She held grudges!"

"NO, you listen! You were angry that your ex boyfriend, *Ethan*, was trying to hook up with your twin sister, Emily." the inspector said, "So you tried making him jealous by hooking up with his *best friend*, Eden."

"The fuck are you talking about?! I don't *care* about Ethan anymore and... Eden kinda looks like a bowling pin." Evelyn argued.

380

"That's not what you said last week, you said you'd do anything for him and that he was *irresistible.*"

"That's what *every* girl says for Eden! Big deal!"

"You were jealous of Mina, every person I interrogated told me you get attached to boys how hooligans get attached to drugs. You were angry they were together so you took the bow and arrow and killed her."

"Bull-shit." Evelyn scoffed.

"Then where the hell were you that night??!" the inspector asked, "Why can't you tell me? It can't be worse than a murder, right?"

"I can't tell you." Evelyn sniffled, "I'm sorry. Can't you just check the security cameras at school?"

"Funny, when we went to check, the footage was missing."

"What?" Evelyn gasped softly.

JULY 17, 2019

"I wouldn't let her tell anyone." Miles admitted, "So then the police thought she killed Mina for you."

I snorted.

"Evelyn with me?? OH PLEASE."

"Any more questions?" Kai yawned.

"No I-"

We were interrupted. We heard something behind us. I swung around and it was a guy on a motorbike.

It was Jules.

"SHIT SHIT SHI-" Parker panicked.

We heard a few arrows being shot. One hit a tire.

"Do we have a spare?!" Kai asked.

"Do you *THINK* we have *TIME* to REMOVE THE SLASHED TIRE TO PUT THE SPARE ON??!" Parker screamed.

"We *could* finish the task." Miles said while laid back on the seats with his arms rested.

"Yeah, IN HEAVEN!"

The car was slowing down and the motor was driving faster towards us. Kai and Parker kept blabbering.

"We're all going to die!!" Kai panicked.

"FINALLY!" Parker yelled.

"NOOO I WANTED TO VISIT ANTARCTICA!"

"WHAT'S SO SPECIAL ABOUT ANTARCTICA!"

Miles and I swung back around from looking at Jules and faced Parker and Kai.

"SHUT UP!" Miles and I screamed.

There was a moment of silence. We were just staring at each other breathing heavily. Suddenly Parker and Kai started cackling under pressure, Parker continued frantically driving. They sat up swiftly and looked around. We were in a neighbourhood.

"Hey I recognize this place!" Kai said.

This is where Parker slowly realized how bad the situation was, like really. She was usually spacy around everyone. This is when her head finally reached earth again. She started panicking.

"EVERYONE OUT OF THE *FUCKING* CAR!" Parker panicked.

We jumped out of the car and ran after Parker. We were all extremely fast, I played six sports, I used the money from Salva to help me join. Miles played soccer and basketball, and Parker and Kai did track.

We ran through houses and backyards and heard old people shout at us.

"SH! Quiet down!" Miles whispered.

Eventually we reached house 13.

Parker banged on the door.

"Silené! OPEN THE DAMN DOOR!!" Parker yelled.

Miles smacked her arm as Kai smacked the back of his head.

"Shut up!" Kai whispered.

Parker couldn't yell loud, we didn't want Jules to find us.

"¡VALE! ¡VALE! ¡COÑO!" Silené answered.

She opened the door and Parker pushed her way in as we followed. We were all exhausted from running block from block.

"¿Qué pasa?" Silené asked, "Why are you guys dressed like that?"

This is when we all remembered we still had our costumes on. I was the only one wearing casual clothes. Parker grunted and took off her vest and removed the stick out of her hair.

Silené was around 5'4, around 24 years old, slim and skinny, she had shoulder length dark brown hair and bangs. She was gorgeous. Her brown eyes were sharp and she had a tiny mole on her top lip.

Parker and Miles started explaining everything to Silené in European Spanish. Kai and I just stood there watching awkwardly.

"¡Este maldito maníaco nos estaba persiguiendo por la calle en una motocicleta!" Miles sighed.

"¡Sin mencionar que este maníaco es el mismo maníaco que mató a Mina!" Parker explained angrily.

```
Translation: "This fucking maniac
was chasing us down the street on a
motorcycle!" Miles sighed.
"Not to mention that this maniac
is the same maniac that killed Mina!"
Parker explained angrily.
```

Arón walked out of a room.
"Oh hi Arón." Kai said.
"Hola."
I sat down on the couch in the middle. I sighed and laid my head on the backrest. I had to process things for a minute, remind myself that this is real.

Jules was rich enough to start a new life. He's a fugitive now. We figured he was trying to kill the rest of us off then run away to Mexico.

Emily's the most vulnerable, that's why she's targeted first.

After Silené finished hearing the story she paced over to the front door and locked it cautiously.

"Arón, lock the windows," she ordered, "and shut the curtains."

"¿Por qué?"

"NOW!"

"Why are you guys all yelling??" a soft deep voice asked coming from the bedroom.

"It's about Mina." Silené answered.

He stepped out of the bedroom immediately, he was tall, 5'10, blue eyes and short black hair. He was 19 years old and slim and skinny like Silené. His socks were the biggest detail about him, they were red with yellow thin stripes.

"Uhhhhh-" he said as he saw us.

"Hi Leo." Parker said as she dug into the fridge to find an energy drink.

Silené and Leo were siblings. Arón was staying at their place because we burnt *his* place down.

Arón and Silené explained everything to Leo. Leo sighed. He was the closest to Mina compared to the two of them. When Mina didn't hang around us as much she hung out with Arón, Marina, Silené, and Leo. Leo was like an older brother to her. He missed her the most out of the three of them.

I remember seeing the siblings at the funeral, they sat with Arón in the fourth row. They all wore Mina's favourite colours. Even Leo made a speech.

They were also with Marina and Jordan the night it happened. They were at the party.

Parker found an energy drink.

"Silené! I'm drinking this!"

"Okay."

Parker turned around and looked at Leo. She noticed that look on his face.

"What's his problem?"

"He's been... up in a knot." Silené sighed, "Ever since Mom died."

"Shoot, your Mom died?" Kai asked.

Leo nodded.

"We've been trying to turn our life back around since then, that's why we moved here."

"We also moved here because your boyfriend died in a shooting." Leo scoffed.

"¡Oye!" Silené snapped, "Not in front of the teens."

Leo sighed and sat down next to me, "Lo siento."

He looked over at me.

"Eden right?"

"Yeah."

"Ha! Mina told me about you."

"She did?"

"Duh."

Leo started opening up to me. He figured since I was Mina's boyfriend, I was just like her.

"My girlfriend, Erla, she was so pretty." he sighed, "She cheated on me though."

"Awe, I'm sorry."

"Meh it's fine, I just pretend she was just any other blonde girl."

Leo sighed again.

"Mom's dead, Erla's gone, Mina's dead. These two weirdos are the only ones I have left!" he said as he pointed to Silené and Arón.

"Is it okay if we stay here? Just for a little bit?" Miles asked as he sat down with us.

"Okay." Leo smiled.

Leo seemed like a nervous person. He was always shaky and stuttering unless he's talking about something that made him happy.

"Miles, we can't stay, we have to keep looking for Emily." Parker sighed.

"Wouldn't Jordan, Marina, and Riah try to find her too?" Kai asked.

"I figure that's what they're doing at the moment."

"Then..."

"No, we need to go and find her before it's too late." I said.

"The car's been slashed, we can't drive." Miles sighed.

Leo looked up at us, "Take my car!"

388

He gave us the keys. He drove a lexus convertible, it was black.

"Don't crash it!"

We got into Leo's car without being seen by Jules. We started driving.

"How are we going to *find* Emily? We can't just drive around!" I said.

"Riah just texted me, she said they're hiding at the 7-Eleven near the middle school right now." Miles explained.

"Did they find Emily?"

"No."

The group has been blowing up Emily's phone, calling her, we only got one text message.

Gas station.

It was sent to Parker. We hurried and drove to the 7-Eleven.

"We don't know which gas station she's talking about." Kai said.

"She'd either pick 7-Eleven or Wawa," Parker explained, "They checked Wawa already, now we're going to check 7-Eleven."

We speeded through the streets, still stressed out and nervous under the pressure. We even got the cops called on us. We heard the sirens and red and blue lights flash.

"Shoot! The cops!" Miles panicked.

"I DON'T CARE!" Parker shouted as she continued speeding.

We were all screaming on the top of our lungs, laughing from the adrenaline as the sirens roared louder.

Parker started cackling while speeding down the streets.

"*Mayyybeee* you should've let me drive." Kai said.

"And what?" Parker replied, "Crash this?"

I ask myself stupid questions a lot. Sometimes I wonder if my friends are batshit crazy and if they're actually okay or not.

This is one of those moments.

"What do we do?!" Kai giggled.

"I don't know." Miles and Parker answered frantically.

Kai huffed and swung around towards me.

"EDEN!" she screamed.

"WHAAT!?" I screamed back, "WE'RE RIGHT NEXT TO EACH OTHER!!!!"

"I KNOWWW!!!!"

"*WHY* ARE WE SCREAMING!!???!"

Miles started shifting around in his seat to look for something to help us. The cops were still coming closer and closer. He found a can.

"What's this?" he asked.

Kai turned and looked at Miles.

"Shit, that's a smoke bomb!" she exclaimed, "It's the kind they use at gender reveal parties!"

Miles widened his eyes and looked at me. We both had that look on our face. We grinned and looked forward to Parker and Kai.

"How many bombs are in here?" Miles asked as he looked around.

"Only three." I answered.

Miles looked up and took a deep breath.

"PARKER! SPEED!"

Parker grinned and stomped on the petal as we all immediately fell back into our seats. We grunted as Parker started cackling again while jumping forward against the wheel.

Miles and I picked up the bombs and rolled down the window. We set them off then threw them out behind us.

"Is that going to work??" I panicked.

"Hopefully!" Miles sighed.

Parker continued speeding and she swung right, Miles and I crashed into each other again.

"Parker, CAN--YOU---QUIT--THAT!!"

We eventually lost the cops. The smoke bombs somehow worked. It was sort of unrealistic, it was normal to us. We were always unrealistic. Everything would take us a while to actually realize what we're dealing with because we never take things seriously. We'd always have to have a reality check. We sighed in relief.

"We're at the 7-Eleven." Parker sighed, "I see it right there!"

We were interrupted by a phone call. It was Riah. Miles picked up.

"Miles! I think we see Emily! Don't do anything stupid! Jules is here too!"

You could hear feedback on the other side of the phone.

"We're all going to die, we're all going to die!" Jordan panicked.

"Jordan, I *swear*, if you don't shut the hell up *I'll* be the one to kill you." Marina snapped.

We started slowing down. Miles and I were ready to jump out of the car and tackle Jules to the ground. We had enough anger to, Jules screwed up our lives, every single one of ours. We saw Emily, she looked exhausted from running away from Jules but we knew she could do it. She was athletic in school.

"How did Jules find us so quickly?" Kai asked.

Parker stopped and laid back to think for a second, "Shoot! Eden! Your smart watch! It's linked to Jules' phone! The location!!"

I widened my eyes and looked down at my watch.

"You need to throw that away!"

"No! Axel got it for me!"

"Shoot!"

Emily was staggering in the middle of the streets. We only saw her back profile, she was facing the other way, it looked like she was yelling something.

"Kai, roll down the window." Miles whispered.

We heard some of it. Miles quickly pulled out his phone to text Riah.

"Shit! My phone died!" Miles panicked as he aggressively tapped his phone, "Kai text Riah to get ready!"

We had to be quiet, we didn't know what was going to happen if we weren't. That's why Parker and Kai didn't jump up celebrating when Miles cussed again.

We were listening to Emily. I was praying she wouldn't do anything stupid. She was breathing heavily and gasping for air, it sounded like she was crying.

"Fuck you." she cried.

Now.

The arrow pierced her chest as her head flew back. She fell onto her knees then collapsed to her side.

"EMILY!!" I screamed.

"HOLY SHIT!" Parker yelled.

Kai and Miles' jaws dropped as they covered their mouths at the speed of light.

I jumped out of the car and ran over to her.

No, no, not again. Please, not again.

Miles jumped out of the car and ran over to Jules.

Pow!

He punched him in the face and he fell down to the ground. The yellow gun fell out, Miles picked that up and immediately pointed it at Jules.

Jules was laying on the ground with a cheeky grin on his face. He sighed and chuckled softly as he rubbed his eye.

"*What in the world* is wrong with you?!" Miles yelled, "Are you deranged?!!"

Miles started hyperventilating and panicked. He was angry too, all he wanted to do was shoot. He didn't have enough strength to look at Emily's body.

This time there was more blood.

Emily was laying on the ground with an arrow through the middle of her chest.

"NO!" I sobbed, "Someone call the ambulance!! PLEASE!"

Carry her this time.

I picked her up into my arms, I didn't want to tear the wound any more. I stood up carefully. Emily was crying and hissing in pain. Blood stained her shirt and was dripping onto mine.

She kept repeating my name.

"Eden."

"It's okay Em, everything will be okay."

Riah ran out of the 7-Eleven calling 911 frantically. The look on her face explained it all. She wasn't fond of Emily but seeing her dying in my arms was still unsettling. Her eyes were widened and the more blood she saw the more flashbacks she got.

The rest of the group ran out of the station, they were in shock.

"I'm sorry Emily, I'm really sorry, hang in there." I cried, "Listen to me!"

She didn't last long.

"Someone get her in the car!" Jordan shouted.

"Drive her to the hospital!" Marina panicked as Parker drove Leo's car closer to us.

"She deserved it." Jules muttered.

He was still laying on the ground rubbing his eyes. Miles was still trying not to pull the trigger.

Soon he reached his breaking point, he grunted angrily and shot the gun up at the sky with tears streaming down his face.

"Shut up! Literally SHUT UP!" I shouted.

All our voices were raspy. We haven't got any sleep and the tears made it worse. It was too late, the arrow went through her heart.

Emily Clarins. Dead at 17.

She was laying there in my arms as her head rested on my chest.

She wasn't breathing.

"Joder." Marina sighed.

"I have to throw up-" Jordan muttered as he staggered over to the curb. He threw up onto the sidewalk.

We were all scattered in front of the gas station, blood everywhere on the pavement, tears on all of our faces, feeling the shock and terror of seeing her dead.

I couldn't stop crying. How did I let this happen again? I could've saved her. Miles was distracted, he turned his head over to me. He was crying, lips quivering and eyes barely shut. I set Emily down on the ground gently and wiped my eyes with my arm.

Jules started shifting up to run away, I shot up and snatched the gun from Miles and cocked it.

"The fuck did you do that for?! What did Emily ever do?!" I sobbed.

My hands were clammy and shaky. I couldn't keep the gun still. Blood on my hands staining the gun, my legs close to collapsing, my heart burning and feeling like it's going to explode any second. I wanted to shoot, everyone did. I couldn't, the tears in my eyes blocked the vision, my heart felt heavy, my back heated up, it felt like the world was collapsing onto me. I always felt like the world was doing that to me, by now I figured I should just start getting used to it.

Miles started freaking out, running his hands through his hair and hyperventilating. He looked over at me swiftly and realized I wasn't doing any better. None of us were.

Riah was over, kneeling down beside Emily, crying.

"I'm sorry Emily." she cried, "I'm so sorry."

I slowly lowered the gun and sniffled. I felt the urge to start screaming. Almost how I did when Mina died. I dropped the gun and Riah ran over. She immediately pointed it at Jules as the cries and whimpers left all our bodies.

"WHAT THE HELL!" I screamed loudly as everyone flinched.

I started screaming louder and louder as everyone was silent, in shock listening. I figured that's the first time they saw me like that. I started screaming at the world, I was only 17. I was so tired, angry, I didn't know if I could do anything anymore. I thought this whole stunt would distract me, running away and solving the case on our own, but it didn't. All it did was create a million new issues to fix.

"WHEN WILL WE EVER LEARN!"

"WE'RE JUST KIDS, DUDE, KIDS."

Miles staggered over and cupped my face with his hands.

"Listen to me, this wasn't your fault." he whispered.

We went through the same thing again. Interrogation, no sleep, trauma. The funeral was one of the worst parts.

Barely anyone was there, people didn't like the Clarins twins unless you include the girls that wanted to be them. It was at a small church around the corner. We couldn't even go look inside the casket, we saw her die. We weren't even sure if we were allowed at the funeral.

We couldn't even say a word, we were too shaken up. Riah was crying uncontrollably into

Miles' shoulder. Marina was hyperventilating softly, she put her hand on my shoulder.

What bothered me most was that Jules had the audacity to show up to the funeral. We weren't in the mood to create a scene but we knew we needed to so the inspector could take action.

We were sitting in the 4th row covering our faces and the only noises coming out of us were muffled sobs and sniffles. None of us were that close to Emily but we knew the death was our fault. We could've prevented it. The answer was right below our noses this whole time and we didn't point it out because we normalized it.

Jules walked into the church, we all turned around swiftly. He wasn't even wearing black. He had a moss green hoodie under a black tee and sweatpants on. He even tried wearing sunglasses and a hat to hide his identity. Marina and Parker shot up.

This is when I knew. I always knew, I just needed a confirmation.

He wasn't going to give up until I was dead.

"You have the fucking nerve to show up here, do yah!?" Marina shouted.

Miles groaned and rubbed his eyes.

"Just get out dude, no one wants you here!"

"You're clearly not welcome." Kai said angrily, "How are you still walking free??"

Jules eyed each and every one of us then put his hood over his beanie. He started pacing towards the door.

Jordan widened his eyes and hesitantly pointed towards him.

"Wait, someone stop him!" he exclaimed.

We started pacing towards him. We wanted him behind bars, once and for all, we needed to do it for Mina and Emily. We didn't need to hurry that big, Inspector Alex handled it for us.

"Hey!" she shouted.

She came out of nowhere. Detective Toby and Max followed her on each side with Aisha, Toby's sidekick, following along beside him. They paced towards Jules.

"Stop right there!" Detective Max shouted angrily as he paced faster.

They eventually catched up to him. Jules was trying to pace instead of run to not look suspicious. Detective Max grabbed his arm aggressively as he swung around.

"You are under arrest for the murders of Mina Willow and Emily Clarins." the inspector said sternly as she handcuffed him.

Detective Toby and Aisha started taking turns telling him his rights as they brought him away.

"You have the right to remain silent," Detective Toby said, "Anything you say can and will be used against you in a court of law."

"You have a right to an attorney," Aisha continued, "if you cannot afford an attorney, one will be appointed for you."

Jules tried to fight back, he didn't deny the murders but he kept screaming at them to let him go and that his parents would bail him out anyway. We all stopped and watched them drag Jules away.

Parker had that expression on her face, she was disappointed. The way her eyes melt and her mouth is slightly open. She took a deep breath.

"It's over now." she sighed, "'It's over."

She turned around and glanced at me.

"We're free."

We all took a deep breath. It's over. The murderer's been arrested. We still had a few tasks to do.

At the end of the funeral I heard a soft knock at the front entrance. It seemed normal to everyone but me. The energy was suddenly different. I turned around slowly and wiped my tears.

"Salva?" I gasped.

I stood up slowly in shock to have a better look at him. The group swung around as well, they had that curious look on their faces.

"Holy shit!" I gasped.

I had that look on my face. I was so excited to see him. I jumped out of my seat and ran up to him at the speed of light.

I stopped myself in front of him. He was the same, same awkward, nerdy Salva. He had a backpack around his shoulder, sticking out of it were a few rolled up posters. I hugged him tightly, just like I did when I was 14. I sighed and laughed in relief.

"You're so tall now!" he chuckled.

"I can't believe you're here!" I gasped, "I thought I was never going to see you again!"

I was so happy tears started falling from my face. I had a huge smile on me. It's the first time I've smiled that big since this whole mess grew on me.

"How are you??" I asked.

"Everythings going fine!" he replied, "How are you!!"

I sighed. My shoulders weren't tense anymore, I felt safe around Salva. Seeing him made me miss when I was 14, with Axel, going on adventures with them.

"You can't believe what has happened." I sighed.

"Eden," Miles said, "Eden!"

I woke up. It was just a dream.

We were in my car driving to the prison Evelyn was kept in. I sat up and frowned, I would do anything for that dream to be real.

"What happened, I fell asleep." I said.

"Jules got arrested at the church," Parker explained, "Then you fell asleep in the car after we left."

"Oh, so... Salva didn't come back??" I asked softly.

"What? No." she said, confused, "I'm guessing you had an interesting dream, sounds like a *you* problem."

I sighed.

We walked into the prison, we weren't exactly sure how to break the news to Evelyn. She had no idea what was going on.

They let us in and I sat down on the opposite side of the glass. The rest of the group surrounded behind me.

Evelyn was sitting on the other side, she looked different, she was less nervous. It looked like time in prison changed her. She had her arms rested on the table and her blonde hair up in a pony-tail.

"What's going on?" she asked.

She hasn't seen us in a while, she was confused why so many people are here. Her eyes scattered across each and every one of our faces.

"Where's Emily?" she asked.

This is where I started tearing up again.

"Did you know Jules was the murderer?" I asked.

Her eyes widened.

"What? No?"

"Did you know Emily was stuck in an abusive situation?!"

"No, what's going on?"

She was clueless. She spoke differently too, almost like she finally got her shit together. She didn't sound like how she was back in school.

"Emily's uhm..." I murmured.

I looked down at the table and rubbed my eyes.

"Dead." Riah cried softly.

Evelyn immediately sat up straighter and her eyes widened. She sat there in shock, it looked like her heart stopped. She immediately started uncontrollably sobbing. We all waited quietly on the opposite side of the glass.

"I told you it wasn't me..." she cried softly.

"We're sorry." Marina said.

That surprised all of us. Marina never apologizes.

Evelyn couldn't stop crying, she lost a twin, a lifelong best friend. Miles was crying along softly too, he felt like this was all his fault for not letting Evelyn tell her real alibi. He didn't want to ruin anything with Riah.

He knew that if he let her spill, there would've been a bigger chance of Jules getting arrested sooner.

He cried because he understood her, he understood how she felt because he couldn't imagine losing Anna.

"You're getting released soon." Riah said, "We're sorry for your loss."

Evelyn sniffled and wiped her nose.

Everyone started to step out of the room.

We don't need to worry anymore, it was over. As we walked out of the prison the air felt new to us. We were still shaken up but it didn't feel like we were stuck in an endless cycle anymore. We felt free. We knew it was over.

We felt free.

17
the end of it all

"Look, you can let go now."

I keep hearing their voices in my sleep. Mina's, Emily's, even Axel's. I've talked to Miles about it. He says I have to learn to let go, for my own sake. It's been a while, the group has moved on, slowly but surely, just how Mina and Emily would've wanted them to.

"You should write a book about what happened, y'know," Miles suggested, "Mina loved writing stories, maybe you should do that to honour her."

I thought it was a great idea.

"It's a good idea Miles... but I don't know how to spell."

"Sure you do!" he chuckled.

It's been a while, things have changed. During senior year Salva wrote me a letter. I was shocked to see it at first, I made sure I wasn't dreaming this time.

I was at my house. I opened my mailbox and expected an envelope from Carla for the bills. I told her I was old enough to start paying them myself but she insisted. I saw the envelope from Salva and picked it up carefully. I felt my heart do a cartwheel and shoot up to the sky.

"HOLY SHITTT!!" I gasped as I broke into laughter.

Parker was on her porch eating licorice like the old times. She looked over at me jumping obnoxiously around my mailbox.

"What is it, Eden?" she asked.

"SALVA'S COMING BACK!!!" I laughed.

Parker's eyes lit up. She was happy for me.

Salva told me we could meet up again, he finished his big heist and was able to go to the United States again. We met up at a local coffee shop. As soon as I saw him I ran up to him at the speed of light and hugged him.

"You look so different now!!" he chuckled.

The hug we gave each other felt like the best hug you could ever imagine.

He was the same, just how he showed up in my dreams. He had the same beige pants and button up shirt, the same glasses, the same smile. I started telling him everything that happened.

Riah and Miles got engaged early, Miles proposed as soon as they both turned 19. It seemed like a thing *they'd* do. As soon as they graduated they got their life together. They even went to NYU together to complete their dreams. Riah coped with her childhood trauma, she hadn't seen her Mom ever since Miles went missing. She wanted it to stay that way. She knew her mother couldn't care less if she got into college.

Miles and Anna were still in touch. Miles' Mom didn't bother him anymore when she found out he got into NYU. He didn't tell anyone the real reason he ran away. His Mom and him got into a fight and he couldn't take it anymore. He fought back and ended up getting a black eye from his father. He didn't tell anyone because he didn't want to make a fuss about it.

Miles and Riah were always the happy ones together. Laughing and pretending nothing was wrong. They were pretty simple in their eyes, they only fought over stuff because they cared about each other.

Miles was like the brother of the group, goofy with everyone, he had his priorities straight but couldn't help but care for others more than himself. He's always been in the dark growing up, he just didn't care anymore, he found what he really needed and it was us.

Riah was the happy hyper girl of the group. She stuck up for others because no one at home did for her. Whenever she got upset or angry she'd get mad at herself for it, in fear of turning into someone she's never wanted to be. Sometimes she'd have us stay up at night wondering if she's actually doing okay or not.

In reality Riah and Miles were just the 17 year old couple who grew up too fast.

Parker finally got her peace. She proved her mother wrong by getting a scholarship for softball. She was so proud of herself she couldn't stop smiling for weeks. Parker was always aggressive because she confused anger with love. That's how she grew up. She pushes people away and never softens up because vulnerability is something her mother used against her. Sometimes if you read her eyes or the way her smile fades when she spaces out you'll picture her sitting in her bedroom at night, wide awake, not able to fall asleep because her parents were fighting two stories below her.

Kai made her dream come true, when she was little and living in orphanages she always wanted to be a dancer. She worked hard and got to perform live performances. She was always clumsy and hyper because that's how she was born. Being thrown into miserable, sad orphanages made her embrace it even more. The workers and care-ladies hated her because they were always sleepy and stressed while Kai was always giggling and jumping around trying to distract herself from the fact she had no one. She escaped the orphanages for the sake of her own.

Jordan continued being a lifeguard, he worked his ass off to buy a private beach near the shore. He'd let us hang out there once and a while. He doesn't mean to be a homewrecker or pissed off all the time. He's always been in the shadow of the group, no one really relies on him unless they need a job as a lifeguard or they want to sneak into a beach at night. He's always either been a second choice or never a choice at all. He messes up and screws around because the attention drawn to him makes him feel real for once.

Evelyn wasn't holding up well after her sister's death. She visited Emily's grave twice a week to tell her how sorry she was. She studied hard to become a doctor to honour Emily. Emily always told us she wanted to be a doctor when she grows up. Evelyn was a little misunderstood, she *chose* to be a bitch but not everyone understood why.

Marina always wanted to become a boxer. She still stayed in college because that's what she promised Mina but she and Silené started making boxing a new favourite hobby. They were amazing at it.

Marina acted the way she did because everyone she met screwed her over at least once. She was always distant with the group, not telling anyone anything because of the fear of being left alone. She loved and cared for all of us deeply, she was willing to defend and take any bullets for us any day. She's always laughing and alert because of her past. Mina and I were the only two she *truly* had a heart for. We were almost like her children even though the year difference wasn't big. The more people relied on her the more it made her feel needed.

Arón went back to Spain to pursue his music career. He came back to the United States once and a while to check up on Marina. Leo and Mina always joked about saving up to travel Europe. So that's what Leo did, he planned a trip to Italy and came back with a bunch of funny stories and memories.

There was Mina and I. We were almost like opposites but we still mirrored each other. I grew up with a neglectful mother and a father who abandoned me in a foreign country and she grew up with abusive parents, a crazy brother, and a family image to cover. Mina always hung around Miles because he was a better brother than Jules. She always wanted the movie feeling because her family constantly reminded her how miserable her life was. I was the cure for that but I wasn't any better. I went through hell, parents weren't really there, fake name, fake life, living in constant fear of someone figuring me out completely. I just eventually didn't care anymore and so did she.

I remember senior prom, all cases were closed, everything was supposed to be okay again. We showed up and everyone was having a good time. I felt bad with anyone I pictured myself dancing with so I just danced alone. All eyes were on me. It was nothing new, girls were checking me out and smiling. I just enjoyed the attention secretly then moved on. I spent most of my time giggling with Parker and Kai. I remember finding Alicia in the middle on the dance floor. Seeing her again made my stomach turn into a knot.

"Hey stranger." she smiled.

I turned to her. We haven't spoken in ages, it's been awhile since I've seen her.

"You're back?" I asked.

"Just for prom." she sighed happily, "Want a dance?"

I hesitated for a second. I nodded. We were giggling and dancing spontaneously together just like old times.

"Friends?" she asked.

I was surprised she'd actually ask that. I looked into her calm brown eyes. I smiled. Her smile grew wide as well. We both shook our heads then giggled.

I smiled lightly, "No."

She raised an eyebrow as I spun her around.

"We're neutral, chill, just strangers with memories." I sighed happily, "If we're anything more then the same thing would happen again."

"Yeah, I understand." she smiled, "We can't start anything, soon you'd get into a hole you can't escape."

As soon as I heard those words my smile faded a little and I had that look in my eye. Those words made me think of something. She grabbed my wrist and danced around. We had a fun time that night. Just like old times. We were older now, 18. I got a chance to tell her how proud of her I was.

I still was having trouble letting go of what happened. Writing a book about what happened seemed to help a little bit but I still felt something was holding me back.

"I feel like it's my fault." I told Salva.

He was sitting on the opposite side of the table stirring his coffee carefully.

"Not necessarily," he said.

Salva was smart, he spoke smart too. What do you expect? He was a mastermind behind big heists.

"Everyone had something kept in." he explained, "It takes courage to actually speak up about these things, we would know, right?"

I nodded.

"Maybe *some* of you guys had a heart for Jules. I can tell some of you guys cared for him *a little* so it was harder to confess," he suggested, "and I'm sure Jules manipulating everyone made it harder."

I sighed, I felt a little relieved but it wasn't enough.

"If anything the inspector and detectives should've been more careful. They should've looked at all angles. Instead of looking at the *unusual things,* they should've learned *your normal.*"

I still had a few questions. I decided to confront that issue instead of running away from it.

How did Jules know to go to the sunflower field at the same time Mina and I skipped 7th period?

I visited Jules in prison.

I was afraid of seeing him again, I never knew who he was, who the real him was. To be honest he didn't seem real, his mind worked oddly.

I walked in slowly and sat down. He was sitting on the opposite side of the glass glaring at me.

"Any visitors?" I asked softly.

"No."

I figured.

"Why did you come here?" he snapped.

"I just need to let go." I sighed.

"Just like Mina needed to."

"Shut up."

He was sitting on the opposite side of the glass, he had eye-bags, he hadn't slept. He wasn't doing well. I didn't care, I just wanted to get it over with.

"How'd you know where Mina and I were that day?" I asked.

"Hm?"

"The day you killed her."

Jules scoffed and rubbed his forehead.

"That boy Miles told me."

I narrowed my eyes and started rethinking things.

"Don't stress it on him though,"

I widened my eyes. I was surprised he'd say something like that. He never defends others when he's the one in trouble, he usually uses anything he thinks of to put it on someone else.

"I asked him where you guys were, he told me we were all going to meet up at the field." he explained, "That's how I knew."

"The hell did she do to you?" I demanded, "The hell did Emily do?"

I was angry.

"Mina had a twisted vision. She didn't know the real you." he snapped again, "I kept telling her, he's a twisted and cursed person, when will you learn that?"

You know that face you make when you want to slap a person's face so hard because of how stupid they sound? Yeah that was me.

I couldn't even look him in the eye. I kinda wanted to hurt him, hurt him how he hurt us.

"You don't know the real me either?" I said, "You could've just left us alone, we were finally happy, you've *always* been against me."

He took a deep breath. The more I looked at him the more he looked like a psychopath.

We were best friends.

"What if you went through another rampage and hurt her like you did during sophomore year!?" he asked.

I narrowed my eyes. Got a *tad* bit more frustrated.

"Well I guess we'll never know if she's DEAD!"

"What if your personality sides changed again?"

"She signed up for it. I warned her about them and she stuck through with me." I argued.

Jules owed us too much, hours of sleep, trauma, loss.

"Hell yeah she signed up for them but was she happy?" he scoffed, "What'd you expect her to do? When she wants something she will go through hell to get it."

I scoffed.

"You try acting like you care but you always make everything about yourself! You only care when it benefits you!" I exclaimed, "Mina was finally happy and you killed her!"

Jules' voice raised.

"I WAS TRYING TO KILL YOU!" he shouted.

My voice raised as well, only louder.

"HOW WOULD YOU THINK MINA WOULD'VE REACTED IF I DIED, HM?!"

"She would've moved on, coño."

"With WHO?!" I giggled, "YOU?! Oh, she hated you. Everytime you said something stupid she'd have the urge to punch you in the face. Everyone had that urge."

"Shut up!" he shouted.

To be honest I was just *joking*. I didn't expect him to take that to heart.

He expected me to flinch. I told him the truth.

"She would've gone fucking rogue if you killed me." I scoffed.

"I was trying to protect her from you."

"From me?"

"She wouldn't stop, she wouldn't give up," Jules argued, "She loved you to death but you were going from *girl* to *girl*. She wanted a turn and she got it. She fucked up everything to get her way, to get you."

"How is that your problem? I'm pretty sure she knew what she was getting herself into."

He took a deep breath and held eye contact with me. He tried looking intimidating but I wasn't scared.

"You're a living lunatic." he said.

"I know."

"She was addicted and you're addictive."

PSA FROM EDEN TO AUDIENCE

I'm not a good storyteller. To be honest, I'm not even half as good as Mina was. I'm still learning though, bare with me, enjoy this book as you wish.

I feel the need to remind you how sarcastic I am. REALLY sarcastic. I clap back to make them feel stupid.

I can call myself a *heartbreaker* or *this* or *that*, I'm only saying what they tease me.

I'm only mocking them.

We all do that. Most of the arguments throughout this book are just us talking in a cocky, obnoxious, sarcastic tone. We don't actually, *seriously*, argue over small things, at least that's what I think. We just mock each other.

You've been told I don't like getting involved in things but I always end up in them anyway, so being the narrator suits me just fine.

Axel was right, I do speak my mind.
This book is living proof.

-Eden B.

Made in the USA
Middletown, DE
26 November 2021